Rocky Mountain Retribution

Kurt James

DEDICATION

I would like to dedicate this book to my children - Eric, Matt, and Larisa. I love you to the moon and back.

ACKNOWLEDGMENTS

Without the help of forever friends from high school Kurt "Wally" Wollenweber and Lorraine "Blaze" Mays, I would never be able to follow my dream of being a storyteller.

TABLE OF CONTENTS

Chapter 1   Page 1
Chapter 2   Page 7
Chapter 3   Page 14
Chapter 4   Page 20
Chapter 5   Page 25
Chapter 6   Page 32
Chapter 7   Page 37
Chapter 8   Page 46
Chapter 9   Page 52
Chapter 10   Page 55
Chapter 11   Page 61
Chapter 12   Page 67
Chapter 13   Page 72
Chapter 14   Page 76
Chapter 15   Page 81
Chapter 16   Page 87
Chapter 17   Page 94
Chapter 18   Page 99
Chapter 19   Page 105
Chapter 20   Page 111

Chapter 21	*Page 119*
Chapter 22	*Page 125*
Chapter 23	*Page 131*
Chapter 24	*Page 137*
Chapter 25	*Page 141*
Chapter 26	*Page 146*
Chapter 27	*Page 152*
Chapter 28	*Page 158*
Chapter 29	*Page 164*
Chapter 30	*Page 169*
Chapter 31	*Page 176*
Chapter 32	*Page 181*
Chapter 33	*Page 186*
Chapter 34	*Page 191*
Chapter 35	*Page 196*
Chapter 36	*Page 201*
Chapter 37	*Page 207*
Chapter 38	*Page 213*
Chapter 39	*Page 219*
Chapter 40	*Page 223*
EPILOGUE	*Page 225*

CHAPTER 1

All that came to mind was "Oh hell! This is not good!" as the six riders slowly emerged from the tree line as they made their way into Jace's and my camp. Our mining claim on Bald Mountain, though not more than a mile from Nevadaville, Colorado, was not on a well-traveled road and was difficult to locate if you did not know exactly where it was, which meant to me that these men now sitting on horseback in front of Jace and me were looking for us. This could not be a good sign, not at all.

Of course, I recognized who these men were and had been hearing about them all over the Rocky Mountain frontier since Jace, my younger 15 year old brother and I had made our way here to Gilpin County, Colorado to look for gold after our folks had caught the fever and died on our dirt and windswept farm south of Dighton, Kansas.

Having seen the Herman Biggers and Rod Hammond gang once before as they were riding hard out of the town of Golden, Colorado after they had secured a withdrawal from the bank there, shooting and killing a deputy sheriff as they left town with guns blazing, I knew who these gents were, and it did not bode well for Jace and myself.

The old man on the far right with the almost white hair that hung down to his shoulders and the grizzly gray beard was Herman Biggers himself, the leader of the gang. As I scanned left to right, I knew each and every one of these outlaws. The tall, lanky man to the left was the second in command of the gang, Rod Hammond. Then came the Indian half breed Rick Alvardo. Next in line with an idiotic grin plastered on his face was Bobby Burke followed by the one-eyed gunman from back east somewhere Dave Edgar, and last in line was a youngster about my age but with a reputation as a bad man already, Chucky Livingston.

Mutt, our half wolf and half something else dog, was growling and showing his teeth at the six intruders. Well, he was not really "our" dog, more like Jace's dog. Mutt loved Jace and barely tolerated me.

Herman Biggers, the old man, leaned forward in the saddle and had his right forearm resting on the saddle horn when he spoke. Looking at me he said, "You best settle down that mangy dog before I put a bullet in it."

Never taking my eyes off of Mr. Biggers, "Jace, calm Mutt down for Mr. Biggers."

Jace reached out and patted Mutt twice and told him "No!" Mutt stopped growling but was still showing his teeth, and the hair was still standing straight up on his back.

Herman Biggers now was looking at Mutt but when he spoke, it was for me to hear since I was obviously the oldest. "Well son, it seems you know who we are, so why don't you introduce yourself to me and my boys."

I tried not to show the fear that I felt, but my voice immediately gave it away as it cracked a reply, "My name is Chance Bondurant, and the little fellow is my younger brother Jace."

Biggers pointed to the youngster in his gang, "Chucky, dismount and check the entrance to that mine shaft to see if anyone else is hiding in there." Chucky dismounted and drew his Colt 44 pistol and slowly made his way to our mine entrance.

Still with fear in my voice, "I can assure you, Mr. Biggers, the only fellas here are Jace and myself and of course our dog Mutt."

Now looking directly at me, Biggers asked, "How old are you son?"

Still unsure of myself and what was happening and still confused why the Herman Biggers gang would have an interest in Jace and me, "I just turned 18 last month and Jace is 15, sir."

Biggers seemed almost fatherly when he spoke again, "Where are your folks, young man?"

My mind was still tangled as I replied, "Died from the fever and buried down south of Dighton, Kansas next to our sod house."

Chucky, after checking out the mine entrance, started to make his way back to the rest of the gang. "Seems these boys and that damn dog are the only ones here, and by the looks of this camp, I believe we were lied to about how successful these two were at mining, and it does not appear they have much of anything let alone a pile of gold dust."

Herman Biggers did not seem pleased to hear this, "Now Chance, I know for a fact yesterday you and that sawed off brother collected $200 after cashing in some gold dust at the assay office. So I know you got at least that much cash and probably a substantial cache of gold dust and/or nuggets stashed somewhere. I suggest you collect that money and gold and hand it to me or this is going to get ugly."

Jace was scared, but the little shit had more nerve than brains as he said his piece, "No way, no how are you getting anything of ours, Biggers, and you best ride on out of here and take your ugly compadres with you before we get mad."

My little brother was all of 15 years old and small for his age about 5' 4" with short, dark hair and weighed maybe a 120 pounds soaking wet. Always talked tough like he was twice as big as he was. I loved my brother, but sometimes he never knew when to keep his mouth shut; this was one of those times.

All that tough talk from my little brother got the Herman Biggers and Rod Hammond gang laughing so hard that Bobby

Burke, the smiling moron, almost fell out of his saddle. Still looking at Biggers, I spoke to my brother, "Jace, shut your trap; this is not a time to be mouthing off."

My little brother, God love him, still mad as all get out, spouted off once more, "We ain't scared of them, Chance. You want me to go get Pa's pistol?"

Pa's Colt 44 pistol was the only weapon we had and up until yesterday, we never had enough money to buy any ammo. Even then we never thought to buy any since we never had a use for the pistol till now. Pa's Colt pistol was as dry and empty as my throat right now.

All six of the outlaws started to laugh once again and seemed to be pleased at my little brother's outburst of bravery as he stood before them so small, yet defiant. Their laughter at my little brother was only pissing me off, and I was praying for a bolt of lightning to fall from the sky and strike them all dead. Looking toward the blue and cloudless heaven and seeing no such bolt of righteous lightning, I tried to decipher out how Jace and I were going to live through the next couple of minutes. I was at a loss for what to say or do.

Herman Biggers finally stopped laughing long enough to utter, "Is that right Chance, you got a six shooter? I guess we will be needing that with the $200 and any gold you got stashed."

Feeling defeated, but seeing no other option, "Over in that leather pouch by the campfire, you will find the pistol and what's left of the $200. That's all there is, Mr. Biggers. We cashed in every bit of gold dust we had. We worked for three months to make that money; take it and leave us be."

Chucky Livingston hurried to grab the leather pouch that had everything that Jace and I owned in the world and started walking back to his horse when I heard Jace say, "Sic em."

That was all the encouragement that Mutt needed as he attacked Chucky Livingston. Mutt grabbed his arm and savagely slung Chucky to the ground and within mere seconds was on his face slashing with his teeth, and the blood started to flow.

The whole attack by Mutt lasted less than ten seconds before Old Man Biggers palmed his Colt and shot Mutt through the hindquarters, which brought the savage and brutal attack on young Chucky Livingston to an abrupt halt.

Mutt, the half wolf, after being shot scampered as fast as he could toward the tree line and away from anymore bullets being flung his way. Mutt, without looking back, disappeared amongst the evergreens and aspens headed in the direction of Nevadaville.

Chucky Livingston, the youngest member of the Biggers and Hammond gang, was bleeding liberally with large drops of blood staining the dirt, his left ear hanging by a thin piece of skin. After gaining his feet with a drunken sway and without a word, he palmed his Colt and shot Jace in the forehead. Jace, my little brother, dropped and was dead before he hit the dirt.

It all happened so fast I wasn't even sure it had happened, like a bad nightmare. Seeing Jace as he lay in the dirt with blood flowing from the wound in his head, I screamed, "NO!!" I started for Chucky, raising the pick ax I had been holding when the gang rode in from the tree line.

As soon as I started for Chucky, every remaining member of the gang still on horseback drew his pistol and started throwing lead my way. The only thing that saved me from getting riddled by bullets was they were afraid of hitting Chucky, and since I was so close to him, they all missed in the first volley except one which took me in the right side above my hip and spun me around facing the mine entrance. Seeing the gaping hole in the mountainside and using Chucky as a shield, I ran as fast as I could toward the entrance. In six strides I was in the gold mine.

Once I was far enough in so the Biggers and Hammond gang couldn't see me, I stopped to try and gather my breath and my wits. I knew if they entered the mine, I was done for; I had no weapon and no place to run. The mine was only 60 feet deep, and I was trapped in a hole in the mountain that Jace and I had dug. I had dug my own grave.

As I began to think about what to do, I tried to not think of Jace lying dead out yonder. Jace, dammit Jace why did you have to sic Mutt on that outlaw? I closed my eyes and tried to put the image of Jace being shot to the back of my mind, but I failed miserably at it.

Biggers' voice echoed down the mine, "Chance, come out here where we can talk. We are not going to hurt you."

Speaking loudly with more than a little fear in my voice, "Biggers, no way, no how am I coming out there; you come get me; I got my fully loaded Winchester here waiting for you."

Biggers chuckled, "Chance, you and I both know you don't have any rifle in there with you."

With a more sturdy voice, "If you are so sure Biggers, you come first."

It was quiet for a few moments, and then I heard Herman Biggers say, "Alvardo, go in there and drag that kid out here."

Alvardo was no dummy because I heard him chuckle, "Hell no Herman! If that kid has got a Winchester, he couldn't miss in such a narrow passage, I say let him be."

I heard Biggers' voice echo down the mine tunnel as he said with some anger, "We can't just let him be! He saw Chucky kill his brother! Someone is going to have to go kill the little bastard!"

Hearing a new voice, I assumed it was Rod Hammond, "Got a stick of dynamite that should do the trick."

Biggers laughed out loud this time, "Sure as hell will, light it and toss it in."

With a heavy thud, the stick of dynamite landed at the entrance of the Bondurant gold mine. I had two choices, and both would get me killed. One, I could run outside into a hail of bullets or two, I could get blown up and buried. I turned to run toward the back of the mine when everything went black.

CHAPTER 2

S napping my eyes open, I blinked them fast trying to recover the light except there was no light to be had; it was complete and utter darkness. I had lost track of time and without any light, I was disoriented on how long I had been unconscious. It could have been just a few minutes or days.

My ears were still ringing from the explosion, and I had the worst headache of my life. I do not recall being blown into the back wall of the Bondurant mine, but I must have because every muscle and every bone of my body hurt. I remembered vaguely getting shot, and I reached down to my side and touched the wound. The bleeding had stopped, and it seemed the bullet had passed on through without doing too much damage. Being shot and wounded was the last of my worries. It was obvious the mine had not completely collapsed or I would have been buried under tons of rocks and sure enough dead.

The air was hot and heavy with dust and with every breath, I started to choke and then spit up dirt. Being a youngster and still a kid, I still was smart enough to know without fresh air coming into the mine, it would not be long before I ran out of breathable air and would suffocate. It might have been more desirable to have died in the explosion than die suffocating on dirt.

Bondurant luck it was. Bondurant kin, or at least the ones I knew, had a streak of bad luck a mile wide. On our farm near Dighton, Kansas, no rain for a long spell withered our crops and they died. Then came winter, and the folks caught the fever and died, leaving Jace and I to fend for ourselves. After hearing the Colorado Mountains were full of gold waiting to be picked up like dirt clods in Kansas and with our future and everything we had known lying in two graves next to that windswept sod house on the plains of Lane County, Kansas, Jace and I packed everything we had and headed for the far Rocky Mountains in Colorado. Now, Jace was lying dead outside, and I was sure to die a miserable death inside. The only future and dream that the two of us had was the Bondurant gold mine. Shaking my head, I should have realized it was a bad omen to name it the Bondurant gold mine.

Trying to stand and falling down several times, I was still somewhat dizzy from the explosion or getting shot, probably both. I was determined if death is what awaited me in this gold mine that Jace and I had spent the last three months digging, that I did not want to lie down and wait to die. Finally finding my feet and in the total darkness, I backed up to the rear wall of the mine.

Standing there resting against the back wall, I started to ponder my way through this and find a way to survive. I needed to survive, because there were six men that needed to pay for what they did to my brother. Speaking to myself, "Chance! Think! You have to live and bring justice to those that caused Jace's death. Think, dammit!"

I closed my eyes, hoping it would clear my head and make me reason more clearly. I was 6'2" tall and weighed about 180 pounds and was all muscle, not an ounce of fat on my body with strength, stamina, and the will to live. I was just going to have to dig myself out of here is all, one rock at a time with my bare hands.

First, I would have to decipher how thick the wall was that the cave-in had caused. Coming up with a simple plan on how to calculate the thickness of the wall and how to gauge my progress, I ran it through my mind once again. I knew the gold mine was 60 feet long, and roughly 6' 5" tall. Knowing my foot with my work boot was close to a foot long or longer, I could use it to conclude how thick the wall was. Starting at the back wall I slowly, but deliberately, placed my right foot heel in front of my left foot toe and counted one. Placing my left heel in front of right toe stepping forward I counted two. Using the same method, I continued in total darkness and silence as I moved one step, one foot at a time toward the entrance of the Bondurant gold mine. Moving cautiously forward, I was on step 39 when I first stumbled and almost went down after tripping on a rock that was almost a foot in diameter. Trying not to lose my place and count, I carefully moved the rock to the side and continued on in my steps and count. I was on step 50 and ten feet from the entrance when I encountered my rubble from the explosion and cave-in. Still, I was able to move forward to step 55 when I hit my head and stumbled at the same time.

Without falling, I reached out in the dark and touched the forward wall of the cave-in that the dynamite had caused. My calculations in my head told me I was roughly five feet away from the entrance and fresh air. This was something I could do; five feet of loose rubble I could move by myself. I would have to put my faith in the Lord that doing so would not cause another cave-in.

I started in total darkness by grabbing hold of the rocks and then turning to toss them behind me. With every rock and small boulder that was removed, I pictured the faces of the six men of the Biggers and Hammond gang. Every one of their faces and how they looked, I planted into my memory for recall later. If fate lets me survive this, then I needed to remember. I needed to be able to serve justice to those that caused my brother's death.

My plan was to start at the top and burrow far enough to get some fresh air into the mine. I had been working for two hours, and I knew the air was being used up fast and I was getting light headed.

I worked as fast as I could, which seemed to be slowing down because my mind had started to drift. Lack of oxygen was playing tricks on my mind, but I was not so far gone that I didn't realize it. I started to think maybe I was not going to make it now, that my quest for justice for Jace was going to die with me here in the gold mine that Jace and I had dug.

Taking shallow breaths, thinking this might help conserve what air I had left, I still was moving rocks, but ever so slowly. Death, when it came for me, at least would say I gave it my all to my very last breath.

I must have passed out or fallen asleep because my eyes snapped open. Seeing nothing but darkness, I closed them again. Wait! There were sounds coming beyond the caved-in wall. A smile slowly appeared on my face because what I heard was a dog barking. It was Mutt, he had survived! At least one of the three of us was going to make it; damn that dog was tough! After taking a bullet, he was still alive.

Then it was there, a muffled man's voice, "Hello, anyone in there?"

Maybe there is a God, and with a voice dry with dirt and dust I gasped, "Yes! Yes! I am about three feet or so from the entrance."

With some astonishment the voice replied, "I will be damned; hang on son, we are going to get some help and get you out of there. Devon, ride back to the Coeur d' Alene mine and gather some help. What is your name, son?"

Not sure who the man was or who Devon was, the thought of getting some help sounded glorious to me, so I yelled as loud as I could, "Chance Bondurant! My name is Chance Bondurant, sir."

I then heard the muffled sound of rocks being moved from the other side of the cave-in, the greatest sound that I have ever heard. "Chance, my name is Lucas Eldridge, I am going to get you out of there."

Working with no fresh air, but with new found vigor, I started moving rocks again. After moving a dozen or so, I tired once again, and my mind started to drift again.

I felt Jace's presence as he started to move more rocks from the top which bewildered me because I knew that Jace was lying dead outside of the Bondurant gold mine. I had seen him shot; I knew he was dead. Knowing I was dying and the lack of oxygen was killing me, I knew somehow Jace was here in the mine with me and helping to save my life. Rolling onto my back with Jace bent over me, I felt bless. Even in the total darkness, I could see his face; where the light that illuminated his face came from, I was not sure. Trying to think and put my thoughts in order; I was still baffled how he was even in here. But, here in the gold mine with me, my brother Jace was. He reached down and touched my face ever so softly. I closed my eyes because it felt like the right thing to do.

My eyes snapped open, and my body convulsed as fresh air made its way into my lungs. Like a man drowning in a river, I gasped for air, trying to fill the void that was in my chest. After several seconds I rolled back onto my stomach and crawled up the collapsed wall to the source of the fresh air. Somehow Jace and the man Lucas outside had made a small tunnel about six inches wide at the top of the wall, and I drank heavily of it. My lungs ached something awful as I coughed up dirt and snot as my lungs once again started to move to some sort of normal rhythm.

The voice that belonged to the man Lucas came from the other arched side and was no longer muffled. "Chance, if you can hear my voice, try to get to the top of the wall. I believe I have broken through and I could feel the air rush in."

I tried to speak to tell the man Lucas that I could breathe again, but my voice gave out and no sound came out of my mouth. Thinking that Jace would find this funny because I was never for a loss of words, I looked behind me - but he was gone. Still confused, I reached back in the darkness to touch Jace, but he was not there.

I could still hear the sound of rocks being moved from the other side, and Mutt was barking up a storm, which only seemed to confuse me more. I closed my eyes once again to concentrate on breathing in the fresh air, which was more difficult than I could imagine after going for some spell without it. How long did I not breathe? How long could a man go without dying or causing some sort of damage to his thinker? Having no answer to my questions and with my focus broken, I heard several horses and more voices in the distance. I heard Lucas say, "Hurry up boys, the boy buried inside is no longer talking to me and I fear the worse."

I lost track of time, but it seemed just in a matter of a few minutes that the sound of more rocks was starting to be moved and at a faster rate. Mutt and Jace most have gotten some more help. Jace? Where was Jace? How did he get outside? My mind was a whirlwind of facts that just didn't add up. My rational thinking told me that both Mutt and Jace had been shot, but I had seen Jace, and I could hear Mutt barking non-stop on the other side of the wall. I closed my eyes again with my thinker in a tumble as I tried to decipher what was happening on the other side of the caved-in wall. The wall that had entombed me was slowly melting away.

I must have passed out or simply fell asleep and as strong arms grabbed me under my shoulders, the voice that belonged to Lucas made its way into my mind snaking its way through the dark cloud, "Dammit kid, wake up, I didn't work my butt off trying to save you just have you die. Let's get you outside into the air." Lucas dragged me by my armpits into the cool night summer air.

Opening my eyes, I looked over to where the campfire stones were and saw that Jace was still lying there, and my brother was very much dead. My head and heart hurt in that moment because that part had been real. Jace, my younger brother, had been killed and I did not stop it. I remembered how I had held Jace when our parents died and swore to protect him and take care of him. I had failed to do that. Jace was now dead to the world and me. Everything in my world was now spinning out of control.

Helping hands loaded me onto a wagon. Lying on my back facing the stars above, I then knew I was in fact out of the mine. Mutt either climbed on board with me or was lifted into the wagon as he lay down next to me with his nose lying on my chest watching me with a concerned look. With Jace dead, I guess Mutt figured he would adopt me as his new owner. I tried to reach out and pet him, but my muscles did not seem to respond; Mutt didn't seem to care, he knew I wanted to pet him.

A woman climbed on board and sat next to Mutt and reached out and touched my forehead as my mother use to do when I was feeling poorly. "Chance, my name is Devon and my husband

Lucas and I are taking you to our home in Central City. We are going to fix you up."

Focusing on her beautiful green eyes with a hint of blue, I finally mustered within myself to actually speak, "Thank you Devon, I don't seem to be myself right now, but thank you."

A powerful looking man with midnight dark hair looked over the side of the wagon, and I could only assume this was Lucas. "Chance, the other boy, who was he?"

Closing my eyes for fear I would start to cry, "My brother Jace. He was shot by the Bigger and Hammond gang."

Reaching and giving me a comforting pat on my shoulder, "Chance, we will take care of your brother proper. For now just worry about yourself."

The mile ride was bumpy and rugged to Central City and to the home of Lucas and Devon Eldridge, but that didn't seem to matter much to me as I fell asleep.

CHAPTER 3

S uddenly waking and gasping for air, I needed several minutes to gather my thoughts and calm my breathing to realize that it was a dream and that I was no longer suffocating and dying a slow death.

I blinked my eyes not from fear, but because of the brightness of the room; sunlight was filtering through the windows that had drapes of lace. Looking around the room, I saw that it was a simple affair with a double bed that I now found myself in with a light blanket and two goose down feather pillows. Across the room, there was a light color wooden dresser with eight drawers and a beveled mirror hanging above it. Two wooden rocking chairs were opposite of the dresser - one on each side of a large metal grate in the floor, which during the cold months served to let warm air rise from the first floor fireplace to heat the room which told me I was on a second floor.

It was somewhat painful to sit up because every bone and muscle ached from being blown back against the back wall of the mine when the Biggers and Hammond gang tossed the dynamite into the entrance of the Bondurant mine.

Remembering getting shot, I reached gingerly to my side and felt the wound, counting nine stitches. My mind was still in a fog from the ordeal, but I vaguely recalled a man named Lucas that dug me out of the gold mine, and his wife Devon said they were taking me to their home in Central City. Eldridge? Yes, Eldridge was their last name. Lucas and Devon Eldridge? The name Lucas Eldridge meant something, and as I pondered it for a few minutes, it struck me who Lucas was. Speaking out loud with some astonishment, "I will be damned; I am in the home of Lucas Eldridge the famous gunfighter that gunned down the bandit brothers Jose and Juan Verdugo a year or so ago."

My little outburst when I realized who Lucas Eldridge was woke up Mutt who had been apparently sleeping next to the bed out of my sight. Mutt jumped up on the bed and lay his head on my chest, looking into my eyes probably wondering if I had lost my mind. Seeing Mutt, my half wolf and half something else dog, brought a smile to myself as I pet him. Remembering he had been shot too, I sat up and pulled him towards me so I could check his hindquarters. Sure enough, I found his wound and it too had probably been stitched by the same hand that stitched me up. Mutt did not seem bothered by the wound and seemed as agile as he was before getting shot. As I held Mutt tight, tears formed in my eyes as the memory of Jace being shot and lying with a bullet hole in his forehead weighed heavily on my chest and shoulders. It was not supposed to be that way. 15 years old was too young to die. I felt guilt that Jace had been killed on my watch because I was the older brother, and it was my responsibility to take care of him. I promised Jace and my mom I would take care of him before she passed away from the fever. I almost wished that death would have taken me in the mine to even the slate with God. Mutt sensed my sadness and licked my face a couple of times showing that he cared.

Hearing the door close downstairs and footsteps, I thought it best to get Mutt off the bed and show some respect for the Eldridges. I patted the side of the bed, indicating to Mutt to get down, and the half gray wolf dog just lay there still looking at me.

With a low, but forceful voice, "Mutt get down before they see you on the bed and patted the side of the bed again."

Mutt wasn't having any of that. It was as if he went deaf or something. With a tad more frustration I patted the bed harder and spoke in a harsher tone, "Mutt! Down!" Still nothing.

Soft footsteps like that of a woman were coming up the stairs now and being a guest in their home, I did not want to get caught having Mutt up on the bed and shedding his fur; this time I tried to push Mutt off the bed while trying to reason with the dog this time. "Mutt buddy, don't get us in trouble. Down!" Still nothing, and it was like he gained 100 pounds or so; I could not budge him. Mutt just lay there looking at my face.

The door opened and Devon Eldridge walked in, and the first thing out of her mouth was, "Mutt, down."

Without looking at Mrs. Eldridge, Mutt jumped down nice and easy. I gave Mutt the ole' stink eye without Mrs. Eldridge seeing me.

Setting down a bowl on the bedside table that had what looked like some elk stew and freshly baked bread, Devon said, "Your half wolf dog Mutt sure does love you. He has not left your side since you were dug out of your gold mine."

Mutt was still staring at me, and I was trying to figure out if he had a smirk on his face and was laughing at me. "Not so sure, Mutt was more of Jace's dog, and he just barely tolerated me."

Mrs. Eldridge was helping me to a sitting position with my legs over the side of the bed so I could eat the stew. She was talking the whole time about Mutt and myself, "Never kid yourself; Mutt may have been Jace's dog before, but he sure is your dog now. He saved your life."

I was starving and could not really remember the last time I had a decent enough meal and just as I was getting ready to dive right into that elk stew that was calling my name with the spoon in mid-air, I stopped and pondered Devon's last statement, "Saved my life? How did Mutt save my life?"

Devon took a step back and with a maternal concerned look on her face, "Chance, I am so sorry; I thought you already knew. The day of your run in with the Biggers and Hammond gang, Lucas and I were at the Coeur d' Alene gold mine just right above

our house across the Gregory Gulch. We have a part ownership in
the mine; anyway, we were outside the office when Mutt came off
the road to the west and proceeded to bark and howl like a wolf
with rabies. He was barking so much that Lucas pulled his
Winchester from his saddle scabbard and was about ready to shoot
Mutt. Lucas has an almost magical way with animals, and he
sensed that Mutt was not a threat to us and lowered his rifle. As
soon as Lucas did that, Mutt started to herd us to the west. We got
settled into our saddles and decided we better follow Mutt as he
led us to your gold mine. Of course we saw your brother Jace right
off and we thought that was what Mutt had wanted us to find.
Mutt then ran straight to the entrance of the mine and started
barking again, forcing us to dismount and check out the entrance.
As soon as Lucas heard you respond in the mine, he started to dig
and then sent me back to Coeur d' Alene mine for some help to
dig you out. So yes Chance, Mutt saved your life."

I tried to hide it, but did not succeed as a tear formed in my
eye thinking of Jace being shot and Mutt saving my life. I patted
the side of the bed to have Mutt come close enough so I could pet
him. Mutt just sat there. The frustration must have showed on my
face as Devon patted the same spot and Mutt immediately
responded and moved to that position. Smiling, but shaking my
head, I hugged and petted Mutt and he licked my face and hand a
few times. Needing to know the answer, but afraid to ask, "And
my brother Jace?"

Devon moved closer and took my hand as she sat down on
the side of the bed next to me. "With the summer heat and not
knowing when you were going to wake up, we buried Jace
yesterday in the Bald Mountain Cemetery just west of
Nevadaville, not far from your gold mine. When you feel up to it,
Lucas will take you to see your brother."

Having said that, Devon stood up suddenly because she had
also teared up and started to fuss around the room straightening
things and cleaning things that really did not need straightening
and cleaning. "Anyway Chance, you must eat now and gather
your strength back. You have been sleeping for three days and
have not had anything to eat."

My stomach also reminded me of that fact as the smell from the elk stew was almost overpowering. Looking at Devon, "Thank you Mrs. Eldridge for everything you and your husband have done for me. And soon as I am able, Mutt and I will take our leave so we are no longer a bother."

Devon gave me a stern look, but with a smile on her face she replied, "Well Chance, we will not have any of that type of talk, and Mutt and you are welcome to stay as long as you want. Now eat that stew before it gets any colder."

As Devon was turning to leave, she remembered something and turned back towards me, "Chance, we do have a telegraph office here in town, and I can bring some paper and a pencil so you can write messages to your folks or any other siblings."

Trying not to tear again and feeling less of a man every time I did in front of Mrs. Eldridge, I shook my head no. "Jace was all I had left; my folks died of the fever, and Jace and I buried them south of Dighton, Kansas next to our sod house. And besides that, I don't know how to write. Nobody in my family knew how."

Devon looked at me for a few moments before she replied, "Well then you are part of our family here in Central City. And for not knowing how to write, we will start your first lesson right after a hearty breakfast tomorrow. Now eat your stew and if you want more just holler, and I will bring you another bowl; we have plenty."

After finishing the excellent bowl of stew, I was still hungry, but I did not want to bother Mrs. Eldridge any more than I had already and was content to wait till morning. Having just had that thought, Mrs. Eldridge showed up with another bowl. "I already know you well enough, Chance; I knew you wouldn't holler for another bowl."

With a big smile Devon left the room so I could finish my supper. With a full belly now and the sunlight slowly disappearing through the lace curtains as the sun melted behind the mountains to the west, I could hardly keep my eyes open. I patted the bed next to me to call Mutt up on the bed, "Come on Mutt."

No Mutt! He just sat there looking at me. Chuckling to myself, I placed the bowl on the floor so Mutt could lick it clean, which he happily did. I closed my eyes and rolled over on my good side that had not been shot. Soon as Mutt was done with the bowl, he jumped up on the bed and cuddled up next to me. Reaching out to pet the half wolf dog, "Damn dog! I guess this is how it is going to be."

Mutt gave one bark as to acknowledge, "Yes, that was how it was going to be." We both settled down and fell asleep.

CHAPTER 4

Waking in the middle of the night to the sound of thunder in the distance and lightning flashes that lit up the room, I knew from past experience that being in the Rocky Mountains and closer to the heavens, the weather could turn quickly for the worse.

Lightning storms that I had experienced so far this first summer in the mountains got my heart racing; the bolts seemed to be brighter and thunder seemed to be louder than on the plains of Kansas. Maybe it was because the lightning had a shorter path from the heavens to the earth or the mountains reflected the light more, and the thunder rolled down the canyons and mountain ranges, gathering a louder roar. I was at a loss why the storms were more spectacular; I just knew that they were.

The first such storm that Jace and I had experienced scared the bejesus out of the both of us. After that we came to love the storms and looked forward to the fireworks show that the Lord put on display as if the Rockies and we were his only audience and the sky was his canvas.

Trying not to wake Mutt and failing, I gingerly got out of bed and made my way to the window that was facing west. Pulling up one of the wooden rockers, I slid open the window and the cool summer air drifted over me. Mutt got out of bed and came and lay back down by my feet as I watched the fireworks show above the mountains to the west. As the rain started to fall in a slant that kept it out of the window, I began to reflect on Jace and all things that had gotten me to this point.

One thing that I knew was that somehow, someway I was going to bring justice to the Biggers and Hammond gang for causing the death of Jace and burying me alive in the Bondurant mine, or I was going to die trying.

I had carved each of the six members of the gang's faces in my memory, and I was sure I would never forget what each of them looked like. Knowing it was foolish to want revenge and the little church going I, had tried to teach me that I should forgive those that had done Jace and myself harm, I could not forgive nor could I forget Jace lying there in the dirt of our camp with his blood soaking into the earth.

A brilliant bolt of lightning lit up the sky and on the either side of the gulch up the mountain a tad was a white wooden cross that seemed to glow in the aftermath of the blinding light. It was some sort of sign from the heavens, but this evening thinking only of revenge and vengeance, I could not decipher what the sign might mean.

Reaching down to stroke Mutt's black-tipped fur, I contemplated my life now and what it will be. I also realized I had no money, horse, nor weapons of any sort to bring about the justice that I wanted to hand out to the Biggers and Hammond gang. What I did have was the will and determination and of course a half wolf dog that would not listen to me. It was a start and for now it would have to do.

I was going to have to figure out a way to make a living and stake myself to start back digging at the Bondurant mine for the ever elusive gold and earn enough money to save to begin my ride for justice against the Biggers and Hammond gang.

Sitting here listening to the thunder as it rolled across the heavens and the mountains and watching the white cross and its eerie glow after each lightning bolt that blossomed in the heavens, I started to think about the area that Jace and I had adopted and called home here in Colorado. As long as Jace was in the Bald

Mountain Cemetery, this now would forever be my home to return to. Central City and the town of Blackhawk, which was just a smidgeon to the northeast of Central City, were so close together that most folks considered them as one town. Both towns and settlements were formed after John H. Gregory discovered a gold bearing vein smacked dab in the middle of both towns. Soon after, a flock of people arrived, which included out-of-work cowboys, miners, saloon keepers, soiled doves, and so many Chinese that it was not uncommon to hear the Chinese language being spoken just about everywhere you went in both encampments. All these folks were searching for the same thing - to acquire wealth that came in one form or another from the gold that was sprinkled across these mountains of old.

Jace and I were a tad late in reaching the area and all the land that could be claimed, for gold that was anywhere close to the original Gregory Lode had already been spoken for and we had to settle on a claim near Nevadaville.

Nevadaville was about a mile or so southwest of Central City. The town had all of the same origins of folks that populated the slightly bigger gold camps of Central City and Blackhawk. For some reason, though it seemed that there was a larger population of Irish in Nevadaville, and most of those were miners working the Burroughs lode and the Kansas lode.

The rain, lightning, and thunder slowly started to taper off as the storm made its way south. The white cross across the gulch I could no longer see in the darkness.

Jace and I had made more money than we had ever seen mining the Bondurant mine, but now I was going to have to start all over again and dig out and stabilize the entrance again by myself. Not an easy task, but it was my only option at this point. I would have to learn to live off the land while trying to make enough money to buy the essentials such as food, horse, and picks and shovels. And I must also buy a pistol with some ammo and practice with it till I was good enough to take down the Biggers and Hammond gang. Maybe Mr. Eldridge could give me a pointer or two. Thinking of Lucas and Devon, I tried to recall what I knew of them besides the obvious that they had and were being so good to me by saving my life and letting me heal up in their beautiful home.

Having only seen Lucas briefly, I could tell he was probably ten years older than I was and powerfully built with ebony hair. He was probably about 6'2" and weighed I am guessing close to 210 pounds. Of course he was famous as a gunfighter being in several shootouts with outlaws. The most famous shootout was when he gunned down the Verdugo brothers. I heard the tale that he tracked them for two years after they had savagely murdered his first wife. He killed the younger brother Jose on top of Boreas Pass in between Como and Breckenridge, Colorado. It was at that time he had rescued Devon after the brothers had kidnapped her. His most talked about shoot out and the one you would always hear around the campfires was with the older Verdugo brother Juan in Silver Plume, Colorado. It was said that a bartender named Bill Termes took a hand in the fight and saved Lucas' life from a relative of the Verdugo brothers who had been lying in wait to ambush Lucas after he had been severely wounded after killing Juan in the Silver Plume Saloon.

It would seem that Lucas and Devon had married sometime after he saved her from the Verdugo brothers.

Devon Eldridge was probably the most beautiful woman I had ever seen. She was so beautiful she seemed out of place in this rugged Colorado Rocky Mountain gold camp. She was small in stature with red hair, not flaming red hair, but subtle like the glow of an evening sunset. Her eyes were something else, and I had to fight myself not to be rude and stare at them. They were almond-shaped and bright green with a hint of blue. Lucas and Devon seemed to be made for each other, and I felt privileged to have met them.

So much thinking of what had been and things that might be had worn me out, and I needed to get back to sleep. Delicately pulling my aching body out of the rocker, I made my way back to the comforts of the bed. After lying back down, I patted the bed beside me and spoke, "Here Mutt, come on buddy."

Mutt didn't seem to hear or he cared less as he did not budge. Chuckling to myself, "Okay Mutt I get it, you have a mind all to yourself. I reckon I am much the same myself and never much liked people ordering me around much."

Rolling over on my good side, I closed my eyes. Just before I drifted off to sleep, Mutt jumped back onto the bed and cuddled next to me and after finding a comfortable spot, it was not long before we were both sound asleep.

CHAPTER 5

Waking up to the sound of Mutt snoring next to me on the bed with his head resting on my right leg, I lay there for a few minutes gathering my senses and trying to take inventory of my body. I seemed to feel better with less soreness in all my muscles, and my bullet wound was healing fast in the high mountain air with no infection.

Slowly getting out of bed and halfway through the motion of trying not to disturb the half wolf dog Mutt, I started to chuckle thinking, "Why am I worried about waking up a dog that does not listen to me?"

Swinging my legs faster, I watched Mutt's wolfish head fall to one side, and his eyes flew open, giving me the ole' stink eye. Now standing with a smile, I reached over and gave him a good ruffle of his fur on his neck, and he rolled over and exposed his belly for a rub, which I promptly gave him. As Mutt was eating up the belly rub, my smile slowly disappeared because I realized up until this moment Mutt would only expose his belly that way for a good ole' rub to Jace. Mutt must have read my mind because his head turned in such a manner that told me he was missing Jace also. With one better rub, I stood up and started to dress, thinking I had been lying around long enough and should at least make an appearance at the breakfast table.

Without speaking a word to Mutt, I jumped out of bed and headed downstairs, and I heard Devon say as she opened the front door, "About time, Mr. Mutt."

Devon and Lucas did seem pleased that I joined them for a hearty breakfast of flapjacks, chicken eggs, and elk sausage.

After breakfast and drinking some hot tea, Lucas explained he had acquired a taste for the British beverage while he was recuperating from a bullet wound at his good friends Bill and Barb Termes' home in Silver Plume after his gun battle with Juan Verdugo and now preferred it over coffee in the morning.

Lucas also went on to explain how Devon and he had ended up living in Central City. He had taken the bounty money he had acquired for the Verdugo brothers and invested in the Coeur d' Alene gold mine and now were part owners in it. As they made some money, they also began investing in other mines in the area. Lucas then set his teacup down, leaned forward, rested his elbows on the table and asked, "So, Chance, what are your plans now?"

I had been up most of the night during the lightning and thunderstorm pondering that very same question, but having it actually spoken to me, it seemed all the planning I had thought of last night seemed rather foolish and stupid. I really didn't have a clue on what or how to proceed. "Well, Mr. Eldridge, I feel like a bother here and I think I should be well enough tomorrow to get back to the Bondurant mine and get back to work and make some money. I feel that I need to do something to make those men in the Biggers and Hammond gang pay for what they did to Jace and that will take money. I really do not have a choice at this point, so that is the best answer I can give you for now."

Having said my piece and hearing it come out of my mouth, I felt foolish because it really was not much of a plan. Lucas and Devon were quiet as I spoke my mind, and I could only wonder how they must think of me now. Lucas looked at Devon for a few seconds, and she slowly nodded her head "yes."

Lucas, still with his elbows on the table and with an even voice, "Well Chance, I see that you have given your future a lot of thought and I admire that. As for wanting to bring justice to those that have wronged Jace and yourself, I can also relate, because I reckon I am much the same myself. Devon and I have a business deal for you. We would like to become your partner in the Bondurant mine and purchase 50 percent for $500. What would you think of that?"

$500? I had never seen that much money, nor did I ever imagine I would ever have that much money at one time. Pondering it for a few seconds, "49 percent for $500 so I can keep the controlling interest in the Bondurant mine."

Slowly Lucas leaned back in his chair with sort of a blank look, seemingly studying me. A smile broke out on his face and he turned to Devon, who already had a huge grin, and she once again nodded her head "yes."

Reaching out his hand to shake mine and still with a smile on his face, "Well Chance, it seems we have a deal - with one stipulation."

Stopping the handshake in mid-shake, "Stipulation?"

Lucas still with a smile, but in an even tone of voice, "Yes, you have to give the Bondurant mine and our partnership two years. You need to learn many things, Chance, before you can seek the justice against the Biggers and Hammond gang. So, the deal requires you spend two years here working the mine. If you decide to leave earlier on the vengeance trail, then you forfeit your 51 percent ownership to Devon and myself. That is the stipulation. Take it or leave it."

Pondering the stipulation, I realized it would take me at least two years or longer to acquire and earn enough money to track down the Biggers and Hammond gang. Plus, there also was another factor - I did not handle firearms very well. I needed to be more proficient in the use of them. I needed time to learn.

It seemed to be a win, win situation and a smile broke out across my face, and I started the handshake again. "Fair enough, Mr. Eldridge, I agree to the two year stipulation."

Devon spoke up for the first time, "Chance, you and Mutt can stay here in the house with us until you feel you want to move.

Also today you will have some errands to run with Lucas to finalize the partnership so you have a busy day ahead, so school for you starts tomorrow."

Somewhat confused at what was going to happen, I questioned, "School?"

Devon still with a smile and nodding her head "yes" several times, "Yes Chance, school. We can't have a business partner not knowing how to read or do his numbers can we? So my stipulation which neither Lucas nor you can overrule is that you have to attend my school three days a week until I am satisfied our partner can read and write and do his numbers."

Looking at Lucas, who kind of just shrugged his shoulders like "What can we do, she has spoken," I felt I had to agree. "Okay Mrs. Eldridge, I agree to that stipulation also."

After breakfast and our first business meeting, Lucas and I headed to the bank in Central City and started two bank accounts. One was my first bank account of my life which Lucas deposited $300 into, and the second account was for the newly formed partnership of the Bondurant Mine. I deposited my remaining $200 from the sale of 49 percent of the mine, and a matching $200 from Lucas was deposited in for working capital.

After seeing and taking care of the first steps in our new business venture, Lucas said it was "time to focus on Chance," and we stopped off at the dry goods store and purchased some work clothes and a set of going around town clothes. After dressing in my new Levi Strauss jeans, boots, and flannel shirt, I felt like a king. I even bought a new black cowboy hat that had a cattleman crease. Not just a hat, but a Stetson "Boss of the Plains" hat. A fellow named John B. Stetson had started his hat making company back east in Philadelphia and now was considered the "Hat of the West" which included the Rocky Mountain region.

After purchasing and trying on my new Stetson, I remarked on how Lucas should buy a new hat for himself because he's had a rather nasty looking hole in his hat. Lucas took off his bullet-riddled hat and stared at it for a moment or two and stated, "Maybe another time, Chance. This ole' hat and I have been through some tough times together, and I have grown sort of sentimental toward this ragged looking head warmer." Having said that, he reshaped it some and snapped it back on his head.

After purchasing my new clothes, Lucas helped me in picking out a new Colt 44 pistol, a leather holster, and a Winchester rifle. He spent more than an hour choosing the right pistol for me. He checked the action of the hammer and triggers of several Colt pistols before finding one that met his approval.

The next stop was the livery stable where I purchased the most beautiful horse I had ever seen, a mare named Storm. She was a magnificent looking animal that showed all muscle when she walked and looked to have a powerful stride. Pure black except for two snow white stockings on her forelegs that stretched all the way up to where her legs connected to her chest, which gave her an almost eerie look of a horse that didn't have any front legs. Mutt had tagged along, and Storm had seemed to take a liking to Mutt and was not bothered by Mutt sniffing and checking her out. Storm even twice in that first meeting between the two bent down and playfully shoved Mutt with her nose hard enough to make him stumble. Mutt responded by crouching in attack mode with his tail wagging feverishly back and forth. Smiling, knowing they were meant to be with each other, I knew my only hope was that Storm would listen to me better than Mutt.

After getting my outfit, Storm my mare, and weapons, I felt ready to take on the world. I could only hope to live up to the expectations that Lucas and Devon had for me. I had agreed to the two year stipulation on our partnership and felt somewhat guilty about it. Feeling selfish in my wants and needs because I needed to first get my feet back on the ground and with the help of Lucas and Devon, I had done that. There was so much for me to learn in the way of mountains and life, and I was smart enough to realize that the two years gave me the opportunity to do that. I knew deep in my heart and mind that the next two years were meant for me to gain courage and the skills I needed to seek the justice and vengeance that the six members of the Biggers and Hammond gang had coming. I would embrace the next two years with all my energy and devotion and work hard at the Bondurant mine and getting the education I needed beyond reading and writing and doing my numbers. The Lord had put me in the path of one Lucas

Eldridge, famous righteous gunfighter, for a reason, and I would not question why. All I could do was learn from the best.

Lucas' and my errands had eaten up most of this cool and sunny summer day. I felt the need to visit Jace's grave at the Bald Mountain cemetery. Lucas made his way to his office at the Coeur d' Alene mine, and I started the two mile climb to the cemetery just west of Nevadaville astride Storm. Without asking Mutt to join me because I knew he would anyway because he had a mind of his own, I turned Storm and headed west. Mutt did not want to be left out and realizing where I was going decided to take the lead in front of Storm.

The ride to the cemetery, though short, seemed to take a long time. I was getting to know Storm more and was pleased with her powerful stride, and I could feel her muscles as she made her way through the evergreens and aspens.

The lateness of the day had the sun just over the top of the mountains full in my face. The warmth felt good and invigorating. The air was cool, but it was always cooler at these higher altitudes when you were closer to the heavens than I was accustomed to on the prairie of Lane County, Kansas.

Finding Jace's grave was a simple affair. It was the only fresh grave amongst the headstones and wooden crosses. Jace's grave was marked by a stone cross about four feet tall and two feet across and read simply Jace Bondurant, Beloved Brother.

Dismounting Storm, I tied her off to a nearby evergreen tree branch fearing that she had not known me well enough yet not to wander off. Mutt, the half wolf and half something else dog, showed his sadness when he lay right on top of the grave and howled to the heavens for a full minute or two. Listening to Mutt's haunting rendition of grief brought more than a few tears to my eyes as I sat down next to Mutt on top of the grave. Mutt, feeling my discomfort, felt the need to reassure me and lay his head in my lap.

I stroked Mutt's fur to ease his grief as much as my own; the memories of my life with Jace flooded my mind. Most of the memories seemed as if they happened yesterday and were full of life and color - swimming and taking a bath in the pond next to our sod house; summer days just like today catching minnows, crawdads and pollywogs; working side-by-side in the hot and dusty fields, helping our father; telling each other our dreams at night watching the stars and the moon; and holding him close and telling him it would be all right after our folks had died. All of these and many more memories flipped faster and faster through my mind like fanning a deck of cards. All these memories hurt; every one of these memories I would forever hold close to my heart, even the ones I would like to forget...forever. The one memory that I had to keep and forever recall at a moment's notice was the one where Jace had been shot in the head. Seeing his body crumble to the ground was something I could never forget. I needed to focus on this image. I had to remember this dreadful image so I could recall what needed to be done in the regards of the Biggers and Hammond gang. Justice would be served. It was going to take time, and the Lord willing I would be the one to serve it on the six men that had caused the death of my little brother.

Darkness had fallen and a slight breeze got the evergreen needles and the aspens' leaves to start the music of the night. I had grown to love the music of the mountains when the wind stirred the leaves and pine needles in the trees that made the trees whisper their songs. Not far off a night owl started to hoot, and the half wolf in Mutt gave into his wild nature and returned a long howl. This eerie howl was hauntingly appropriate for the night and the situation as Mutt and I both mourned the loss of Jace.

Lying down next to the grave as the moon made its arc across the cloudless sky, Mutt gathered up close with his big grayish wolf head lying on my chest, and we both fell asleep.

CHAPTER 6

T he next two years went by in a whirlwind. I never did move out of the Eldridge house at 225 Hooper Street in Central City. I worked and studied hard at everything that life presented to me in the form of schooling and running the Bondurant gold mine. Not only could I read and write and do my numbers thanks to Devon, but I also discovered the world in the numerous books that I read that included the bible, but also from some great authors such as Charles Dickens, Edgar Allen Poe, Walt Whitman, and my favorite author, Ralph Waldo Emerson.

The Bondurant gold mine under the leadership of Lucas and myself made a moderate, but good living. The mine that Jace and I had discovered and started would never make me a rich man but gave me enough to live a fine life in the mountain towns of Central City and Blackhawk.

Storm and Mutt became my constant companions wherever I went. Storm and I connected so well; she knew my mind and listened to me with the utmost attention. I could not have asked for a better horse than Storm. Mutt, well Mutt is Mutt! In the two years following Jace's death, the half wolf and half something else dog developed into my best friend. I never became his master, for Mutt had a mind of his own. I never scolded him nor did I ever call him to me. Mutt seems to know my mind and most times would anticipate my moods and feelings and either comfort or stay away from me, depending on how he read my mood. Mutt and Storm were one of a kind animals, and I found them both to be more intelligent than most people I ran across.

In the two years I lived at the Eldridge house Devon, even though she was only ten years older than I was, became almost like a mother figure to me. I trusted her judgment and valued her friendship like no other woman in my life. Her physical beauty was beyond question; she also did not seem to know how beautiful she really was. Lucas told me numerous times that was what made her so special on the inside. Devon Eldridge would become the woman against whom I would gauge all women in my life. Thinking that last thought, I chuckled to myself, for it hardly seemed fair to the other women that I might meet in the future.

Lucas in two years became my mentor and teacher of how men should be. He was a gentle and loving man unless you crossed him or took something that he valued highly; then he became a man not to be trifled with, a very dangerous man.

Every free moment of my time, I spent with Lucas as he taught me the way of the Rocky Mountains. We took many trips to the land of forever snow above timberline and to the top of the world called the "Great Divide" where all rivers began as droplets as they made their way downward the west slope or the east slope of the divide to form the great rivers of Colorado. The Colorado River, Platte River, Clear Creek, Yampa River, Blue River, Gunnison River and the Cache la Poudre River all started somewhere across the Rocky Mountain spine called the "Great Divide" that stretched clear across the territory of what now was being called Colorado Territory.

Lucas taught me how to survive in the mountains in all four seasons - summer, fall, winter, and spring. He also told me the old joke that the mountain men would tell of how the mountains really only had three seasons - summer, winter, and mud. When he would tell me that joke, it was always followed with a smile because it was so true. He told me that most men fought the elements and the mountains, which he said, was a mistake. He told me the trick of survival in the high mountains was not fighting the elements and the altitude and weather, but instead learning to love it and to understand how it all was part of the Lord's master plan - that you had to realize that the mountains were here long before I was and will still be here long after I was dead and buried.

Lucas taught me wilderness skills, and I was a willing pupil. Through his teaching, I learned many things such as swimming, mountain climbing, unarmed combat skills with a knife and tomahawk, hunting, sign reading, horsemanship, trapping, and survival under extreme conditions. It was not long before I became a master of all and an equal to that of Lucas, my teacher.

As a young man Lucas spent time living with the Ute Indians that called the Rocky Mountains home long before the white man ever set foot in them. Lucas' religious belief was based on Christianity, but he realized that the Ute Indian spirits were also a strong force in nature. The Ute Indians had many nature gods that controlled weather, rain, animals, people, and harvests. Lucas told me he learned his way with animals when he lived among the Utes and had a sixth sense with all animals which was true because I had seen him with his horses. He had a way of communicating to them without ever speaking, and wild animals seemed to be drawn to him and Lucas had a way with them also. He told me of the spirit of the crow, which was associated with all life's mysteries, but also of death.

He taught me how to rely on animals for danger signs and also told me of a heartbreaking killing of a beloved horse named Misty when trailing the Verdugo brothers because he didn't heed his horse's warning. Lucas was patient with me as he taught me the way of the Utes. He respected them and their teaching and passed that respect on to me. I knew I was a better man for it.

Lucas and I never spoke of it, but we both knew that I was getting ready for an encounter with the Bigger and Hammond gang. Under Lucas' tutelage I became proficient in the use of firearms, namely my Colt 44 and my Winchester rifle. I learned how to care for my weapons in a professional manner and how to draw my pistol with the speed and accuracy of gunfighters such as

Wild Bill, Johnny Ringo, and Jake Slade. My speed in palming my Colt pistol was even on par with Lucas himself.

Toward the end of that second year in the spring Lucas, Mutt, and I had stopped on top of Rollins Pass, which was part of the "Great Divide" and topped out halfway in between 11,000 and 12,000 feet. The top of the pass was roughly about 24 miles northwest from Central City. We had dismounted and had a lunch of elk jerky and some butter biscuits that Devon had sent along for our journey. The sun was at its highest arc in the sky that was filled with huge clouds that floated in the forever blue sky. As we looked toward the east, we could see down below into the high mountain plateau that some had started to call Middle Park. I would never get accustomed to the grandeur of the view from this lofty position on top of the world; it was always awe-inspiring and made me feel so trivial in the world. We watched an eagle's flight in silence as it flew toward the west and Middle Park, and I realized it had covered more ground in just a few minutes than any man on a good horse could cover in a day. It was at this moment when Lucas told me the difference between life and death in a gunfight.

Lucas, who was a man who had killed men in gunfights several times in his past, went on to explain no matter how fast of a draw you are or how accurate you are with a Colt pistol, there will always be someone faster, more accurate, or just plain luckier than you are. The difference all came down to if you had a "killer instinct" or not - the ability to put your mind outside of your body and focus on the only thing that mattered at that exact moment of time before you drew your weapon. You had to have the ability to place your fear of death aside; you had to have a black heart; and you had to be able to focus on all things that could affect the outcome, such as the placement of the sun, the wind, or even a droplet of sweat. All this focus had to happen in the mere seconds before, during, and after you drew your weapon. You had to become a killer in all sense of the word and go against everything you had ever read in the bible. The bible taught us we are supposed to forgive those that have harmed us or the ones we loved. As much as we wanted to believe this, we had to realize that man was and always will be a predator. As in the way of the world and nature, only the strong survive. In the wild in the Rocky Mountains, the bear, mountain lion, and the wolves were king because they were stronger than the rest. It was the same for man. If you were not tougher, stronger, or did not have the killer instinct, you were just a future victim of men such as those that rode with the Bigger and Hammond gang. Having a "killer instinct" gave you the advantage to survive when everything else was equal.

During those two years that I took learning my trade as a mine owner; learning how to read and write; learning the way of the mountains; and learning to hone my "killer instinct," I never lost track of the Bigger and Hammond gang. They still were robbing and stealing and murdering folks from Arizona to Colorado. They always kept on the move, staying a step ahead of any law. The governor had placed a dead or alive bounty on all six heads of the famous gang.

I felt the day of retribution was fast approaching. I was ready as I ever was going to be.

CHAPTER 7

Mutt woke up first and started to fidget on the bed. It was his way of telling me it was time to get up. I had left the window open last night and my room had grown cold. Standing and walking to the window, I pulled out the block of wood that had been propping up the window and slowly lowered it so it was shut and to keep the cold out. Looking through the broad glass window, I got a wavy and distorted view of autumn fast approaching in the mountains. Looking west across Gregory Gulch, I saw that the aspen trees had started their turn of color and the green leaves now were a mixture of green sprinkled with gold.

As I always did when looking out this window, I spent a minute or two looking up the hill to the white wooden cross that I had seen glow eerily the first night I was in this room two years ago during a lightning and thunderstorm. That old white wooden cross had become a symbol of peace and solace to me. Somehow just looking at it from time to time gave me strength; it was comforting to me.

Today was Sunday and I dressed quickly because I knew Devon was expecting Lucas and me to accompany her to the Lutheran church service today. Devon understood that Lucas and I during the summer months would be spending most of our free time in the mountains, but it was also understood when it started to cool off during the fall and winter that we were expected to attend church with her.

Mutt led the way down the stairs and was their routine, Devon opened the front door for him as the half wolf headed outdoors. Breakfast was already on the table, and Lucas was already seated reading the Gilpin County newspaper.

Already digging into the eggs and bacon and butter biscuits that Devon had prepared, Lucas laid down the newspaper in front of me and without a word he pointed at an article on the front page.

I read the paper as I finished eating my breakfast; it reported of recent sightings of the Biggers and Hammond gang. Two weeks ago, they were involved in a robbery and shoot out with Anton Stark in the main street of Saint Elmo, Colorado just a couple of miles south of Buena Vista. Anton was wounded but expected to live. No one from the Biggers and Hammond gang seemed to catch a bullet. Four days later the gang had been seen in Fairplay, Colorado, which was roughly 60 miles northeast of Saint Elmo in the South Park region. A couple of days later it was reported they had robbed some gold miners at the base of Webster Pass still further north of the towns of Como and Jefferson. It was evident that the Biggers and Hammond gang was heading north in their quest to rob and steal what they could from hard working folks. They were headed north in my direction.

Lucas was watching me read the newspaper after he had finished his breakfast and was sipping his hot tea. "Seems that you may have to choose the direction of your life soon, Chance."

Without saying a word I nodded "yes" as a response to his statement. Lucas added, "You have grown into a man the last couple of years that most men would be envious of. You have a fine life and a bright future in front of you if you stay here in Central City. You also have acquired a set of unique skills that will make you better than most men in either path you choose. If after two years you still feel the need to right the wrong that was inflicted on your family, I reckon I can understand that better than most. Devon and I just wanted you to know that whatever path you choose, be it to serve justice on the Biggers and Hammond gang or simply to forgive and let the Lord in the end serve the righteous justice they have coming, we support you no matter what."

Not sure how to respond and what to say, I said nothing. Lucas understood the conflict that was pulling at my soul. Feeling slightly uncomfortable, I stood to help move the dishes off the breakfast table when Devon started her daily fuss over me as if I was her five year old son. She started to use her fingers to comb my shoulder length brown hair. This fussing always got a smile and chuckle out of Lucas. Of course I just let her fuss. What else could I do? After combing my hair and straightening my collar of my shirt, Devon took a step back and remarked, "Chance, you have grown into a right handsome young man that any woman would be proud to call her own."

Growing up here in the high mountains with hard physical work, I had gained a good 30 pounds of muscle that made me weigh about 210 pounds that was stacked on my 6'2" frame. I knew I was much stronger than most men and could work harder and faster. I had gained the respect of the older miners when I worked right alongside of them at the Bondurant mine.

Lucas leaned forward with a look of concern and pointed at the front of my shirt, "Chance, are you sure you have your shirt buttoned correctly?"

Of course that was all the encouragement that Devon needed to go into full mother mode again as she started to pull and straighten out my shirt as she inspected my buttons to make sure they were lined up and buttoned correctly. I gave Lucas the ole' stink eye that was meant to convey that he was an "asshole."

With a full grin Lucas stood and strapped on his holster and tied it down to his right leg. Still grinning, he snapped on his hat that had the bullet hole in it and headed out the door.

After Devon was satisfied, I did indeed have my shirt buttoned correctly, I did the same and followed Lucas. After I helped Lucas saddle Devon's horse Diamond, his horse Breeze, and of course my horse Storm, Lucas started to laugh, "I am sorry Chance, it just tickles my fancy to watch you stand there while Devon fusses over you."

Laughing myself, I replied, "Doesn't make you any less of an asshole Lucas."

Still laughing Lucas said, "I reckon not."

Once we arrived at church this cool autumn morning, Mutt decided as he always did to remain outside lying by the front door. Everyone in town knew Mutt and talked to him and pet him as they made their way into the church. Mutt was a popular fellow around town and seemed to enjoy all the attention.

After we were planted in our pew, I looked back toward the front entrance and watched the people as they went about their normal Sunday routine of visiting and finding their seats.

I was a little surprised to see the Dutchman, James Balkema as he entered the church. He was new to the Central City and Black Hawk area and lived in Russell Gulch, which was south of the Eldridge house and Gregory Gulch. Mr. Balkema sold hardware and mining equipment, and we just started to do business with him buying such things as shovels and sluice boxes. I was even more surprised when the rest of the family entered. The older woman with her hair starting to turn gray was obviously his wife, and two stout looking boys probably 14 and 15 entered following their mother and looking a little peevish that they had to attend church this morning.

What really caught my eye was his daughter who was trailing the rest of the family as they found a pew that would seat them all. She was probably 17 or 18 and beautiful with long blonde hair tied into a simple ponytail in the back with a pink and blue ribbon. She smiled as her Dad introduced her to the Patton family. Her smile lit up the room. Devon caught my gaze and with a smile gave me a friendly jab in the ribs with her elbow, "It would seem Chance Bondurant you are smitten."

Lucas caught the action of Devon giving me an elbow and looked back and saw the Dutchman's daughter too. He looked at me and smiled and rolled his eyes, "I am not saying anything Chance, and you are on your own on this one."

Feeling embarrassed and slightly peevish myself that I got caught staring at the Dutch girl, I turned toward the front and picked up the hymnal and pretended to read.

After the sermon and the service, I made the mistake of stopping to speak to a man about my age that worked at the Bondurant mine, which slowed down my quick exit out of the church. Devon, with Lucas in tow, made a beeline for the Dutch family, the Balkema's.

Trying to plan an exit so I would not have to walk by the Eldridge's and Balkema's as they exchanged pleasantries and seeing none, I tried to wait them out. They talked so long I was finally the last person still in the church and feeling like a fool because it was obvious I was trying to wait them out. Lucas was getting a kick out of this by his noticeable grin as he kept glancing back my way. Even Mutt, my half wolf dog who was sitting at the front door watching me, seemed amused.

Devon finally glanced my way and started to wave me over, "There you are Chance, come over here and meet the Balkema's."

With no way to retreat I slowly made my way to where everyone was standing. When I got closer, Devon grabbed my arm and moved me even closer and positioned me right in front of the blonde Dutch girl. "This is Chance Bondurant, a business partner in the Bondurant venture."

Reaching out and grabbing Mr. Balkema's hand to give a firm shake, I mumbled something along the line, "it was good to see him again."

Mr. Balkema began to introduce the rest of his family and started with his wife and boys; their names did not register with me as I was mesmerized by the young girl's stunning blue eyes. When it came time to introduce his daughter, I sort of snapped out of the fog I found myself in and actually caught her name. Gesturing toward the blond hair beauty, Mr. Balkema said, "And this is my oldest Ronda Joy."

On hearing Ronda's name Devon replied, "Joy, isn't that a beautiful name. Is that a family name?"

Mr. Balkema replied with a smile as he was looking at Devon, "Family name? No, it just seemed fitting since she was my bundle of Joy!"

I was looking right at Ronda when her father said that, and Ronda sort of smiled and rolled her eyes. Of course she did that so her father couldn't see it. You could tell she was over the embarrassment of hearing that tidbit, probably, been hearing it all her life. I liked her immediately.

In a few moments with all the introductions and pleasantries out of the way, the Balkema's made their exit followed by the Eldridge's and then myself. Mutt, my half wolf and half something else dog, gathered up alongside me and gave me a quizzical look like, "What the hell was that all about?"

After stepping into the stirrup to mount Storm my mare, I spun her around to get one last look at Ronda Joy as her family loaded into their wagon. Ronda looked over her shoulder and gave me one of her smiles that in just a short time I had learned to love. Not missing a beat, Devon caught the whole exchange as I gave Storm some rein and a slight jab of my spur and galloped down the road before Devon could say anything.

Trying to get my mind off of the Dutch girl, Ronda Joy, and the inevitable teasing that I knew would be awaiting me at home with Lucas, I headed to Russell Gulch which was just south of the Eldridge house just over two miles.

Russell Gulch was a gold mining town that was founded when William Russell discovered placer deposits of gold, which were quickly worked out. Gold recovery quickly shifted to the vein deposits that were the source of the placer gold. Russell Gulch was located at the top of Virginia Canyon and five miles to the bottom of the canyon was the mining camp of Idaho Springs. Most of the locals called the Virginia Canyon road the "Ole' My God" road, either for its spectacular views or sheer drop offs of the canyon sides as you rode your horse to the bottom. It was not a horseback or buggy ride that was for the faint hearted.

As was Mutt's custom, he was out in front of Storm as we rode down Main Street. He already knew where I was headed - the "Tommy Knocker" saloon. Lucas and I from time to time would stop here while we were doing business in the camp for lunch and a hand of poker or two.

As I dismounted Storm, I took the rawhide thong off the hammer of my Colt to free it up. Lucas had taught me "trouble comes when you least expect it and you better be ready."

As Mutt and I entered through the bat wing doors of the Tommy Knocker Saloon, we stopped to survey the room for any potential trouble. Jake the bartender was alone at the bar and restocking the whiskey bottles. At the card table sat four gents and Lorraine "Blaze" Mays, the card dealer and owner of the saloon. "Blaze" was a middle aged woman with long dark hair with a streak of gray, which seemed only fitting for her. She still was a good looking woman that turned the head of any man who saw her. The rumor was she got her nickname "Blaze" for setting fire to her old boss's saloon back east somewhere before she headed to Colorado and Russell Gulch. I asked her about the name one time. "It was like this, Chance; my boss was my lover and I caught him cheating on me with a new gal that he hired and I decided it was time to leave him and head to Colorado as I always wanted to do. I just left him something to remember."

I always liked "Blaze." Hell, I was half scared not to.

Thinking I would sit in for a hand or two, I took a step toward the table with Mutt in tow. Mutt stopped and started growling and the hair stood up on his back. Knowing Mutt was never one to growl unless there was a good reason, I started to study the four men a little more closely. Three I had never seen before and did not know. The fourth man, when he turned his head to see what the ruckus was with Mutt, I noticed was minus one ear below his sweat stained cowboy hat, his left ear.

Chucky Livingston, youngest member of the Biggers and Hammond gang, was sitting at the table. He was about my age, maybe a little older with a thin build and dirty short blonde hair. As he turned, I could see his gun rig and it was a Colt with a tied down holster with the butt turned back for a conventional draw. The one that pulled the trigger and killed my brother was sitting not more than 30 feet away.

I had not forgotten what he looked like. I had etched his face into my memory.

When Chucky spoke, I could see his teeth were stained from too much chewing tobacco. "Calm that flea bag down or I will put a bullet into it."

Quick as can be "Blaze" pulled her one shot derringer pistol and stuck it in Chucky's ear, well if he had an ear, "I don't like you much mister and I like that dog."

Chucky was taken by surprise with "Blaze's" move, but that would not be the last of his surprises here today.

Everything - the tick of the clock, the sound of the wind outside, the smell of the whiskey in the shot glasses - flooded my senses. Controlling my anger and focusing on all things around, I spoke with an even voice, "Thanks Blaze, but that won't be necessary. I have something I need to discuss with Mr. Livingston."

Blaze looked almost as confused as Chucky and reluctantly withdrew her derringer from the ugly side of Livingston's face. Chucky was not happy to hear I knew his name as he stood slowly. Looking bewildered, "How do you know me, boy?"

Blaze and the other three men wisely decided it was time to move to the other side of the saloon.

Looking into Chucky's eyes and speaking in a level tone, "Not surprised you don't remember me since I have grown a little and added some muscle since the last time you saw me. I am surprised you don't recall the dog that chewed your ear off."

Chucky's face first went blank and then it tensed as the recognition of who Mutt and I were, "You both are dead! Both of you!"

The moment was close at hand as I spoke again, "No Chucky, you and the others failed in killing Mutt and myself. The only thing you accomplished was killing my unarmed and helpless brother. Today, you pay the price for that!"

The tick of the saloon clock sounded like thunder in the silence of the room for six ticks. Chucky went for his gun. Instinct and all my training went into action as I palmed my Colt and my first shot caught Chucky about a foot above his belt buckle; my second landed just below his throat; and my third was placed nicely in between his eyes before he ever even cleared leather.

Chucky was dead before his body thumped to the floor in a puddle of ever growing blood.

I didn't feel anything. No hatred or happiness, absolutely nothing. At that moment I was empty of any human feeling other than I had done what needed to be done. The slayer of my brother was now dead, and I was the one who had served the righteous justice on him.

Mutt, after seeing the one that had killed Jace lying dead on the floor of the "Tommy Knocker" saloon, walked over and sniffed Chucky Livingston's now very dead body and promptly lifted his leg on him. Seemed like a proper send off to me.

CHAPTER 8

S till looking at Chucky Livingston, I reloaded my pistol not knowing if there were any more members of the Biggers and Hammond gang in town.

The saloon started to fill with folks that either heard the gunshots or just found out about the shooting. Mutt, satisfied that justice had been served to the killer of his former owner and friend, took a stand at the door. I knew that he would alert me to the presence of any or all of the remaining Biggers and Hammond gang members. Mutt, like myself, would never forget what each one of them looked like. In Mutt's case I was sure he also would be able to smell their outlaw stink.

The next several hours were spent with Russell Gulch's young, newly appointed Mexican sheriff Daniel Sierra. This was the new sheriff's first big happening in town, and he seemed to be handling it with the professionalism of a much older sheriff. Sheriff Sierra had Blaze and the three men who had witnessed the gunfight write down and record the account of what had happened. He had his deputy and right hand man go back to his office to retrieve the dead or alive wanted poster on the now dead Chucky Livingston.

The deputy in a short time returned with the wanted poster, and Sheriff Sierra was convinced that the drawing of Livingston on the poster matched the dead man lying on the floor of the "Tommy Knocker" saloon. He told me he would wire Denver for the release of the $400 dollar bounty and have it sent to his office.

I was still not feeling any emotions at all. I felt as if only part of the job had been completed, knowing that there were still five members of the Biggers and Hammond gang still alive. All five of the outlaws were probably close; I had never heard of them not being bunched together.

After the sheriff was done with his investigation into the shooting, all I wanted to do was go home and go to sleep, knowing in that moment I drew my weapon and killed Livingston that my life and how I lived it was forever changed. I needed time to think and be alone.

Slipping a $20 gold piece in the hand of the Tommy Knocker owner's hand, I gave her my apologies for what had happened. Lorraine "Blaze" Mays tried to refuse the money, saying, "It was part of the business."

With nothing more to say, I squeezed Blaze's hand with the gold coin, meaning she had to keep it. I turned and walked out of the saloon through the bat wing doors right past Mutt, without saying a word to the half wolf who fell in behind me as I made my way to the hitching post and Storm.

As I was about to mount Storm, the Dutch family, the Balkema's and Ronda Joy were just now entering Russell Gulch's main street from the east. Taking my foot out of the stirrup and placing it back on the ground, I looked at the beautiful blue-eyed blonde and tried to think of the pleasure that I felt in seeing her earlier in the day at church.

Mutt started to growl again and was looking past me to the west to the center of Main Street away from the Balkema's. Knowing this was probably a sign that more trouble and bullets might be headed my way, I pushed Storm to the side hoping to get my mare out of the way from catching a stray bullet. Storm seemed to sense the danger and pawed the ground several times with her hoof and snorted a couple of times.

Turning to the west and walking in the middle of the street, I saw the eastern one-eyed gunman Dave Edgar standing there. Not much was known about the small gunfighter other than he was deadly accurate with both of his Colts. Taking up a position about 30 yards in front of Edgar, I took a moment to size up my adversary. He was small, about 5' 6" tall and weighing about 140 pounds. He had short dark hair that matched his black eye patch over his left eye. His stance spoke of a man who did not fear anyone or anything. He wore a black gun belt that matched his cotton pants and shirt. He wore his pistols in a cross draw manner with the handles facing forward.

Lucas always said that men who wore their guns in such a manner thought they were fast on the draw and always looking to prove it. Edgar's voice when he spoke sort of surprised me how deep it was for a man so small in stature. "I heard you beat Chucky in a fair fight; that does not impress me much; Chucky was a tad slow on the draw. Who are you, kid?"

My mind had once again started to focus on all things that could change the outcome of this gunfight. The new autumn air was slightly chilled, but not cold. The wind was still and the sun was overhead and to the west, but still high enough in the cloudless sky not to be a factor. All these things I noticed in just a tick of seconds. "My name is Chance Bondurant. You might not remember me, but my dog and I remember you, Edgar."

If Dave Edgar was surprised I knew who he was, he did not show it. "Humor me Chance, and refresh my memory on how you know me."

Speaking in an easy tone, but with a strong voice, "Not far from here near Nevadaville, Chucky killed my younger brother. You and the rest shot my dog and blew up my mine and buried me alive. So tell me Edgar, are any of the rest of the Biggers and Hammond gang here to back your play? Seems to me you cowards stick together."

A deadly smile appeared on the eastern gunfighter's face. "Hell kid, you are looking good and the dog too. Nope the others have already headed to Grand Lake. Chucky and I stayed longer because we both had too much to drink last night. So it is just you and me."

Having said that and with no more to say, the one-eyed Edgar started his draw with his right hand first, then his left hand. He was fast and just as fast as I was. Palming my Colt, I fired at the same time as Edgar. His first shot went wildly to my left and on down Main Street, and his second shot punched a hole in my shirt sleeve on my right arm, but never found flesh. My first shot found his right shoulder and as I squared my feet fanning my Colt, my second and third shot were center mass in his chest. Dropping both his Colts in the dirt, Edgar's knees buckled as he stopped momentarily on his way down on his knees before flopping backwards into the dirt. Walking up with my pistol still on Edgar, I got close enough to see his eyes. I wanted to watch his life seep out of them as he died. He looked at me, not with any emotion at all and spoke in his deep voice, "You are fast kid." That is all he said before he died. Once again I felt nothing at all, and it started me to wonder - maybe I was empty on the inside; maybe something of me died that day that Jace was killed.

Mutt had wandered next to me as I made my way to the now very dead body of Dave Edgar and as if he had to make sure he was no longer alive himself, Mutt decided to do what animals do and lifted his leg and peed on the very dead gunfighter. I reckoned I understood that. Mutt was satisfied with the end result of the last gunfight. Mutt, the half wolf and half something else dog, now sat down and looked back east down the Main Street of Russell Gulch and let loose with more than a few loud whimpers. Quickly reloading my Colt pistol, I turned in the direction he was looking and there was some sort of commotion going on at the Dutch family wagon.

Confused and not really sure what was going on, I stood my ground for a few seconds and that is when I saw the Dutchman lift a body out of the back of the wagon. Moving faster now as I made my way toward the Dutch family wagon, re-holstering my Colt as I got closer, I realized the body that they had laid onto the ground had blonde hair tied with a pink and blue ribbon into a ponytail. Twenty feet away I heard the mother cry out, "NO!" The father, James Balkema, was more than frantic and the look of grief had already taken hold of his face as he bent over Ronda Joy holding her hand. I had been mistaken thinking that Dave Edgar's shot that went wild to the left had not found flesh. I was mortified to realize it had indeed. Ronda Joy, the young, attractive blonde Dutch girl had taken the stray bullet. The mother's wail of disbelief and the father's loving touch of Ronda's hand brought a tear to my eye.

I knew that everyone that is born to this life in time will die. If it is minutes, days, or years, we all are trapped by the same fate. Everyone that dies leaves behind a family and a story of how they lived. Ronda was taken too early with her story nowhere near completed. My heart was heavy, just like on the day that Jace was killed. I felt the guilt as if I was the one that had shot and killed her. She would still be alive if I had not made the trip to Russell Gulch after church. James, the father, turned to me as he bent over his daughter, and there would be no retreat from what his face and expression told me. With only one look, I could read what he would forever think in his face. He believed I was responsible for his daughter's death. In his grief he would never understand that I would also bear the burden of knowing I was partly the cause of Ronda's death. I was devastated as I looked upon the very serene face of Ronda Joy in death.

The sheriff Daniel Sierra and his deputy had finally made their way to the Dutch family wagon. James Balkema stood up and faced me, not more than two feet separating us. In a voice, filled with grief, but only in a whisper, "Chance, you better leave before I can't control what I want to do to you."

The sheriff stepped in between us and faced me, "Chance, I think it best you head on home for now. It was a fair and legal fight and you have nothing to fear from the law. I know where to find you if I need you, but I need you to leave now so my deputy and I can concentrate on bringing an end to this sad state of affairs today."

Looking into the young sheriff's eyes for a moment, I realized he was right. My presence here in town would just complicate what he and his deputy needed to do. Shaking my head with a slow "yes," I started to back away and after about 30 feet, I realized the whole town had turned out and now was lining the street. Looking at all their faces, I felt the sadness and grief that everyone was feeling for the death of someone young and innocent. I gave Storm my "come to" whistle and within seconds was standing by my side.

Mounting Storm and squaring myself in the saddle, I gave one last look at the Dutchman. With a heavy heart, I gave Storm some rein and with a slight jab of my left spur, she broke into a trot and headed down the road toward Central City.

CHAPTER 9

Not wanting to go home just yet and tell Lucas and Devon what had happened in Russell Gulch, I just started to ride with no destination in mind. Storm and Mutt seemed to understand my need to be alone and away from people just now.

In just a few minutes, my whole life and the course it would take forever changed with the death of three people in Russell Gulch. I was having difficulty trying to wrap my mind around that. Livingston and Edgar were men I wanted to see pay the price for what they did to myself and Jace. It was one thing to wish and want them dead; then it was completely something else to be the one that caused their death in such a violent manner. Everything happened with instinct and training I had learned from Lucas during the gun battles. I never once thought of the aftermath of how I would feel. Of course I wanted the two members of the Biggers and Hammond gang dead; hell, I wanted them all dead. I thought I would feel some sort of happiness in what had happened. I did not feel any type of happiness, just remorse and sadness. I could not help but think that maybe I was not much different than those in the gang. Maybe I was cut from the same cloth as those evil men. I guess in the end it will be the Lord who will decide my final fate. It was now too late to change that, what's done is done. I had no regrets in the killing of Edgar and Livingston. My regret was how an innocent blonde-haired Dutch girl got caught up in the madness that was now my life. I will never forget her father's face as he looked at me. I will be forever haunted by the death of Ronda Joy.

Riding down the trail, not really thinking or having a thought on where I was going, but in the deep parts of my mind, I guess I did. Rounding a stand of aspen trees, I sat on Storm looking at the wrought iron arch that marked the entrance into the Bald Mountain Cemetery. In my confused state of emotions, I had ridden without thinking to the one place and person that might understand it the most, my departed brother Jace.

Mutt had stopped when Storm and I had stopped, and he was looking at me and waiting for me to do something. Thinking maybe I had gone soft in the head from the recent ordeal, Mutt the half wolf dog, took matters and the thought process away from me and headed under the arch and towards Jace's grave. He knew the path well. I often thought when Mutt would disappear for half a day or so, this is where he headed, to spend time with Jace.

Storm was wanting to follow Mutt as she snorted and tossed her head a couple of times and pawed the ground with her hoof. I gave her some rein, and she followed Mutt to the graveside.

I reached Jace's grave, seeing that Mutt was already lying on top of the grave. Dismounting, I did not tie off Storm so she could graze at will through the last remaining grass before the autumn cold killed it off. I knew she would not wander far and would come as soon as I gave her the "come to" whistle.

Mutt moved over so I could sit down with my back to the stone cross that bore the epitaph "Jace Bondurant, Beloved Brother." After I had found a comfortable position, Mutt lay down again and placed his head into my lap. After I stroked Mutt's gray wolfish head, he promptly went to sleep.

The air was chilled, but I was not cold since Mutt was lying next to me, putting off enough warmth to keep me content as the day started to turn to night. The sun was starting to dip below the western skyline above the evergreens and aspens. As darkness started to blanket its way from east to west across the cloudless sky, the wind picked up some, and the autumn gold and green leaves of the aspens started their song of the night. My mother called it the "Tree Whispers." All I know it seemed right for the night. I loved the music of the aspen trees here high in the Rocky Mountains; it soothed my soul and right now I needed the music. I focused on the sound of the mountain melody and once in while the hoot of a faraway night owl.

Trying to find answers this night at the grave of my brother amongst the aspen trees and gravestones of the ones that had died and were buried, I found none, just more questions.

I realized that maybe my path in life was already chosen and it flowed just as a mountain spring that bubbled up from the depths of the Rocky Mountains. I was just going to have to go with the flow and see where it led me.

Settling down into a lying position, I watched the stars above as they twinkled in the heavens. The stars seemed brighter here in the mountains compared to the western plains of Lane County, Kansas, where my folks were buried. I think being closer to the heavens brought me closer to the mysteries of life. Knowing now that the answers were not going to present themselves to me tonight, I cuddled up to my half wolf dog for warmth, and sleep soon followed.

CHAPTER 10

Mutt woke me up before dawn by just standing up and leaving. I watched him as he moved down the road and out of sight. That dog truly had a mind of his own; never knew when he disappeared like that if I was ever going to see him again?

Standing up, I tried to get the ache out of my bones from sleeping on the ground in the cold. Stretching several times to relieve the ache, I then gave Storm the "come to" whistle. It wasn't more than a few minutes when I could hear her working her way through the evergreen and aspen trees as she made her way back to me. Seeing her still saddled, I felt guilty for not unsaddling her before falling asleep. Lucas would have my butt if he knew I had done that. Grabbing hold of Storm's reins and pulling her close and rubbing her nose and combing her midnight black mane with my fingers, I told her, "Sorry Storm, and I promise never to do that again." She seemed to accept my apology and nuzzled up close, accepting my grooming of her mane. I loved this horse more than anything in the world, except maybe that half wolf dog.

Stepping into the saddle and giving a hard push, I was able to mount Storm in the first attempt even though my muscles were aching from the cold from sleeping on the ground.

I stopped Storm, reining her around so I could get one last look at Jace's grave. Having spent the night here looking for answers on where my life was headed, I would be leaving the Bald Mountain Cemetery with still not a clue on how to proceed.

The next two weeks slowly passed. After reaching the Eldridge house after spending the night at the cemetery, Lucas and Devon had already heard about what had happened in Russell Gulch. They asked if I was okay and if I wanted to talk about what had happened. I told them I needed time to sort it all out in my mind and for the time being I would prefer not to talk about my encounter with the two members of the Biggers and Hammond gang and the subsequent death of the Dutch girl Ronda Joy.

I did, however, attend Ronda Joy's funeral as she was laid to rest in the Bald Mountain Cemetery, not far from Jace's final resting place. Well, when I say attended, I mean from a distance. Knowing that Mr. Balkema was still grieving and blaming me for his only daughter's death and not wanting to upset the family, I had ridden Storm with Mutt following to the top of Bald Mountain and watched from there. Even though the Balkema's had not been in the area for long, there was a huge attendance for Ronda Joy's funeral. People always went to the funerals of the ones that had died way too early in life for some reason. Maybe it showed how short and unexpected life could be. Ronda Joy's was no exception.

It was a sad affair for a chilled autumn day. The music was the usual affair of hymns from the bible. I always get goose bumps when "Amazing Grace" and "Rock of Ages" were sung. I waited in the cooling autumn air until all the mourners had left before I rode down to Ronda's grave to give my respects to one that had died too early in life, still feeling guilty and remorseful that the Dutch girl probably would still be alive if not for the course of my actions of the day she was shot. There were no do-overs in life and what had happened could never be changed and at the young age of twenty, I had already seen more death than most did in a lifetime.

The newspaper in Gilpin County ran several articles about the before, during, and aftermath of the shootout in Russell Gulch. Reporters came and went from towns such as Fairplay, Grand Junction, Colorado Springs, and of course Denver, all trying to interview me. I avoided all without giving one interview. The reporter from the Denver Post was so rude and pushy that Lucas even pulled his Colt and threatened to shoot him. There were more than enough willing witnesses to be quoted that each reporter left with some sort of story to be told in their newspapers. Each story had its own spin on what had happened and some were so outlandish and had zero truth in them, it was like I was reading a fictional novel. Jace's and my story and our encounter with the Biggers and Hammond gang had been well known in and around Central City, Blackhawk, Nevadaville, and Russell Gulch, but the shoot-out with Livingston and Edgar made our story well known outside of the area I now called home.

With so much coverage and how the gunfights were portrayed in the newspapers across the state, it was obvious that I now had a reputation as a gunfighter having learned my trade at the heels of the famous gunfighter Lucas Eldridge, killer of the famed Verdugo Brothers. Just as Lucas had warned me would happen and just like Lucas before me, it was a reputation that I did not want nor need. The reputation, just like the death of Ronda Joy, was something that could not be undone no matter how much I wanted to.

I went back to work at the Bondurant mine and tried to do my best, but my mind was no longer interested in the mining of the elusive gold dust and nuggets. It was if I was waiting for something to happen or a sign of what to do from here on out. Most days following the shoot-out in Russell Gulch become a blur to me without any direction or focus.

A short time after the Dutch girl's funeral, Sheriff Daniel Sierra stopped by the Eldridge house at 225 Hooper St. to present me with the bounty money for Livingston and Edgar, $400 each for a total of $800. With the $800 and what I had in the bank and a steady income from the Bondurant mine, I was not hurting for money nor would I be anytime soon.

I could see the frustration building in Devon as the days wore on as she tried to get me back to the same old Chance Bondurant that she had grown to love - the easy-going fellow who let her fuss over him like some five year old, but not in Lucas. Lucas, without even talking about it with me, seemed to know my mind and confusion better than I did. Hell, he had lived it already in his life. I reckon he already knew what direction my life would take before I even did.

Two weeks to the day of my shoot-out with Livingston and Edgar, Lucas, at the breakfast table, handed me the Gilpin County newspaper and pointed to an article. According to the article which had been taken from the Denver Post, the four remaining members of the Biggers and Hammond gang had reportedly been seen in the Middle Park region, south of the new supply town of Grand Lake.

Pointing at the newspaper after I had laid it down on the breakfast table after reading it, Lucas said, "If this is true Chance, then we need to come up with a plan of action."

With a slow nod of my head indicating "No," I told Lucas with a voice filled with no emotion, "There is no "we" to this Lucas. This is my fight and mine alone. I wanted vengeance for Jace's death when I was eighteen and with recent events I still want it. For the Biggers and Hammond gang, there must be a retribution - a Rocky Mountain retribution. Men such as these only know one thing and that is death and killing. You have done enough in teaching me the skills I needed to fight this battle. I have been waiting for some sort of indication on what to do and it seems the Biggers and Hammond gang have just given me that sign. I need to finish this on my own terms, you taught me that. I am not going to hide behind fate as it is presented to me. I am going to challenge it and take it straight on. I am going to track down the last four remaining members and serve the righteous justice they deserve. I do realize in the end, I might be assigned a seat in hell right along with the Biggers and Hammond gang. I might even deserve it with what happened to the Dutch girl Ronda Joy. All I know is that any happiness that may be in store for me in the future can't happen until I have served justice on these evil and cowardly "men".

Devon tried not to, but she shed a tear or two. Lucas looked at me for several minutes before he spoke, "I guess Chance, I have always known it would come to this. I reckon I was much the same myself when the Verdugo Brothers slaughtered my first wife. Remember son what I taught you; until this "Rocky Mountain Retribution" as you call it is done and all those that needed the justice that you will serve on them are dead, you must bury your heart. You need to be a cold killer; you can't care and you must be prepared to die in your quest. Only then, with the physical skills that you have learned, will you be able to come home here to Central City."

That night was a cloudless night, and the stars and a full moon shone bright in the heavens above after the first snow of the autumn, which left two inches on the ground. I awoke about midnight and pulled the wooden rocker in my room over to the window so I could look out through the wavy glass across Gregory Gulch. I had already decided to leave in the morning for Grand Lake, Colorado in the high plateau called Middle Park. Grand Lake was the last reported sighting of any of the Biggers and Hammond gang. It was a long shot, but I had to start my hunt somewhere.

Mutt had joined me at the window and sat next to me peering out the window, and I wondered if he knew what was on my mind about leaving. Scratching his wolfish head, "I am leaving in the morning to track down and kill those that were the cause of Jace's death. You are more than welcome if you want to come along."

Mutt looked at me, but gave no indication that he heard or cared for that matter what I was going to do. I never had any type of control over the half wolf, and I should expect none now. He would decide on his own fate in the morning. Mutt would join the vengeance trail or he would not. As it always was with him, it was his decision.

Before going to bed, I took one last look up the gulch to the white wooden cross as I did every evening before going to bed. Tonight with the full moon reflecting off the fresh blanket of snow, the white cross seemed to glow as it did on my first night in this room when the lightning from the thunderstorm cast an eerie radiance. Somehow I felt it was the Lord trying to talk to me. And try as I might, I could not understand the meaning of this sign from the heavens.

Crawling into my bed, maybe the last time ever in this house on Hooper Street, Mutt and I soon fell asleep.

CHAPTER 11

Mutt woke me up before dawn and I stretched while getting out of bed, making my way to the window facing Gregory Gulch. The window faced west, so I could not see the sun as it started its daily arc across the sky but could see the sky turning lighter as the morning wore on. Autumn was now in full swing as the aspen leaves were quacking across the gulch as a slight wind stirred them into their mountain melody song. It seemed it would be a good day to start my travels in search of the Biggers and Hammond gang.

After getting dressed, I sat back onto the bed and ran through the plan for the day. It was a simple plan to go to the last known sightings of any of the gang and try and pick up their trail. Heading to Grand Lake, I would take the shortest route possible over Rollins Pass into the Middle Park Basin country. My first day's travel would be 15 miles to Rollinsville where I planned on picking up a packhorse and more supplies since winter was coming. This trail was well known to me since Lucas and I spent several days each summer up on top of Rollins Pass during our mountain trips together.

Petting Mutt's wolfish head, I wondered if he would make the trip with me. I wanted him to, but you never knew which way the half wolf and half something else dog would go.

Breakfast with the Eldridge's was awkward because Devon kept tearing up as she went about getting Lucas and I fed some bacon and eggs. Lucas was quiet with a look of concern on his face. All three of us knew this may be the last time we saw each other. It was not like I was going on a business trip; there was no question that I would be riding into harm's way.

Looking at the two people who now were the most important people in my life, I could not help but think how much I owed both of them. They gave me a home, job, schooling, and love when I needed it the most. If needed, I would take a bullet for either of the Eldridge's. I loved them both and had never said those words, and being the man I now was, it would also be difficult to say those words now even with the aspect of never seeing them again.

After breakfast as I stood to leave, I let Devon fuss over me like the "Chance" before the gun fights in Russell Gulch. It was different now and we all knew it, but for this moment in time I gave into Devon and let her fuss. Of course she made sure my collar was folded correctly and my shirt was buttoned properly. There were no laughter or smiles from Lucas on this day of my leaving.

After saddling Storm and putting my Winchester into my rifle scabbard, I hugged Lucas and then Devon, and while still holding Devon, I wanted to tell her and Lucas I loved them. Devon, who probably knew me better than any woman would ever know me, saw me struggle to do so and reached out with two fingers and placed them gently on my lips to silence me and said, "No need to say it, Chance. Lucas and I both know your heart. Save it for when you come home."

Turning as fast as I could so they both could not see the anguish in my face, I stepped into the stirrup and with one push mounted Storm. Riding about 30 feet, I stopped and turned in the saddle to see what Mutt was going to do. Mutt, deciding, lay on his belly at the feet of Lucas. With no indication he was going to follow, I turned back around and gave Storm some rein and a slight jab with my left spur, and she started a slow trot towards the camp of Blackhawk to the north. A huge smile crossed my face as Mutt caught up and was leading Storm. In my mind that was the way it was supposed to be.

After the mile or so to Blackhawk, I hit the well-worn trail to the northwest towards Rollinsville, Colorado. The camp of Rollinsville was in between Nederland and Blackhawk and was still in Gilpin County. The camp was named after a successful, prominent mining executive named John Rollins.

The weather on this day of leaving everything I had grown to love was a beautiful, partly clouded sky. I loved watching the shadows from the clouds as they passed over the evergreens and the now golden aspens, making the mountain landscape seem alive as the shadows moved from darkness to the light. The wind was slight and the air had a slight chill. I felt so alive this morning in the wilderness. Storm and Mutt seemed to be enjoying it also as both of their heads were held high as we moved through the valley.

It had not snowed north of Central City; thus, the trail was clear. I did not pass anyone on the trail, and I was able to make the 15 miles in record time to Rollinsville with still enough sunlight to be able to secure the purchase of a pack horse and sway back pack saddle. The horse was a strawberry roan that stood 16 hands tall and had the look of intelligence in her eyes. Storm had walked right up to her in the livery stable corral and seemed to make friends, which was all I needed to know. I now owned a pack horse with the unlikely name of Strawberry.

After paying the livery stable man $70 for Strawberry and the pack saddle, I left Storm and Strawberry at the livery to get better acquainted. Mutt and I then headed down the street to the hotel and saloon named the "Rollins" to secure a room for the night and hopefully some decent grub. I already missed Devon's cooking.

Stepping up onto the boardwalk with my Winchester in my left hand, I slowly eased the rawhide thong off the hammer of my

Colt with my right hand to free it up. Trouble had a way of finding me, and I needed to be prepared.

The "Rollins" hotel had two entrances, one in the saloon and one off the hotel side. The saloon doors were the bat wing doors that you would see in most saloons, or at least the ones that I had been in. The hotel doors were a fancy affair that were at least ten feet tall with wavy broad stained glass windows that looked like something you would find in your local church. I walked through the fancy doors just to see what it felt like. Standing just on the inside, I decided fancy doors were nothing to be impressed with; they opened and closed just like a saloon door. Seemed to be a waste of wood and fancy glass if you asked me. Mutt must have thought he would try out the fancy doors too as he followed me right on in as if he owned the place, which did not please the fat, bald-headed man behind the hotel clerk counter, and in a louder than needed voice, "Hey you, get that damn dog out of here."

Looking at Mutt, I knew he had heard the man, but Mutt didn't seem to care much what the hotel clerk was saying, and in a level tone I replied, "I reckon he wants to stay with me."

The clerk's face now turned a shade of red as his anger was mounting, and in a louder voice, "No dogs are allowed in the hotel, so kick his mangy butt out of here."

Mutt was now giving the now red-faced clerk the "ole stink eye" and was sitting as quiet as he could be. Wondering where this standoff might be headed, I sort of chuckled to myself as I spoke, "Mister, I am not that half wolf and half something else's dog master; he has never listened to me and I do not reckon he is going to all of sudden start today. If you want to shoo him out, give it a try."

The "Rollins" hotel clerk stepped out from behind the counter, and I realized he was a big man, probably 6'3" and weighing 300 pounds and what really caught my eye was a three foot long club in his right hand. Mutt, without a sound, moved into an attack crouched position with his right paw forward, his black tipped gray fur standing straight up on his back, and showing his pearly whites in a snarl. Looking at Mutt all primed and ready, I could not help but think what a grand looking creature he was. "Mutt does not look like he wants to leave. In all fairness, I should warn you the last man that Mutt took a disliking too, he chewed his ear off."

The hotel clerk had quit moving forward and stood his ground, not liking one bit that Mutt did not scamper off as he thought he would. Never taking his eyes off of the half wolf dog and in a more quiet and subtle tone, "His ear? Where is that man now?"

In an even tone, I replied, "Dead, I shot him in Russell Gulch a couple of weeks ago."

The clerk started to sweat, and I could almost hear the gears working in his mind as he was trying to decide if the story was bullshit or the truth. Having decided not to test Mutt's or my resolve any more, he slowly stepped back behind the counter and dropped the club into whatever nook it was before we entered the hotel. In a more defeated tone of voice, "I guess we can make an exception for the dog this one time, but you will have to pay extra for him."

Looking back at Mutt who by now had seated back on his behind and no longer looked as if he was pissed, and then back at the clerk, I laid 50 cents on the counter. "I guess you did not hear me when I said, 'I was not the dog's master.' If you want more money for his stay, you need to take it up with him. The sign says 50 cents a night, I am staying one night."

Finally resigning himself that Mutt was not going anywhere but with me, the clerk spun the hotel register around for me to sign, which I did. After handing me the key to room 201, the clerk took one look at my name as I had written it and looked at me again and stuttered as he spoke, "Chance Bondurant? I have read about you and heard of your fight with some of the members of the Biggers and Hammond gang. I apologize if I have offended you today."

Trying not to laugh, "Mister, I was not offended, but Mutt over there might be a different story. I don't think he likes you much."

Heading up the stairs with the key to room 201 in my hand, Mutt and I heard the clerk say, "I apologize to you too, Mutt."

After getting settled into the room, Mutt and I headed down to the saloon to order some grub. Mutt was not really welcomed, but nobody else tried to shoo him outside. I had a decent meal of rare beef steak and taters and a slice of peach pie and some warm beer. Mutt just had a rare steak, which the waitress placed on his own plate on the floor next to my table.

I left a generous tip because the waitress seemed to warm up to Mutt, and he even let her pet him for a spell whilst I finished up my supper.

It wasn't long before we were back in the room. After claiming my side of the bed and Mutt claiming his side, we both fell asleep to the sound of an off-keyed tinny piano in the saloon.

CHAPTER 12

Waking before dawn, I quickly dressed and then looked out the window to the west of the "Rollins" hotel. It was still too dark to see Rollins Pass in the distance nine miles as it towered above the valley. I would simply head west along the side of South Boulder Creek as the creek flowed east until reaching the bottom of Rollins Pass. Rollins Pass was part of the "Great Divide" and topped out about 1,000 feet above where the trees don't grow anymore above timberline in the land of forever snow. As far as high mountain passes, Rollins Pass was an easy one to travel because simply it was not as tall as most of the passes along the "Great Divide" in Colorado. I had heard tales of wagon trains using it on their way west to the land of California. Lucas had told me the Ute Indians had been using the pass as their means to travel back and forth across the divide since the beginning of their time, long before any white man had ever set foot in these mountains of old.

After strapping on my holster and tying it down to my right leg, I practiced my draw for several minutes. The Colt pistol slid easily into my hand each time I palmed it. I knew I was faster than most men when drawing my weapon because I had learned from the best. Grabbing my Winchester and the few possessions that I had brought with me into the room and snapping on my Stetson black cattleman creased hat, Mutt and I headed downstairs for some breakfast.

After a hearty breakfast of elk sausage and chicken eggs, Mutt and I had to wait an hour before the dry goods store opened. I needed to purchase supplies for travel during the winter months. Old man winter and the cold snow was not far off. I noticed that Mutt, as he finished off his elk sausage, already had his full winter coat.

The extra hour of wait gave me time to think about the last remaining members of the Biggers and Hammond gang. The day that Jace died on Bald Mountain and I was buried in the Bondurant mine, I etched each member's face into memory.

Since that day I read every newspaper article that was written about the gang so I could learn as much as I could about the men I was hunting.

Herman Biggers was the leader and the oldest member of the gang. It was said that old man Herman rode with the likes of Jesse and Frank James when Bill Quantrall's Raiders sacked and burnt Lawrence, Kansas to the ground. Over 180 people died that bloody day in eastern Kansas. Biggers was obviously a man that saw life as cheap and had no misgivings about taking it. Last time I saw him two years ago, he had long white hair that touched his shoulders and a short grizzly gray beard. He was not a tall man only about 5'7" and weighed in the neighborhood of 170 pounds. As for being fast on the draw, I had never read any account of the man in one-on-one stand up fights with anyone. It seemed he always had those under his command do his dirty work and actual killing.

Rod Hammond was the second in command of the outlaws. Hammond was also with Biggers and a member of Quantrill's Raiders during the Lawrence massacre. By all accounts Hammond, unlike Herman, knew how to use his Colt pistol effectively, having read more than once of his killing more than six men in stand up gunfights. It was widely reported in the papers that Hammond had an addiction to the opium spiked alcohol Laudanum, which would explain the dark circles I saw under his eyes on that day of Jace's death. Hammond was a tall man about 6'3" and lanky and probably weighed no more than a buck eighty. Last time I saw him, he had long gray hair tied into a pony tail.

Bobby Burke was from Texas and had been on the run from the law since he was 13 after he supposedly killed his Ma for overcooking his steak. It was said that Burke was dumber than a box of rocks and if you told him to pee in a corner of a round barn, his mind would lock up and he would not move for hours. He always had a smile plastered on his face as you would see on some folks whose minds were simple. It was also said as dumb as he was, he was also an expert marksman with a Winchester rifle and deadly with the Colt pistol he carried on his left side with the handle pointed forward in a cross draw manner for his right hand. Last time I saw him, he was wearing an old beat up gentleman's derby hat with a bullet hole in it. He had no facial hair of any kind, not even eyebrows and shaved his head bald all the time.

Rick Alvardo was sort of a mystery man. He was half Ute Indian and half Mexican. Lucas warned me he was probably the most dangerous because of his Ute Indian upbringing. He was a quiet man most of the time and did not brag as the others did. It seemed his Ma was captured by Mexican renegades left over from the American and Mexican War. The story goes that his Ma was eight months pregnant with him when she was able to slit Alvardo's father's throat and make good her escape. His story goes cold there with not much about his upbringing or how he ended up in the Biggers and Hammond gang. It was widely reported he was a deadly adversary with all types of weapons such as tomahawk, knives, bow and arrow, and of course the two Colt pistols he carried with the handles pointed backwards in a standard draw. He was a hard looking man about 170 pounds and 5'10", and the last I saw him on Bald Mountain, he had long midnight black hair drawn into a ponytail down to the middle of his back. He was chiseled with muscle and looked very powerful in all his movements.

All four remaining members of the Biggers and Hammond gang were dangerous men and skilled in the death of others. I had no illusion that it was more than likely I would not survive on this vengeance trail. It was my intention that if I were to die that I would take all or as many of these assholes with me.

The clock on the wall showed 7 am and that meant that the dry goods store was open so leaving a tip on the table, Mutt and I headed out the saloon doors and on down the main street of Rollinsville. The Kyriss and Adams dry goods store was right next to the livery stable that Storm and Strawberry had spent the night. Stopping for a few minutes to give them both a pinch of sugar, I could see that both had been brushed down this morning and seemed to be in good spirit.

Inside the dry goods store the proprietor, a man named Kevin, was more than happy to fill my order of ten pounds of elk jerky, five pounds of fat backed bacon, three pounds of sugar for the horses, five cans of peaches, two pounds of salt, three pounds of flour, and he also happened to have some tea that I had grown to love at the Eldridge's, and I bought all that he had which was three pounds. I also bought six boxes of 44 ammo, two canteens, a new gun cleaning kit, 10' bowie knife, two heavy wool blankets, two boxes of stick matches, one new flint stone, two flannel shirts, a pair of rawhide pants, a pair of jeans made by that fellow Levi Strauss, three pair of wool socks, a pair of elk leather moccasins, one set of snow shoes, a wooden curry comb to brush down Storm and Strawberry with, grain for the horses, and last but not least a money belt that went around my waist for my cash money, coin, and gold.

With all the store shopping and packing of the horses, I was not able to get on the trail headed due west towards Rollins Pass until one hour before noon. Making my way to the edge of South Boulder Creek on the edge of Rollinsville, I finally felt geared up enough to head into the wilderness and any battle that the good Lord sought to put in front of me. Stopping to let Storm and Strawberry and Mutt get their fill of water, I took off my hat to survey the weather and what was before us on the trail. The air was cool, but not too cold with not one cloud in the forever blue sky as far as I could see. The aspens along the creek were in their full golden splendor as the river stretched the nine miles to Rollins Pass. With no air to stir their leaves this morning, there was no quaking and I missed that. I loved the sound of autumn in the high country.

After I squared up my hat back on my head, my small army of animals and I moved out and headed west. After I gave Storm some rein, she set the pace at a slow trot while Mutt was content to stay in front of Storm, and Strawberry was tied off to my saddle seeming to enjoy the pace that Storm had set.

With most of the day shot preparing for the trail, I was only able to make the base of Rollins Pass an hour or so before nightfall. Mutt had been able to catch his own supper on the trail, a big fat jack rabbit which he was not going to share with me as much as I tried to take it away from him. I was still laughing at Mutt for his stingy way as he ate his dinner as I brushed down Storm and Strawberry and gave them some grain and a pinch of sugar.

Deciding on a cold camp tonight, I ate some Elk jerky and a can of peaches for my supper and drank a half of a canteen of cold creek water. Mutt tried to coax some jerky from me, but I showed him I could be just as stingy as he was for a spell. Of course he gave me that sad puppy dog look, and I ended up giving him a piece of jerky anyway. Rolling out my bedroll and using my saddle as a headrest, I lay looking at the stars in the heavens above and even saw one shooting star that went from the east to the west. If I had been an Indian, the shooting star would have been some sort of sign. Thinking about it some, I could not decipher what it could be.

It was not long before Mutt cuddled up to me and quickly fell asleep. I listened to the sound of a faraway great horn owl hoot to the sky; the hoot was music to my ears as were all the night sounds and it was not long before I was out too.

CHAPTER 13

Waking before dawn, I was cold because Mutt had wandered away during the night and still had not returned. As always I wondered if he was gone for good; maybe he had found a lady love and now was off on his own adventure. I never knew what that half dog mind was going to do. It must have been the wolf and wild side that made him that way.

I stood and stretched trying to get the night kinks out of my muscles and in doing so decided I would start a small fire and fry up some fatback bacon for my breakfast.

Starting to warm up some as the cook fire took the chill off my bones, I pondered today's activities as I ate my bacon. Rollins Pass was not a difficult pass to travel and was used often by wagon trains headed west and cattle drives. I had read or heard somewhere that it topped out at about 11,600 feet - more than a 1,000 feet above timberline where the trees no longer grow. Here on the eastern side of the pass I reminded myself it was still autumn, but on top of the "Great Divide" it might already be winter. Approaching yesterday in the daylight, I could see the high peaks were covered with snow either with freshly fallen snow or snow that never melts at those altitudes. From east to west of the pass was roughly 20 miles, which would take more than a day to make into the Middle Park basin country on the western side.

Burying what remained of my cook fire to put it out so a spark could not start a wildfire, I looked toward the heavens as the orange of the rising sun in the east spoke of the birth of a new day. As the sun rose, so did the wind from the north, not much of a wind, but enough to start the golden leaves of the aspen trees to start their quaking, which brought the song of the "tree whispers" or so my Ma called it.

I fed some grain and a pinch of sugar both to Storm and Strawberry as I rubbed them down as I got them packed and ready for the trail. I asked both of them if they had seen Mutt or if he spoke of where he was headed, and both horses gave me that look like, "That dog is a strange one." Chuckling to myself I thought, "I couldn't agree more."

Checking to see that my Winchester was fully loaded and that my Colt pistol had one empty chamber under the hammer for safety, I felt it was now time to start moving, for the remaining members of the Biggers and Hammer gang needed to be dealt with and time was a wasting.

After making sure the canteens were topped off with fresh water from South Boulder Creek, I stepped into the stirrup on Storm and after squaring myself into the saddle and leading Strawberry, I started west.

By mid-morning the trail had been a steady upward climb, but not difficult. The sky above was starting to fill with darkened clouds that spoke of possible snow. It would not be a pleasant journey to be caught on top of the pass at this time of year in an autumn blizzard. Weather at these high altitudes could change in a heartbeat and has killed more than a few un-expecting folks that were not equipped for the sudden change.

Not wanting to stop to eat at midday, I ate some elk jerky in the saddle as I kept moving up the pass. The higher I got, the colder it became; the wind had picked up some and I had to put on my winter duster to ward off the cold. Mid-afternoon found me on top of the world sitting on top of the "Great Divide," knowing I could never count in miles as far as I could see looking west. The air was chilled, and the forever blue sky now was cloudless as far as I could see. I always marveled at the beauty of it all as I looked west, north, east, then south turning in my saddle as I took in the Lord's creation.

A mountain man named Matt Lee, who had helped teach me along with Lucas the way of the mountains, once told me that he had told his folks, "I am heading to the Rocky Mountains to become a mountain man."

Matt Lee's Pa told him, "You need to stay here son, this is where you belong amongst people. The Rocky Mountains are full of savages and wild critters and snow that never melts. Those mountains are a difficult and dangerous place to live and men, strong men, die an early death there."

Matt Lee's answer was, "That is exactly why I am going; the Rockies speak to me as if the Lord himself is calling me home. There is no place more stunning than the high country. The Lord built the mountains for men like me, those that seek the answer to the meaning of life."

Matt Lee's eyes sparkled as he continued his story, "Hell Chance my boy, the folks acted as if they had been shot out of a cannon, but by God I was right."

Looking out into the splendor of all that was before my eyes, I thought of that old mountain man and knew he was right. I tipped my Stetson in honor of him and those like him that dared to go where no white man had dared to go before.

I knew I needed to keep moving to make it down below timberline so I could camp amongst the trees for some protection against the wind tonight. I looked back hoping to catch a sighting of Mutt but not seeing him, I wondered if he had decided to make it on his own. I tipped my Stetson to salute him in his adventure.

Giving Storm some rein, I headed her and Strawberry down the trail on the western side of the Great Divide.

I was able to make it down into the aspens and evergreen trees just as the sun was starting to dip down on the western horizon, leaving the sky ablaze with orange as the darkness slowly started to engulf the fading light.

I tried not to worry about Mutt, knowing full well he was capable of taking care of himself. I had always known that the half wolf dog had a mind all of his own and decided what he wanted to do according to his needs. Having grown attached to the half wolf ever since Jace's death, I was just used to having Mutt by my side.

After I unsaddled Storm and took the packsaddle off of Strawberry, I brushed down both horses and fed them some grain and a pinch of sugar. Both of them snorted several times and pawed the ground with their hooves, and I took this as they enjoyed the grooming and sugar.

Never could I have dreamed of having two better horses. After a supper of some fried bacon and beans, I polished off a can of peaches and watched the embers of the fire float lazily in the air as they drifted skyward until the cool night extinguished them. Above the fire I watched the stars twinkle in the heavens and once again was reminded how beautiful they were when you were this close to the heavens. I wondered if that old mountain man Matt Lee was still alive and had found the meaning to life.

The night was turning colder and the temperature had already dropped below freezing, so I grabbed another wool blanket since I would not have the extra heat provided by Mutt this evening. I was hoping he was warm and comfortable wherever he was spending the night tonight.

Listening to the night sounds of the mountains, I felt sleepy and was soon sound asleep.

CHAPTER 14

Waking to the sound of both Storm and Strawberry snorting ferociously, I snapped my eyes open and grabbed my Winchester, standing as fast as I could. Both horses had moved in close to what remained of the fire, and both of them were scared and on high alert.

It was still dark with clouds blanketing the sky, and there was very little light from the stars as I tried to see into the forest. Storm and Strawberry were looking down the trail into the darkness. So what had disturbed them was in that direction.

Concentrating on the sounds of the night, I tried to hear anything out of the normal. Both horses were still snorting and pawing the ground with their hooves when I heard something moving through the trees; it was big and did not fear anything, for it was not trying not to make any noise. I jacked the lever action of the Winchester to place a shell into the firing chamber and after having done that, I took the leather thong off the hammer of my Colt to free that up also.

It had to be a grizzly bear. The fear the horses were showing and the sound of something that huge moving through the trees, the only thing it could be was a bear. Somehow by making camp in this spot, I had interrupted the bear's normal routine and it was not happy about it.

It had gone quiet and it stood still just beyond the edges of my eyesight in the darkness. Lifting my Winchester to my shoulder, I slowed my breathing and tried to take in everything - the darkness, the sounds of the horses, and the chilled air that could affect the outcome of this encounter.

With a bone chilling roar, the bear started its charge, crashing through the trees, breaking into the edge of my eyesight. And it was a grizzly all right as it stopped about 30 feet away and stood up on its back legs and let out an unnerving roar. And she was a magnificent creature for sure, probably 8 feet tall and 800 pounds of pissed off mama bear. Just before I could pull the trigger, a gray flash jumped in between the grizzly and myself. Mutt had joined the fray and was trying to protect me. The grizzly was not sure what to think of this new adversary that had joined the fight. Mutt was all fluffed up with his hair standing straight up and showing sharp teeth that seemed to sparkle in the fading light of the campfire. The bear dropped to all fours and started a slow approach this time. Just when I had a bead on the bear's head with my Winchester, Mutt attacked by going straight at the bear and before the bear could react with those massive paws, Mutt slashed and tore a huge chunk of meat from the bear's right shoulder. The bear now wounded let out an even more frightening roar as it took its focus off me and started to concentrate on Mutt.

Everything was happening so fast that I was not able to get a clear shot at the grizzly without possibly hitting Mutt. Mutt attacked twice more and each time was able to dart away before the bear could catch him, swinging those gigantic paws with dagger like claws. I knew full well if Mutt caught one of those swipes, he was done for. After the third straight attack from Mutt, with the bear taking a beating and bleeding huge drops of blood from three different wounds that had been inflicted by Mutt, the grizzly decided enough was enough and turned and high tailed back into the darkness and the trees.

The whole Mutt and Grizzly bear encounter could not have lasted more than a minute, but in my mind it was all in slow motion like walking in the fog just after dawn.

I was astonished not only that the bear decided to attack our camp, but also that Mutt had come to the rescue seemingly out of thin air. Mutt was just starting to calm down as he looked in the direction that the bear had fled. His black tipped gray hair just moments ago that was standing straight up was now lying back down on his back. Still in a high state of excitement, I said to Mutt, "Not sure where the hell you have been Mutt, but I am glad to see you. Next time at least give me a little advance warning you are close so I don't put a bullet in your ass."

Mutt's ears lay down as I was chastising him. Feeling bad now, "Come here you big dummy and let me give you some loving."

As was Mutt's custom he just sat there looking at me, not wanting me to seem that I might be in control of him. Laughing to myself, I walked the 20 feet and reached under his belly and rolled him over for a good ole' belly rub. It did my heart good to have the half wolf and half something else dog back.

After giving Mutt some welcome home loving, I saw to the horses, who by now were just starting to calm down. I brushed them both down and worked their manes until they were silky smooth. Seeing that both horses were no longer afraid, I fed them some grain and a pinch of sugar each.

After getting the animals settled, I watched the sun start to make its appearance in the east as the sky started to light slowly with a burnt orange color that the chilled autumn air seemed to make even more spectacular.

No use trying to go back to sleep and not wanting to stay any longer in a place for some reason that had upset the grizzly, I packed as quickly as I could and ate a good pound or so of elk jerky for a quick and cold breakfast.

Stepping into the stirrup on Storm and with one push, I got settled into the saddle and headed west down the western side of Rollins Pass and into the Middle Park Basin.

Middle Park was roughly a flat high plateau at around 8,000 feet at the bottom of the narrow basin. It was called Middle Park because it was in the middle of three such high mountain plateaus - the one to the south was called South Park; the one to the north was named probably by the same genius that named all three, which was North Park; and to the south and east of the Middle Park Basin was "The Great Divide," the spine of mountains that run north and south and determined which way the rivers flow.

With Mutt leading the way, we made the bottom of the pass and looking to the northwest of the narrow Middle Park Basin, I was guessing it was maybe 40 miles to the northern tip of the basin and Grand Lake. It was of course a long shot that any of the Biggers and Hammond gang still remained there, but it was all the information I had for now. Giving Storm some rein, I headed in that direction. Grand Lake was where the headwaters of the mighty Colorado River started as a mere stream barely a couple of feet wide. Inside of the narrow basin of Middle Park, there was plenty of water from numerous unnamed lakes and ponds and small tributaries of the Colorado River such as Fraser River, Williams Fork, and Willow Creek. I, along with my traveling companions of Storm, Strawberry, and Mutt, would not be lacking for any water.

The day had been excellent for traveling with a slight wind to our backs and a clear blue sky above with not one cloud as far as I could see. Traveling the flat plateau of Middle Park, I saw very few trees, but on the snowcapped mountains surrounding the park in the distance and below timber line, I could see the golden slashes of the aspens amongst the dark green of the pine trees. It was a handsome sight to behold.

In my travels with Lucas, I had never made it this far and all of what was before me was a new adventure. I welcomed it as I also welcomed the chance to settle my family feud with the Biggers and Hammond gang. It was a righteous ride for justice, but I was not sure if the Lord saw it as such and imagined I would not find that out until the day of my last breath, seated at his feet for my final judgment. I was prepared for whatever outcome he would choose for me.

After traveling another 15 miles from the base of Rollins Pass, I watched the sky begin to darken with the advent of night bullying its way across the sky. The sun was now settled at the top of the snowcapped peaks to the west and was fading fast.

Finding a place to camp near a pond with a few trees, I stepped off Storm, unsaddled her, and dropped my saddle heavily to the ground. After unpacking Strawberry, I fed both horses and rubbed them down before a pinch of sugar, which they both were craving. After locating some stones to build a ring and using what little wood that could be had, I started a campfire for some heat and warm food.

Mutt supplied his own supper after disappearing for a spell, returning with a slow plumb squirrel that was to his liking. I fried up some fatback bacon and beans, which I deposited in my belly in no time at all. After a good thumping on my belly to see if there might still be some room, I followed it with a whole can of peaches. Feeling content after a nerve racking start of the day with the bear, I rolled out my bedroll and used my saddle for a pillow.

After Mutt finished his supper, he stretched out next to me and it was not long before we both fell asleep, listening to the sounds of the darkness.

CHAPTER 15

Waking to a snowflake landing on my face as it started to melt and looking towards the heavens, I could see the ground was covered with a dusting of very small flakes, just a reminder that winter was not far behind and that autumn was almost done here in the high country.

Mutt had evidently already gotten up and was nowhere to be seen, once again leaving me to wonder if I would ever see him again.

Sitting up, I found a long stick and started to stir the remaining ashes from last night's fire, and it was not long before I had coaxed them into a flame, adding the remaining wood until I had a fire large enough to warm my hands.

The sun had not yet found its way above the snowcapped mountains to the east, but the sky had already lightened enough to see that it was going to be a foul day. Dark clouds now filled the sky above the high plateau of Middle Park. The air was cold this morning and close to freezing, and it felt like more snow.

I could see Storm and Strawberry grazing not far to the south on the tall grass. It would not be long before the valley floor would be a blanket of snow and there would be no grass to be had for the rest of winter.

Thinking of the tasks for the day, I thought I was maybe two days away from Grand Lake. From what I remember, it would mostly be easy traveling since the Middle Park Basin was mostly flat terrain. Grand Lake was at the northern tip of the Basin.

As I fried my bacon and beans for my breakfast, I tried to recall what I had read and heard about the newly formed town of Grand Lake. Grand Lake was set on the shores of what has been said to be one of the most gorgeous lakes in the high country in Colorado. The lake was said to be over 300 feet deep and crystal clear, so clear in fact, you can see all the way to the bottom. Grand Lake had become the main outfitting and supply point for the mining camps of Lulu City, Teller City, and Gaskill in the more rugged mountains to the north. The mountain man Matt Lee told me once that north of those mining camps the mountains were so harsh and remote that no white man, maybe not even the Indians, had ever traveled there.

As I was finishing up my bacon, Mutt walked back into camp and was eyeballing the last two pieces of bacon. "Hmmmm, you didn't share that fat squirrel you had last night. Why should I share my bacon with you?"

Mutt took three steps forward and sat down, looking at me with that puppy dog look. "Seeing how you saved my butt from the grizzly yesterday, I guess I could spare a couple of pieces of bacon."

I tossed the bacon one piece at a time, and Mutt caught each one in mid-flight and with one gulp each one disappeared. He looked content for now. Smiling, I could not help but think how much I enjoyed and loved the half wolf and half something else dog.

After burying the fire, I gave Storm and Strawberry the "come to" whistle and knowing they had their fill of mountain grass, I just gave each one a pinch of sugar as I groomed them and saddled them. After getting settled into my saddle on Storm, I pointed her north and after I gave her some rein and a slight jab with my right spur, she took off in a slight trot with Strawberry tied behind and with Mutt leading the pack.

By mid-morning the sun never did find an opening in the clouds, and the sky remained overcast with the hint of more snow. It had been lightly snowing all day, and the ground now had about an inch of fresh snow covering it. The air smelled fresh and clean. Even without the sun, it was a fine-looking day to be alive.

At noon I crossed some tracks of a lone horse that now was heading in the same direction I was. The snow had stopped about two hours earlier; these tracks were made before then since no new snow covered any part of the track. Not long after discovering the tracks, I heard a single gunshot in the distance. I thought it came from the same direction that the tracks were heading, but in the high mountains it was difficult sometimes to tell the direction of gunshots, because the sounds would ricochet off the jagged rocks and mountain sides.

Palming my Colt, I loaded the empty chamber which I normally left empty beneath the hammer for safety. I was not sure what or who I was going to run into on the trail before me.

Not long after hearing the gunshot, I came upon a dead horse on the trail, a beautiful black mare that had a broken foreleg after stepping into a foxhole. She also had a bullet hole between her eyes as the rider had put her out of her misery. That explained the gunshot, but not the who. The rider had taken the saddle and was walking toward the north, and according to the rider's tracks, he or she could not be more than a mile ahead. I had to be wary now; a man or a woman without a horse would be looking for a new horse and not too picky about how they went about getting a new one.

Topping the next small rise, I could see the man not more than a quarter of a mile in front of me as he was carrying his saddle and still walking north. I thought about giving him a wide berth and just keeping on my way to Grand Lake, but then I thought differently and rode straight toward him.

Closing within 50 yards, I stopped and studied him. He must have sensed me because he turned to look in my direction. He did nothing but stare at me; he did not go for a gun or seem startled. He stood studying me. Speaking as loudly as I could, "I am not here to harm you, nor do I want you to harm me. Drop your saddle and place your firearms on top of the saddle."

The man stood still for a few minutes trying to decide what to do. He dropped his saddle and then raised his rifle above his head so I could see it, and then he slowly put it on top of the saddle. He then pulled his six shooter from his holster on the right side and once again raised it above his head so I could see it as he slowly placed it on his saddle with his Winchester.

Giving Storm her head and some rein and a slight jab with my right spur, we headed in the direction of the one man. Riding within 25 feet of the stranger before me, I could tell he was of Spanish or Mexican descent. He was at least ten years older than I was with ebony short hair with a black handlebar mustache. He stood about 6 feet tall and weighed in the neighborhood of 180 pounds. He was dressed for the cold with a fox fur hat that covered his ears and a black winter duster almost exactly like the one I was wearing.

Mutt was standing next to Storm, and his black tipped gray fur was standing straight up. With his teeth showing and a growl, he advanced on the stranger slowly. The Mexican fellow did not like this one bit, and he suddenly reached for a belly gun he had hidden. I palmed my Colt pistol with lightning speed and pointed it straight at his head, "You shoot my wolf dog and I will have to take a disliking to you and put a bullet in your head. I love that dog."

Mutt had stopped advancing, and the Mexican took his eyes off of him and looked towards me with a slight chuckle and in a Spanish accent, "You are fast amigo, maybe the fastest I have ever seen."

Motioning with my Colt for him to lose the belly gun, I replied, "Lose the Colt pistol and open your duster and show me you have no more hideouts."

Slowly taking out the belly gun and placing it on the saddle with his other weapons, he then opened his duster and slowly turned in a circle as he spoke in a loud and proud clear voice, "I am Rey Chavez from Tlaxcala in southern Mexico; I am the body guard for Kellie Shawn Arriaga, the sister of my benefactor Chucho el Roto. You have heard of him, yes?"

Looking at Rey Chavez with a huge smile on his face and his proud bearing, I liked him immediately. "I have read stories of this man Chucho el Roto, whose real name is Jesús Arriaga, a thief and robber of the wealthy that is said to give to the poor of Mexico - a modern day Robin Hood. This all may be true Mr. Chavez, but you are a long way from southern Mexico. What the hell are you doing smack dab in the middle of the Rocky Mountains of Colorado?"

After buttoning his duster, Rey Chavez balled his fist and put them on his hips as if he was a king or at least a nobleman and still with a massive smile replied, "Amigo, what is your name? I wish to know the hombre that has a pistola faster than el relámpago."

Laughing out loud now, I holstered my pistol as I spoke, "My name is Chance Bondurant from Central City, Colorado. I am on the trail looking for a gang of outlaws that killed my brother and tried to kill me. I guess I am going to trust you, Rey Chavez; pick up your weapons and throw your saddle on my pack horse Strawberry"

Rey was still smiling as he picked up his pistols and placed one behind his belt to be used as a belly gun and the other back into its holster. Mutt seemed to sense everything was okay now as his fur settled back down on his back. Rey, after reclaiming his weapons and as he was packing his saddle on Strawberry, spoke, "I feel sorry for those el bandido on the day you catch them. Any man as rápida con su pistol and can tame a wolf is not hombre that I would want hunting me. To answer your question of why we are in your Colorado, my benefactor Chucho el Roto has sent his sister Senorita Arriaga, the most beautiful woman in all of Mexico, north to buy land to build a hacienda to retire far from those that would like to take his head."

Reaching out a hand to help Chavez up to ride double on Storm, "I take it that the Senorita Arriaga and the party you are traveling is north of here. I guess I can give you a hand making it back to them. What were you doing out here all on your lonesome?"

˙ Grabbing hold of my offered hand and hopping up and getting settled in behind me, "I was hunting some carne for supper tonight."

With a chuckle Rey Chavez added, "It is obvious I am a better bodyguard than a hunter. Yes?"

Laughing out loud again I replied, "I reckon so, Rey."

Giving Storm a slight jab with my right spur and giving her rein, she headed north as Mutt the half wolf dog once again took point in front of Storm.

After about two miles I could smell wood smoke of a campfire up ahead and after topping a small rise, I spotted a campsite. Rey Chavez spoke in a loud and clear voice, "That, my new American friend with a pistola faster than any vaquero in all of Mexico, is where the most beautiful mujer in all of my country Senorita Arriaga is waiting for my arrival. I was supposed to be bringing carne for our supper, but I bring something better - my new friend Chance Bondurant, lo más rápido pistolero in all of the Rocky Mountains. Yes?"

Smiling, I could not help but like the strange Mexican that I now had riding double on Storm. He was an interesting fellow for sure. "Not sure what all that meant Rey Chavez, but I reckon that Ms. Arriaga was hoping for a steak rather than a drifting cowboy hell bent on revenge."

CHAPTER 16

fter we reached the camp, two very stout and serious looking men pointed Winchesters in my direction. Both men were of Spanish or Mexican ancestry and looked to be about the same age as Rey Chavez. They both wore matching winter dusters and fox fur hats such as the ones worn by Rey Chavez. They had the look of tough and capable men.

As serious as those Winchesters and the men holding them looked, I could not help but notice the woman standing in the middle of the two bodyguards. If, as Rey Chavez had claimed, she was not the most beautiful woman in all of Mexico, she had to be in the top three for sure.

Rey Chavez dismounted and with a flourish that only he could do, looked at the woman and the two men and pointed in my direction, "This is my savior from a certain muerte in the wilderness, when dumb luck and a snowed over foxhole broke the leg of my now departed caballo. Please welcome my new amigo and King of the Montañas Rocosas, Chance Bondurant."

Dismounting Storm slowly, I stepped over to pat Mutt on the head to signal everything was okay. One of the bodyguards kept his rifle pointed at me, and the other pointed his rifle at Mutt.

As the woman walked forward, Rey Chavez with an open palm and sweeping arm pointed at her, "May I present to you, Senor Chance, the most beautiful mujer in all of Mexico and now Colorado Senorita Kellie Shawn Arriaga, the sister of my benefactor Chucho el Roto."

Rolling her eyes in the direction of Rey Chavez, she reached out her hand to shake mine, Ms. Arriaga spoke in perfect and unaccented English, "You must excuse Rey for all the dramatic words and gestures; he joined my brothers' cause when the theatre he was working in as an actor was burnt down during a riot against the government of Mexico."

I could not believe how striking Ms. Arriaga was; she was petite, but not frail or fragile looking. She had the look of a strong woman who knew her own mind. She of course was Mexican, but with an unusual color of eyes that were blue with a hint of green. She wore a fox furred hat and her ebony hair was long and tied into a pony tail that reached the middle of her back. She wore man leather pants and a fur lined leather jacket to ward off the cold of the mountain air. She moved with agility and swiftness. She was stunning. The Senorita was simply beautiful. Rey Chavez was dramatic in his description of Senorita Kellie Shawn Arriaga, but he could not have been more spot on in his narrative. I tried successfully not to stare or stutter as I replied, "I reckon that explains it Senorita Arriaga, I was starting to wonder if he was all right in the head."

That brought laughter from the Senorita Arriaga and two men pointing their Winchesters at me. Even Rey Chavez had his normal huge smile still plastered on his face.

Senorita Arriaga motioned for the two men to lower their rifles and as they did so she said, "Please call me Kellie; it is what all my friends call me. You of course already know Rey; the other two men are the brothers Martinez, Glen, and Daniel. You must be an interesting man, Chance, to have a trained wolf as a companion for the trail."

Mutt turned his head sideways, because he knew we were talking about him, and it looked like he was trying to catch every word.

Stifling a laugh, I pointed at Mutt, "Mutt, is half wolf and half something else. And don't let his quiet demeanor fool you. He is not trained and never listens to me. He has a mind of his own and comes and goes when and wherever he wants. I reckon that is why we get along. I never tell him what to do, and he never tells me what to do."

With a smile on her face, Kellie bent her knees to lower herself and said, "You are a handsome gent Mutt, just like your friend Chance. Come here and let me give you some loving."

That damn dog went over to Kellie Shawn and flopped on his back like he had known her all his life. In just over 24 hours Mutt went from fighting a pissed off grizzly to being a lap dog. I didn't know if I should be amused or ashamed. One thing it did was bring a smile to my face.

Kellie stood and walked past me looking to the mountains to the west. "You and Mutt must stay for supper tonight, Chance. The day is short and the night is long here in the high mountains. It will have to be a meatless supper of beans and tortillas."

Reaching behind the pack saddle on Strawberry, I pulled out three jack rabbits already gutted and skinned that I had snared last night and handed them to Rey Chavez. "Let's see if Rey can roast rabbit as well as he can act."

Rey, with a grand gesture, held the rabbits above his head as if he had killed them in some mighty battle, "I am the best rabbit roaster in all of Mexico; unfortunately, I am not in Mexico, and then Chavez turned and handed them to the Martinez brothers."

That brought a laugh from everyone, hell, Mutt even seemed amused.

As the Martinez brothers took the rabbits and started our supper for the evening, I joined Kellie Shawn as she stood looking toward the west as the sun was starting to settle down behind the mountains, leaving its last golden hue to light up the remaining golden leaves of the autumn aspen trees. It was a perfect moment in time, watching the encroaching darkness with her. Not wanting to disturb her as she was lost in her thoughts, I waited until the last moment of sunlight finally blinked out and the darkness engulfed the mountain side before I spoke, "Autumn sunsets in the Rockies are something to behold; of course, any sunset is beautiful. My brother Jace and I would watch every one near my home in Kansas, but these in the high country are somehow more special. I don't question why; I just watch, observe, and revel in what the Lord has put before us."

Kellie Shawn Arriaga turned to me and smiled. I was once again taken aback by her beauty. Maybe it was the serenity of the sunset or the just being with her in the high mountain wilderness on this cool crisp autumn night, but after looking at her, I knew I would always remember this moment in time when Senorita Arriaga and I crossed paths. Kellie looked at me without talking for a minute or so as I wondered what she saw, what her thoughts were. "In Mexico near my home the desert heat makes the sunsets spectacular to view, but I agree there is something special being this close to the heavens and watching the sun dip behind the mountains. I have only been in Colorado for a couple of months looking for a home for my brother and our family of misfits far away from the troubles in our native country. My brother has been here before and loved the beauty of the mountains and sent me and my three loyal bodyguards here to purchase land and start our ranch for when he retires. Senor Chance, just in the few short months I have been here, it now feels like home, like I have been gone a long time and just returned back to where I was supposed to be."

Kellie seemed lost in thought, so after she spoke I tended to Storm and Strawberry without saying anything. As I was unpacking them, Kellie grabbed my curry comb and started to brush and groom their manes and help me rub them down. She had grabbed some grain from the sack I had just unpacked and fed my horses, while talking to them gently. She pitched right in helping me as if we had done this a thousand times before. I was amazed at how natural it felt having her by my side, helping tend to my horses. Mutt even sensed the togetherness because he followed her every move staying just to her right side, but never in her way as she moved smoothly, going about taking care of Storm and Strawberry. We released both of my horses to the Arriaga remuda of nine horses. It seems that Chavez would not be wanting for a mount tomorrow when the Mexicans broke camp.

Glen Martinez, the taller of the two bodyguard brothers, broke the tranquility of the moment by announcing supper was ready. Just as he said that, the smell of roasted rabbit spilled over me, reminding me that I had not eaten anything since breakfast that morning after stopping to eat after I found Rey Chavez on the trail.

Our supper that evening on the floor of the high mountain plateau of Middle Park consisted of tortillas, beans, and roasted rabbit. The rabbit was the finest I had ever eaten; the Martinez brothers had seasoned it with some dried Habanero chili they had brought from Mexico. As we ate, Chavez entertained us with his obvious talent for the theatre with a quick, hilarious parody of Romeo and Juliet with him playing both parts.

I felt at ease with these wandering folks far from their native land. I tried not to look at the Senorita Kellie Shawn Arriaga as I felt like I was staring at her, but every time I did cast a glance in her direction, I found her to be looking my way. She would smile each time when this happened. Kellie made me nervous, but in a feel good way, which, as I thought about it more, made me think about what Lucas had told me, "Until this 'Rocky Mountain Retribution' as you call it is done and all those that needed the justice that you will serve on them are dead, you must bury your heart. You need to be a cold killer, you must not care and you must be prepared to die in your quest." As beautiful as Kellie Arriaga was, I could not let her turn my head, but for this evening I would enjoy her troop of bodyguards and the most beautiful mujer in all of Mexico. Tomorrow I would once again focus on my quest for justice. Tomorrow the hunt for the remaining members of the Biggers and Hammond gang would begin again.

The rest of the evening we all spoke at length about what brought us all to the same trail here in the high country of the Rocky Mountains. I told them about my life in Lane County, Kansas and the death of my parents. I spoke of Jace's and my trip to the mountains and finding and filing our gold claim. I spoke of finding Mutt when he was just a pup all alone on the mountain side and how we had adopted him as our own. I told them of my life before the Biggers and Hammond gang had changed the course of all that I had known. I tried, but failed in not shedding a tear when I spoke of Jace's death. I was so at ease with these people I told them everything of my rescue by Lucas and Devon Eldridge, the death of Ronda Joy the Dutch girl, and of course of the two gunfights with two members of the gang that had killed my brother, and now my ride to settle all accounts against those that did my brother and myself wrong.

They all of heard of Lucas Eldridge and were impressed that I knew such a mighty avenging warrior.

Kellie and her bodyguards told me about their life and how they came to be in Colorado. Much of their lives were centered on Kellie's older brother Jesús Arriaga known as "Chucho el Roto." Rey Chavez did most of the talking and explained that Jesús' nickname "Chucho" literally means "mutt" and "Roto" literally meant "broken, discarded or ragged." They explained that the Arriaga, Chavez, and Martinez families were strong Catholics and the President of Mexico, Benito Juárez declared "Juarez Law," which professed that church land was now owned by the government, and the complete subjugation of all bishops, priests, nuns, and lay brothers. The government seized all land held by Catholics. Jesús Arriaga declared war on the Mexican government and became a bandit and with an army of a few true believers in his cause, started to rob the very wealthy in Mexico and give money and valuables to those that had lost so much because of "Juarez Law." Like all bandits though, they kept the biggest portion of the loot for themselves.

When Benito Juárez died a few years ago of a heart attack, the new President Sebastián Lerdo de Tejada had instructed the army that Chucho el Roto and his bandits would become their first priority. Chavez went on to explain that Jesús Arriaga knew his days were numbered in their native land and sent his beloved sister with three loyal men to serve as bodyguards north to secure land and to build a ranch far away from those that wanted them all dead.

The moon was directly overhead and the night had grown longer as stories of our lives were told around the campfire. It was a pleasant night with folks that I had grown to care about and trust. It also helped that one of the group was one of the most beautiful women I have ever known. She was right up in the front of the line with Devon Eldridge. I would miss my new friends when we would have to say goodbye in the morning.

The night air was cold enough so you could see your breath as we all said our good nights. As I lay down, Mutt joined me to add his warmth to me. I could not get the vision of Kellie Shawn Arriaga out of my mind as she slept not more than 20 feet away from me. The chilled night autumn air picked up and started the "tree whispers" above my head and finally gave my mind the mountain music to fall asleep to.

CHAPTER 17

I woke before the sun had broken above the snowcapped mountains to the east. The night sky was slowly turning blue and gave enough light to see by, and the first thing I saw was Kellie Shawn with a huge smile as she lay on her side giving my half wolf dog a belly rub. Sometime during the night Mutt had abandoned me and decided to join and keep the most beautiful mujer in all of Mexico warm. From the look of pure joy from both Mutt and Kellie, I could not find fault in Mutt's move. Hell, it was probably the smartest move I had ever seen by man or beast. Watching them both brought a smile to my face. Mutt, like myself, had realized that Kellie Shawn Arriaga was a distinctive type of woman.

Slowly standing to get the night kinks out of my joints from sleeping on the cold ground, I could feel the wind as it picked up some and brought the scent of the dying aspen leaves, which reminded me once again that ole' man winter was just in the north and ready to bring snow and cold. Looking to the heavens, I decided winter would not start today because the sky was clear of any clouds and the temperature was already on the rise for a beautiful day in the high country.

The Martinez brothers already had the cook fire going and had a fresh pot of coffee boiling. And they also had more than a dozen chicken eggs that they were scrambling up to go along with some fresh campfire tortillas and beans to make breakfast burritos. It all smelled wonderful.

Rey Chavez was still asleep and did not seem to be an early riser; Rey was probably one of the most interesting men I had ever known, and I could count them on one hand - Lucas, Matt Lee the old mountain man, and now the actor turned bandit Rey Chavez.

Walking to the edge of the campsite, I gave my "come to" whistle, and both Storm and Strawberry trotted right up ready to start their day. Brushing them both down, I gave them some grain from my supplies and a pinch of sugar each. While packing Strawberry and saddling Storm, I watched as Kellie Shawn walked down to the small stream to the west to fill their canteens with water. As she was walking, I could not help but notice she was wearing a pair of blue jean Levi's today, and she wore them like no man ever could. She was a stunning woman, and Mutt had taken a liking to her. Of course Mutt was leading the way for her and it seemed they would be friends for life. Grabbing my canteens, I decided to join them.

After filling my canteens, I stood next to Kellie as we watched the morning sun finally as it rose above the mountains to the east on its daily arc across the sky. It was peaceful, and it was times like this I wished these fleeting moments would never end. It was Kellie who broke the calm and tranquility of the moment when she spoke, "I have been thinking Chance, Mutt and you are more than welcome to join us. You seem to be a man of many talents and the men enjoy your company; I know my brother would love you. You would be a wonderful addition to the house of Arriaga. You could put your ride for justice aside for now, and in time my brother could even send some of his men with you to finish what I know you need to do."

Turning my body to look at her before I replied, "This is sort of unexpected and a surprise, and of course I am tempted to take you up on your offer. I do feel at ease with your men and your brother sounds like a remarkable fellow. As for Mutt, he may stay. He seems to have taken a shine to you. I have no hold on him; he does whatever he sets his mind to. I do wonder Kellie Shawn Arriaga, what thoughts do you have of me?"

My reply brought a smile and set off what looked like sparks in the eyes of green with a hint of blue. Kellie reached out and grabbed my empty left hand and slowly rubbed her forefinger in the palm of my hand before she spoke, "You should know Chance, I am a woman that speaks her mind clearly and straight forward. That being said, I asked you to join us for selfish reasons. I am attracted to you and have been from the first moment you rode into camp. As last night wore on, I was saddened by the fact that we would part ways today and probably never see each other again. I think I would like to get to know more about the man Chance Bondurant. I realize part of the attraction is that you will probably say "no" and that your sense of honor will make you ride out this morning to finish your ride to avenge your brother. I understand that and admire that, but I had to say something to let you know how I felt. Of course, if all I get is Mutt the half wolf dog, that is fine for now; he is more than welcome to stay."

Being this close to Kellie and holding her hand brought my blood to a boil. There was no denying that. I was more than attracted to this female Mexican bandit, but the destiny of my life followed a different road for now. Fate and justice dictated that I stay my course and finish what the last surviving members of the Biggers and Hammond gang had started. I would never be able to look in the mirror or visit my brother's grave ever again if I didn't see that justice was done the Bondurant way. Lucas told me I had to have a cold heart to end this with those heartless outlaws, that I could not care about anyone or anything and that I was willing to die to bring about a "rocky mountain retribution." As much as I wanted to be with this woman who had graced my life, I knew she would never respect me if I did not do what I had set out to do.

Leaning in close to look into her eyes, knowing I could lose myself there and be a happy man, I spoke, "Kellie, there is no denying how I was attracted to you from the first moment I saw you. I know this will sound strange, but I feel that I have always known you and your heart. Even Mutt senses how extraordinary you are, and your bodyguards are loyal to you and no one else. I could only hope to have a life with a woman such as yourself, but the time is not right. I swore a blood oath on my brother's grave and knowing what I already know about you, Senorita Kellie Shawn Arriaga, you would never respect me if I did not follow through with that."

Kellie responded, still holding my hand, "I knew the answer before you spoke. I see your struggle in your eyes. Hear this Chance Bondurant, when you have finished with the Bigger and Hammond gang, find me no matter what, look for me amongst the high mountains, for there will always be a place in my heart for you, no matter how long it takes."

With no more words to be spoken, she gathered her canteens and headed back to camp and the others. I watched her walk away with regrets. There was no doubt I could love this woman, no doubt at all.

After finishing packing Strawberry with the freshly filled canteens, there was nothing else to do but head toward the northwest and Grand Lake. Kellie and her band of bodyguards were heading west through Byers Canyon along the Colorado River towards Hot Sulfur Springs looking for land for her brother.

I was reluctant to leave and waited for everyone to get settled into their saddle to say my final goodbyes to Glen and Daniel Martinez. Kellie Shawn rode up next to me and without saying a word leaned over and kissed me, a passionate kiss and one I would never forget. It surprised me so much I almost forgot to kiss her back, almost. As she spurred her horse, she spoke in a loud and clear voice, "Chance Bondurant, when you have avenged your brother, look for me amongst the high mountains and I will be looking for you."

Having said that, she followed the Martinez brothers to the west with one glance over her shoulder and a wave goodbye before I could say anything. Rey Chavez rode up and with a huge smile stuck out his hand to shake mine. "I would say my amigo that she is the best kisser in all of Mexico, but I and no one that I know has ever been that close to Senorita Arriaga. I believe she sees the goodness of your corazón and knows you are a mighty guerrero. I think we will meet again, but until then remember Rey Chavez is your amigo."

With that Chavez spurred his horse into a trot to catch up with the rest of his party.

Mutt seemed torn for a few minutes and looked like he might sprint after Kellie. He looked back at me as if he wanted me to say something. "If you feel the need Mutt, you can follow as you know I would never stop you from following your heart."

He looked at me and finally sat down as if to say, "Let's get moving; adventure is before and not behind us."

Chuckling, I spurred Storm into a light trot to the north leading Strawberry, Mutt took one last look at Kellie fading into the distance and sprinted ahead of the horses to lead us into Grand Lake.

I had not ridden more than a dozen yards before an ebony crow appeared above my head, flapping its wings and heading west in the same direction of Kellie and her bodyguards. I got an eerie feeling seeing this crow heading in the direction of the ones that in short order I had learned to care about. According to those that had taught me all about survival in the mountains - Lucas and Matt Lee - this was a unique sign that the Ute Indians believed in. The crow symbolized life's mysteries and death, and somehow today it might mean something. As I rode north pondering this, for the life of me, I could not decipher what it meant.

CHAPTER 18

As the ride to the north started and a few miles were left behind, I realized I needed to put any thought of the girl Mexican bandit in the back of my mind, abandoning any and all thoughts of her because she would only cloud my judgment and make me confused about the next step in my life to take. As much as I had enjoyed meeting Senorita Arriaga, I needed to forget her for now, for I had an oath to fulfill and there was a good possibility I would not survive my upcoming encounter with the Bigger and Hammond gang. It took over two years for Lucas Eldridge to complete his revenge on the Verdugo brothers after they had slaughtered his first wife. It may take that or much more to bring this "rocky mountain retribution" to a finish. Yes, no way, no how, could I let Kellie Shawn Arriaga fog my judgment.

My mood darkened some as I realized I may never see Kellie ever again. So went my mood, so went the weather. Dark clouds started to form in the north and were rolling down the valley in my direction. The clouds had the menacing look of an autumn snow storm. Stopping at the headwaters of the Colorado River about midday to let the horses and Mutt water themselves, I tried not to think of Kellie heading west to Hot Sulfur Springs, but instead, I thought about the mighty Colorado River. Here, where I stood in Grand County, the river was only a couple of feet across, but I had heard as it flowed and gathered more water and rapids that it had cut a magnificent canyon down Arizona way that some called the "Grand Canyon." Matt Lee and Lucas both had told me it was nature at its finest and it was something to behold. Maybe someday I would head south and see it for myself. For now my trail was headed north to the newly formed supply town of Grand Lake.

Late afternoon brought Mutt, Storm, Strawberry, and myself to the outer edges of Grand Lake. I sat for a spell in the saddle overlooking the new town to get a sense of what I might encounter in the supply depot. From this vantage point, I could see a town with a few tents, but mostly a settlement of cabins and businesses built with lodgepole pine logs which were in abundance along the mountainsides. I had heard or read somewhere that the town was about 8400 feet in altitude and a couple of thousand feet below timberline where the trees never grow any more. I am sure the camp inhabitants try to get their cabins built as soon as possible since at this altitude, the summer and warm months were so short. Looking further to the east, I could see the lake that the town was named after. Grand Lake seemed busy with its everyday activities and did not appear to be a town in fear of the remaining outlaws that formed the Biggers and Hammond gang.

Slipping off the rawhide thong from around my Colt's hammer that held it from falling out on the trail, I palmed my colt and added a 44 shell to the empty chamber that was usually kept empty for safety. I also checked the loads on my Winchester to make sure it was fully loaded. Even if the gang was not still here in Grand Lake, I wanted to be ready for any and all encounters. As the sun started to go behind the mountains to the west, I felt several snowflakes land on my cheek and melt. Looking to the heavens, I watched the sunset as it peeked through the clouds and as always was amazed by the magnificence of a high mountain sunset. Feeling the chill of the coming night air, I spurred Storm in the direction of Grand Lake.

The livery stable and corral was on the western edge of the settlement, and I thought that was a good place as any to try and pick up any information of the Biggers and Hammond gang. After unpacking Strawberry and unsaddling Storm, I let them loose in the pole corral with about 20 other horses in it. I paid the liveryman with a suspiciously common name of Howard Smith the going rate plus two dollars more for some extra care for my horses. Mr. Smith was a quiet man and did not reveal much of himself during the exchange. Some folks headed to the Rocky Mountain frontier to start a new life far from troubles from wherever they were from. I suspected Howard Smith was one of those. I got very little useful information from Mr. Smith other than the location of a suitable hotel to rent a room for the night.

Heading down what served as the main street of the town of Grand Lake, Mutt and I passed several saloons and more than a few drunken cowboys, mountain men, and miners. I knew this was a rough and rowdy settlement with little or no law and that life was cheap here. All took notice of me and my half wolf; no-one said anything to me. It would take a lot of liquid courage to buck a man with a half wolf by his side.

As the night finally took hold and the sun disappeared, the stars started their nightly dance across the sky, and Mutt and I watched them for a spell before heading to the Baldwin Hotel to see if they had a room for rent. The Baldwin was a simple one floor lodgepole cabin affair with six rooms and owned by a no nonsense man named Roger Baldwin and his wife Sherol Roy. Roger was an older man of medium height and build with gray hair and a white goatee, and he wore a tied down Colt this evening as he checked me in like a man who knew how to use it. His wife Sherol Roy was a small and pleasant enough woman with short graying hair and a smile as big as the whole outdoors. Mutt seemed to take a shine to her as he trotted right up to her and flopped over on his back for her to give him a belly rub, which Sherol was more than happy to oblige. I did not have to be a Ute Indian to know that was a sign that they were good folks.

After I paid for the room, Sherol asked if I had eaten yet this evening and finding out I had not set me up with a heaping bowl of elk stew and some butter biscuits to wipe up the drippings with. She even produced several elk bones with generous portions of meat still attached for Mutt to savor on. After polishing that mighty fine stew and a piece of apple pie, I asked both Sherol and Roger if they had ever heard of the Biggers and Hammond gang and if they were still in Grand Lake. Both Sherol and Roger looked at each other for a minute with questioning looks as if they were trying to figure out if I was maybe a member of the gang myself. I thought I should clarify at that point. "My name is Chance Bondurant and my half wolf, half something else dog is named Mutt, and we are looking for them to settle an old score. They killed my younger brother, shot Mutt, and almost killed me near Nevadaville, Colorado several years ago and just recently I ran into two of the members Chucky Livingston and Dave Edgar in Russell Gulch. I had read in a newspaper that the remaining members were in these parts, and I am here to find them or their trail."

Sherol spoke first, and I had a feeling she did most of the talking for the pair, "Chance Bondurant? If you mean by run in, you shot those no good outlaws down, then Roger and I are glad to know you. You have become a famous man here in Colorado. As for the members of the Biggers and Hammond gang for the last couple of months up until yesterday, they all skedaddled except one. They had been here and made the Lake Saloon their headquarters. They never really bothered anyone here, more like they were resting up and waiting for something. The one that looked part Indian, Alvardo had been gone for over a month and returned early yesterday morning and after speaking with the boss outlaw, Bobby Burke, Rick Alvardo, and Rod Hammond packed up and left in a sort of a hurry."

Why would they leave in such a flurry one day before I got to Grand Lake? It would have nothing to do with me, because they would have had no way of knowing I was heading this way, nor would it panic them. They were ruthless and dangerous men and a lone man trailing them would not have made them want to leave. It had to be something else that made them leave in such a hurry.

The interesting tidbit was the boss, Herman Biggers was still here in Grand Lake. Pondering all that Sherol had told me and putting it in some sort of order in my mind, I asked, "Am I correct in my understanding Sherol that Herman Biggers is still here in Grand Lake?"

Nodding her head, "Yes, as far as I know, Roger and I were taking our coffee on the front porch when we saw the gang ride out minus Mr. Biggers."

After a full meal and a day of traveling, I felt more ready for bed than an encounter with Herman Biggers, but I could not take the gamble that he might slip out during the night. Standing slowly with my Stetson in my hand, I shaped it somewhat before snapping it back on my head. "If you would be so kind Sherol and point me in the direction of the Lake Saloon, I would be much obliged."

Sherol's face now showed apprehension and uneasiness, not for herself, but for me. It took her a full minute and several glances in Roger's direction with him nodding "yes" before she spoke, "I feel awful now telling you about Biggers being in town still. I could care less about that old bastard, but I see the goodness in you and I know your heart is true. I would not want any harm to come to you because of something I said."

She was a principled woman, and Roger was a noble man, and it humbled me to know such people had found each other in this life. Smiling as I spoke to calm her fears and reservations, "Sherol, I was hunting these men. It would have mattered not if you told me about Biggers' whereabouts or not because destiny and fate is in play here, and I was going to find them one way or another. I do thank you for your concern."

Roger spoke, knowing his wife was struggling with all that had transpired, "You will not need your horse, Chance; the Lake Saloon is just about 50 yards down the road to the east on the north side. Biggers always sits at the table with his back to the north wall facing the room so that he can see all who enter. He will see you enter. There will be no surprise."

Having said that, Roger stuck out his hand to shake mine. "We will build a fire in the fireplace in your room for when you and Mutt return."

I grabbed my Winchester from the wall by my seat I had been sitting on when I was eating my supper, and then Mutt and I headed out the door.

CHAPTER 19

Stepping out onto the front porch of the Baldwin Hotel, I palmed my Colt to once again make sure it was fully loaded with six. Re-holstering my Colt, I then drew it again checking my speed. The Colt slid fast and easily into my hand. Re-holstering my Colt once again, I then jacked the lever on my Winchester to make sure I had a shell in the firing chamber. Now I felt ready for anything that I may encounter this evening.

Mutt was standing by my side, and he knew something was up. He was alert to everything around us. I took a minute standing there feeling the cold autumn night air. It also smelled like snow, and I would not be surprised by morning that we had a couple of inches, maybe more. The death of autumn was near as ole' man winter was just down the road. Just as I was thinking that, a couple of snowflakes fluttered by my face.

Stepping off the front porch, I headed east toward the Lake Saloon. The saloon was not hard to find, for it was the only business of its kind on the north side of the road. Once I was on the boardwalk, I noticed two sets of doors for the saloon - one set of full double doors that opened inward and one set of batwing doors set in front of the double doors for when the weather was nice. Mutt and I had to open both sets of doors to enter the Lake Saloon this evening.

There were four men in the saloon besides myself. Biggers, of course, a bald headed bartender with a walrus mustache that was half asleep, and what looked like two older freighters that were too busy playing cribbage and drinking whiskey to really notice Mutt or myself.

Roger Baldwin was correct in that Herman Biggers was sitting just as Roger had described it. Herman had his back to the north wall with a half full bottle of bourbon in his right hand. He was in the middle of pouring as I walked in, and he took one look at me before finishing topping off his shot glass. What Roger failed to mention was that he had a 12-gauge Greener double barrel shotgun lying on top of his table with the barrels pointed toward the front door. I would bet my last dollar it was loaded with double-ought buckshot. He also had a shoulder pistol rig hung on his left shoulder with a Colt 44 in the holster with the grip pointed outward in a cross draw manner. Since he was sitting down, I could not see if he was also armed with a conventional holster.

The saloon smelled of stale tobacco, damp whiskey, and sweat. Walking slowly to the bar, but keeping Herman and the two freighters in my eyesight, I laid my Winchester on top of the bar pointed not at Biggers, but in his general direction. The sound of laying my weapon on the bar startled and woke up the bartender who asked me, "What can I do you for stranger?"

Not taking my eyes off of Biggers and in a level voice, "Whiskey if you have it and not the watered down version."

The bartender set a clean shot glass in front and began to fill it with a generous amount of whiskey from a filthy bottle. "That will be 2-bits."

Still keeping my eye on Biggers, I laid 4-bits on top of the bar and ordered another. Biggers was starting to get irritated that I was staring at him; Mutt was standing by my side and giving him the ole' stink eye too. I did not get the feeling he remembered me, but he was eyeballing Mutt and myself something fierce. Biggers looked much the same since the last time I saw him, maybe a tad older with shoulder length almost pure white hair under what looked like a new black cowboy hat with a cattleman's crease. I could see a blue flannel shirt that sported polished bone buttons under an ebony leather vest. His grizzled gray beard was cut way shorter than I remembered. Since he was glaring back at me, I got a good look at his eyes this time and saw the evil that lived there. His pupils were almost black; I had never seen black eyes before. Outside the pupils they were a dirty, milky white. I imagine that most folks would shy away from Biggers when he just gave them one look. On that day that Jace was murdered, I feared this man. On this day of Herman Biggers' retribution, I no longer feared the man; I loathed him. Herman Biggers was going to die today.

Sipping my whiskey with my left hand, I left my right hand free so as to not impede the time when I drew my weapon. Biggers spoke first, "Do you and that flea bag dog have a problem with me, boy? I don't reckon you are giving me the eye because of my beauty."

With a clear and confident voice, "I was just thinking how you haven't changed much since the last time I saw you is all. I reckon Mutt thinks much the same; we both recognized you right off."

My mind focused on all that surrounded me at this moment in time. I could smell the whiskey in the shot glasses and the staleness of tobacco smoke that lingered in the air. I could hear and feel the stillness of the room as the bartender and the two cribbage players stopped what they were doing after feeling the tension mount in the closed room. Knowing what I knew about Biggers, the Colt pistol in his shoulder rig would not be his weapon of choice in this close up battle, but rather that Greener double barrel 12-gauge sitting in front of him on the table. I could see in his eyes that he was confident in his ability to use that weapon against me. I knew that he had no chance; yes, Herman Biggers was going to die today in that chair. All that matters now was the timing. I could hear the tick tick of the clock behind the bar and out of my sight. Little did Biggers know that clock was now counting down the last final minutes of his life!

Biggers' eyes narrowed as he tried to figure out how I might know him. "I guess I don't recall any asshole with a wolf. So if you got business with me boy, get on with it."

With a smirk on my face and still in a clear and confident voice, "Do you think I admire your toughness in the wake of you are here all alone without those that do your robbing and killing for you? You still talk like a man in charge even though your boys are not here. I wish they were here in Grand Lake, because it would save me some considerable time in hunting them down. Where are they? Where have Alvardo, Hammond, and that idiot Burke ridden off to?"

That put a smile on Biggers as he spoke, "You speak boldly for a skinny no-account kid still wet behind the ears; must be that wolf dog that gives you courage. What are you, some wannabe bounty hunter looking to get killed by one of his betters?"

This was maybe escalating faster than I wanted, and I needed to know where Alvardo, Hammond, and Burke had gone. I needed to keep stringing it out some to get that information. The problem with that was I could see in Biggers' eyes, he was tired of the talk and I might have to kill him prior to finding that out.

Looking him in his eyes and never wavering, "$1500 is a lot of money, Biggers. I have no doubt that I will collect that bounty on you, but what you need to know is that I am not here to collect the bounty. I am here for another reason. My name is Chance Bondurant, and the half wolf and half something else dog is named Mutt. Do you remember us?"

That knocked that smile off his face. "Oh Hell, I should have known it was you. My mind is not as clear as it once was due to the booze and age. You are that kid that killed Livingston and Edgar." Another smile started to spread across the man's face I intended to kill this evening. Biggers said with a half laugh, "It seems I now have a couple of openings in the company. Are you and the dog applying for the job?"

Knowing that the other three outlaws were not in Grand Lake, pushing him again I asked in a stern voice, "All I need to know Biggers, is this between you and me, or is one of those other cowards hiding in the shitter out back or behind the bar?"

The smile quickly evaporated off Biggers' face as he replied, "The others are heading toward Hot Sulphur Springs; it seems there is some Mexican gal with a shit load of gold looking to buy land hereabouts, and the boys are seeing how easy it will be to take it from her. Soooooo... I guess it's just you and me and my Greener."

Having said that, Biggers started for the shotgun, and I palmed my Colt with lightning speed. Biggers' eyebrows raised as he saw the speed with which I drew my weapon - he had not counted on that.

I fired once with the bullet catching Herman dead center in his throat. With the advent of the bullet punching a hole in his throat, then out the back, Biggers instinctively stopped reaching for the shotgun, and his hands flew to his throat trying to stem the blood from flowing. His attempt to staunch the flow was to no avail. His blood was squirting through his fingers. I walked closer so he could get a good look at the man that had killed him. Herman's eyes were wide open, and he was still alive when I spoke, "That was for my younger brother your boys killed, and this is for shooting my dog." I placed a nice round hole in his forehead with my second shot. The momentum of the last shot sent Herman slamming into the wall behind him, his legs kicking out knocking the table over, dumping the Greener shotgun on the floor. Biggers, who was still holding his throat, but very much dead, did a slow slide down the wall into a growing puddle of blood on the floor.

Mutt had been standing by my side the whole time content to let me handle the situation. Seeing Herman Biggers down, Mutt paid tribute the only way Mutt could, and he promptly walked up and lifted his leg and peed on the now cooling body of the dead outlaw boss.

Looking at the man that I killed and knowing there was no man more deserving of dying a violent death than Herman Biggers, I once again felt nothing - no happiness or remorse - nothing at all. There was no sense of accomplishment. I again wondered if there was something wrong with me and how my mind worked. It was as if all the innocence of my youth had been sapped out that day when Jace had been murdered.

Biggers' words were now starting to sink in. The rest of the outlaw gang was tracking down a Mexican woman with lots of gold looking to buy land and that could only mean that Senorita Kellie Shawn Arriaga and her bodyguards were in harm's way. I would have to finish up any investigations into the shooting and make arrangements for the bounty to be received and be back on the trail. It seems my fate and what was to be with the remaining members of the Biggers and Hammond gang and my possible destiny with the beautiful Mexican bandit might now be in the same place. I needed to leave for Hot Sulfur Springs as soon as possible.

CHAPTER 20

As much as I wanted to leave at first light to Hot Sulphur Springs, I was held up in Grand Lake since they did not have a sheriff or even a jail yet. Sherol Roy was able to help me out and wired the mining camp of Lulu City to the North which happened to have a Federal Marshal named Eric Robert picking up a prisoner for transportation to the federal courthouse in Denver. Marshal Robert replied in a wire that he would swing by on his way back to Denver to get the testimony from the witnesses and to make sure it was in fact Herman Biggers that had been killed. If he determined it was Biggers, then he could notify the courts about the $1500 bounty and where to send it.

After the shoot-out with Biggers, I had all three witnesses write down what had happened and sign their names to it. One of the freighters could not read or write, so the bartender wrote it down for him, and the freighter made his mark on the paper. I thought about just leaving the three witnesses' testimonies with Roger Baldwin and be on my way. Every time I would get antsy to leave, my thoughts would return to what Lucas had always told me, "When things go south and you kill someone in a fair fight, don't leave town because you know you were in the right; leave town when the law knows you were in the right."

Try as I might, I could not stop thinking of Senorita Kellie Shawn being in peril from the last three remaining members of the outlaw gang. I tried numerous times to convince myself that the outlaws would see how protected she was with her bodyguards and leave them well enough alone. I knew the Martinez brothers and Rey Chavez were capable enough, but the outlaws may figure out a way to ambush the Arriaga party. I needed to try and warn them if I could.

The day after the gunfight with Biggers while I was waiting for Marshal Robert, I decided to take my mind off of worrying about Kellie Shawn and her bodyguards by riding around the actual lake of Grand Lake. After saddling Storm and with Mutt leading the way, I made my way from the livery stable past the Baldwin Hotel toward the lake. The sun was out and not a cloud in the forever blue sky, but the air had that autumn chill to it. As I approached from the northwest, I could see all of the lake from this vantage point. It seemed to me that the lake was in between 500-600 acres.

The settlement of Grand Lake was on the northwest shore, but the remaining three sides were surrounded my snow-peaked mountains. According to Roger Baldwin, it was the deepest lake in the Colorado Territory at 300 feet, and it was said to him that it was formed by a glacier long before man ever stepped into these mountains of old. As Storm, Mutt, and I skirted along the edge, we could see all the way to the bottom. The water was crystal clear on this day and one of the most gorgeous sights I had ever seen. There were more than a few aspens dotted among the evergreens lining the shore, and the slight wind had the aspen trees doing the "tree whispers" which I loved so much. The shoreline was only about four or five miles long and would not take me long to travel and see it all.

Mutt, Storm, and I were taking our time as we explored along the shoreline, recalling the history and stories that the mountain man Matt Lee had told me about this lake. The Grand River Ute Indian tribe had laid claim to this lake, which they called "Spirit Lake" and most of the middle park region. The legend of how the Utes' name for the lake came to be was told to Matt Lee by an elder in the tribe.

One summer evening long ago a thunderstorm rolled in and over the Never Summer Mountains when a small band of Utes was camping on the shores of Grand Lake. In the midst of the storm, the Utes were attacked by a war party of their ancient enemies of the Arapahoe and Cheyenne. As the storm raged, so did the battle; the Ute warriors loaded all the women, children, and elderly in their rafts and set them adrift on the lake for their safety. Numerous warriors had fallen in the battle on both sides, but the Utes drove off the attacking tribes and were victorious in the battle. The chief of the Utes at that time looked to the white-capped lake and saw the rafts had been capsized during the storm and all the women, children, and the elderly could not be seen.

After a night of grieving for their dead, the next night it was said that the Ute warriors could see across the now calm waters the spirits of the dead families rising in the mist. The Ute chief and the warriors were so shaken by seeing the spirits that they never returned to Spirit Lake again.

Looking across the now calm and motionless lake, I tried to envision what the Ute warriors must have felt after losing their loved ones. It had to be a challenging day and night going from victory on the battlefield to losing the ones that they fought so hard to protect. I could relate somewhat. I knew that feeling of helplessness the day that Jace was killed back in Nevadaville.

Thinking of Jace got me thinking of Kellie Shawn and her body guards, not knowing that the remaining members of the Biggers and Hammond gang were hunting them. My only hope was the Federal Marshal Eric Robert would be here soon so I could be back on the trail and headed their way. Not that there was anything I could do about it at the time, but I felt somewhat foolish not knowing that Kellie Shawn Arriaga was carrying a lot of gold. Of course she would be carrying some sort of payment for the land and to build the ranch for her brother. I just had not thought about it; it worried me now that others had.

We were about three-fourths around the edge of Grand Lake when an eagle appeared out of the forever blue sky and with one powerful flap of his wings, he soared overhead almost faster than my eyes could follow him. I stopped Storm so Mutt and I could watch the glorious bird in flight as he turned in a soaring wide circle as he seemed to take an interest in myself and the half wolf dog. I wondered if it was significant that an eagle appeared this autumn morning as I was remembering the tale of how "Spirit Lake" had gotten its name. Matt Lee had told how the Ute Indians saw the eagle as their most powerful spirit animal. The Utes believed the eagle signified courage, wisdom, and strength and spoke to their creator the "Great Spirit." The Utes, like most Indian tribes, used eagle feathers in their dress to symbolize their courage and willingness to battle their enemies. They also used the bones of eagles to make flutes and whistles to use in their religious ceremonies. I thought of this and much more as I watched the eagle as it watched us. The eagle must have tired of us as he moved out of the circle and headed east. He was heading for the spine in the mountains that was the "Great Divide," and I could not stop thinking that distance would be a three day ride for me, and the eagle would take…well, hell, he was already there. As the eagle faded over the mountain top and out of my eyesight, I once again gave Storm some rein and headed back to the settlement of Grand Lake.

After taking Storm back to the livery stable, it was about midday and Sherol Roy was serving up some roasted chicken, butter biscuits, fried taters, and apple pie for her guests. Sherol even had a few leftover elk bones for Mutt. After a second piece of pie, my belly felt content, and Mutt and I joined Roger and Sherol on the front porch for a cup of coffee. With Mutt now sound asleep at my feet, I tried to be sociable, but was failing miserably at it because my mind was wandering, anxious to get after the rest of the outlaw gang. It worried me that the outlaws were gaining so much time and distance on me that I was afraid of what I might find when I finally caught up with Senorita Arriaga and her bodyguards.

Two days had gone by, with time passing slowly, as I waited for Federal Marshal Robert. It seemed almost like an eternity. It was mid-afternoon on the second day as Roger, Sherol, and I were having coffee and tea on the front porch when the Marshal rode into town with his prisoner and made their way to the front of the Baldwin Hotel. The prisoner was a small, dark haired, and dirty man almost dressed in rags with his hands tied to the saddle horn on the horse he was riding that was tethered to the Marshal's horse.

Federal Marshal Eric Robert was a different matter altogether. He seemed ageless like my friend Matt Lee. He looked like he was about 6'2" and weighed about 190 pounds. As he dismounted, he did so with agility and grace that you might find in a dancer. His hair was short and gray and he had a week's worth of an almost pure white beard. He was armed heavily with two rifle scabbards, one hosting a lever action Winchester like mine, and the other with what looked like a double barrel 12-gauge Greener shotgun like the one that Herman Biggers tried to use on me. His side arm was just like almost everyone else in the Rocky Mountain region - a Colt 44 pistol that was tied down to his right leg with the grip pointed backwards for a standard draw, and the metal shined like the owner knew how to take care of his weapons. Marshal Robert looked like a very hard-hitting and capable hombre that knew his law business.

Marshal Robert was all business and after we introduced ourselves without even letting his prisoner off his horse, he read the three witnesses' testimonies and decided that would be sufficient enough and would not have to interview the three men that were in the Lake Saloon at the time of the gunfight. After viewing Herman Biggers' face and body that was being kept cool in the creek behind the Lake Saloon and comparing it to a likeness on a wanted poster that the Marshal had brought from Lulu City, he was satisfied it was in fact Herman Biggers. He wrote out a voucher just in case something happened to him before he got back over Rollins Pass and to Denver for $1500 for the bounty and signed his name to it. He explained as soon as he delivered his prisoner back to Denver and the territorial courts that he would contact the Marshal's office and the Governor's office about what had happened here and have the money sent to my bank in Central City.

After returning back to the Baldwin hotel, Marshal Robert pulled his prisoner off the horse as gently as he could and proceeded to shackle him around the ankles and handcuff him to the railing on the front porch of the hotel. He then pointed to indicate that he should sit on the porch, and having done all of that, he then took off his hat and faced Sherol and asked, "Madame, I know it is not yet supper time, but could you be so kind and rustle up some grub for myself and my prisoner. I am authorized to pay top money for meals. I need to be back in the saddle and on the trail this evening. I received some other unpleasant news while I was in Lulu City. We may have some trouble with the Ute Indians forthcoming."

This of course was news to all. Sherol spoke in her pleasant voice, "Of course Marshal Robert. I have some roasted chicken and taters for supper and will get both of you a large plate while you tell Roger and Chance what the troubles we all may be facing with the Ute Indians."

Roger spoke before me, but we both were thinking the same thing, "I thought the Ute Indians were heading to the government reservation out west in Utah?"

As Sherol went into the hotel to fetch the Marshal and his shackled side kick some food, the Marshal pulled up a chair on the front porch and laid his hat alongside of it before he spoke again, "You can all call me Eric. To answer the question so did everyone else. It seems that Chief Piah of the Grand River Utes had a different idea and decided not to live up to their side of the agreement and broke off with about thirty of his warriors and their families and headed to the remote and rugged mountains north of the mining camps of Lulu City. And to make matters worse, about the same number of warriors and their families joined him from the Yampa River Utes. With winter fast approaching and the nearest troops stationed at Fort Sheridan south of Denver, it would be impossible to first locate them and convince them to go to the reservation anytime soon. No military commander worth his salt would ever agree to a winter campaign in those isolated and almost inaccessible mountains. If the Indians didn't kill them, the cold and snow would. That means any miners, ranchers, or mountain men might be at the mercy of some very pissed off Indians. Until the snow melts during the spring, they all will be on their own if the Indians decide to become hostile and take out their anger on folks they believe are taking away their land and hunting grounds. I have just been assigned that territory and I need to get back as soon as possible."

Sherol returned as Eric spoke with some heaping plates of hot food and fresh water for him and the shackled prisoner. Sherol said in a confused voice, "I have lived here for quite a spell and the Ute Indians have always been our friends and have never caused much trouble. I guess I am sort of ashamed that I really do not know much about them or their culture."

Ute Indians were something I knew a little bit about even though I had never really known any of the tribe. As Mutt sat beside me on the front porch, I tossled his hair on his head some as I spoke, "The word Ute means "Land of the Sun" and there were six original Ute bands - Parianucs, Yampa, Capote, Weeminuche, Tabeguache, and the Uintahs. The Utes were some of the first Indians to use horses after acquiring them from the Spanish and have become excellent horsemen. They also are a very religious and spiritual people. Religion aside, they are warriors to the highest degree. Grand River and Yampa River Utes are the names we have given them since we cannot speak their language. The Grand River "the elk people" and Yampa River "root eaters" Utes are of the northern tribes, and I am sure that the Grand River Utes and Chief Piah would consider that all the folks that live in Grand Lake, Hot Sulphur Springs, Lulu City and Teller City - as squatters in his territory."

Marshal Robert seemed a little alarmed when he spoke, "How is it Chance that you seem to know so much about these renegade Indians."

Looking at Eric Robert, "I have no allegiance to them if you are wondering that. I was raised by a man and mentored some by another who had lived with the Ute Indians for a spell. I was taught some of their way of life, and through these two men, I learned to respect how they live and their beliefs."

Still questioning my motives, "Are these two men Indians themselves? Maybe renegades?"

That almost made me laugh out loud, with a smile on my face, "No, the two men that raised and mentored me are Lucas Eldridge and Matt Lee."

Eric's face now was starting to show some understanding. "Impressive, two of the most famous men in the Rocky Mountain frontier. So I reckon Chance, you must be the same man that killed Chucky Livingston and Dave Edgar in Russell Gulch not long ago. I heard there was a young girl killed with a stray bullet in the gunfight with Edgar."

That last thought of the Marshal's took the smile right off my face. "All true, and the bullet that killed the young girl was from Edgar and not me, but I will have to live with that for the rest of my life. Her name was Ronda Joy Balkema."

Marshal Eric and his prisoner had finished their supper and made ready to leave after handing a five dollar gold piece to Sherol. After both were in the saddle, Marshal Eric pointed toward the man he had handcuffed and said one more thing to me, "I understand how you feel about the girl that was killed Chance, and like you I have had a similar experience. Just remember what you did was for the good folks of the Rocky Mountain frontier. As long as there are skunks like this one and the ones in the Biggers and Hammond gang, innocent folks will suffer beyond description. Men like us need to be the guardians that protect those that struggle to protect themselves. These folks that are innocent didn't bring this upon themselves. Even though sometimes it's hard to see, it's important to understand that these people exist. They are the victims of the sins of assholes like this. Remember Chance, you and I need to be the wolves that devour the evil."

Having said more than I am sure he intended, Federal Marshal Eric Robert then gave his mare some rein and a slight jab of his spur and headed down the trail with his prisoner into the encroaching darkness.

I felt the need to be on the trail too and headed toward Hot Sulphur Springs and Kellie Shawn and her bodyguards, but realized it was too late in the day to pack my horses and would have to wait till morning.

CHAPTER 21

Waking before dawn, Mutt sat next to me and stared at my face. When I returned the half wolf's stare, he tilted his head as if he was wondering what I was still doing in bed; it made me feel all lazy like. Shaking my head, trying to knock the cobwebs out, I reached out to give Mutt a good nuzzling on top of his head before standing up. Walking over to the broad glass window that faced toward the lake, I could see that clouds had rolled in during the night and looked somewhat menacing. I reached out to trace my finger on the glass, and it was very cold to the touch. It seemed it was going to be a chilly day to begin my trek towards Hot Sulphur Springs.

After strapping on my holster and money belt, I began to gather what few belongings I had brought into the hotel with me. Before I stepped out of my room, the smell of frying bacon found me and made my belly rumble.

Sherol Roy had indeed gotten up earlier and was frying up some chicken eggs and bacon. She was hard at work adding wood to the cast iron stove when I walked into the hotel kitchen. "Sherol, is there anything I could do to help you?"

She turned towards me, her face red from the heat of the stove, but she had that Sherol Roy smile, which made me grin. "Oh no Chance, but thanks for asking. Roger went to the livery stable to grain your horses and get them ready for you to saddle and pack. He should be back in a few minutes, and then we can eat our breakfast. I didn't feel right sending you off without a full belly."

When Roger returned, we ate our breakfast and both Roger and Sherol thanked me for ridding the town of Herman Biggers. Biggers and his men had bullied the town into giving free booze and food while they were here. They wished me well in my quest for justice against the remaining outlaws of the Biggers and Hammond gang. Roger went so far as to tell me that he thought that Rick Alvardo was the most dangerous. He thought the other outlaw members were a little bit afraid of the quiet half breed. It reminded me that Lucas warned me also about Alvardo, even without ever meeting him.

Since I had never been to Hot Sulphur Springs, I had asked Roger for the best route and distance. He explained there was only one southwest trail and it forked 12 miles from Grand Lake. The southeastern fork would take me back the same way I had come towards Rollins Pass while the western fork would take me through Byers Canyon where the upper Colorado River flowed along the southern edge of Elk Mountain all the way to Hot Sulphur Springs. He went on to explain it was close to 25 miles and easily traversed since I would still be traveling in the high mountain plains of Middle Park. If the weather held, I could in a long day make it all the way. Roger seemed to be a wealth of information and I also inquired about the trail west of Hot Sulphur Springs in case my quest took me that way. Beyond and due west once I got through Gore Canyon, there was a new supply depot along Muddy Creek owned by a man named Rudolph "Kare" Kremmling. The total distance between Hot Sulphur Springs and this store was roughly 17 or 18 miles. Roger continued in his telling and explained west of the supply depot on Muddy Creek he had never been, and that way was all new territory to him. He did mention though when he was a young man, he prospected for gold 30 miles northwest of Kare Kremmling's store on the southeastern side of Rabbit Ears Pass with little or no success. After barely surviving the winter on the remote and rugged mountain pass that straddled the "Great Divide," he headed here to the Grand Lake area, and this was where he and Sherol Roy had met.

Sherol had made a plate of eggs and bacon for Mutt and set the plate next to my chair for him. Mutt all of a sudden had gotten some manners in the presence of Sherol Roy and would not start to eat until Sherol gave him the okay. Sherol even commented on this, "That Mutt is the most pleasant and well trained dog I have ever seen." Mutt and I looked at each other and I just rolled my eyes. I would have sworn that half wolf smiled and had a smirk on his face.

After I paid my bill for room and board, Roger shook my hand and Sherol gave me a big hug and a sack containing some sandwiches that she made for lunch to eat on the trail. I would miss these two for sure. Roger Baldwin and Sherol Roy may not know it, but they had a friend for life in one Chance Bondurant.

Stepping off the front porch of the Baldwin Hotel, I had to turn my winter duster collar up to help ward off the cold and the damp air. It felt and smelled like snow. The sun was up, but hiding behind the dark clouds on this overcast morning.

I stopped about halfway to the livery stable to take in a lungful of fresh, chilled autumn air and looked to the surrounding mountains and the aspens dotted in among the evergreens. Since I had been in Grand Lake, the aspens had lost at least three fourths of their remaining golden leaves and had probably sung their last song of the "tree whispers" for the season. Fall was my favorite season; I do not believe I would be happy in a world without autumns.

Standing there thinking of autumns past and present, I looked at the half wolf and roughed up the hair some on the top of his head. "Mutt, you no longer have to be on your best behavior anymore; it's just you and me again."

After I said that, Mutt took off at a fast pace headed for the stables. He was restless to be back on the trail. I pondered if he understood the danger his new found friend Senorita Kellie Shawn

Arriaga could be facing. I reckoned it would not surprise me much if he did. Sometimes I wondered who really the boss of this outfit was. I truly loved that dog.

In short order I had Strawberry packed and Storm saddled, and they both were throwing their heads and snorting in contentment. Both horses, just like Mutt, were animals of the wild and loved the mountains and were ready to be back on the trail. Stepping into the stirrup and after squaring myself into the saddle, I turned Storm toward the southwest and gave her some rein, and we were off at a quick trot.

About three miles from Grand Lake, it started to snow, not a hard snow, but a lazy snow. The flakes were small and floated to the ground in a teeter-totter motion as the autumn breeze moved them up and down. The air was cold enough that I could see my breath and that of the horses as we made our way in the direction of Hot Sulphur Springs and Senorita Kellie Shawn Arriaga and her bodyguards.

At midday I stopped long enough to water the horses and Mutt with fresh water from a bubbling brook just along the trail. Taking out the sack that Sherol had given me for lunch, I discovered four roasted chicken sandwiches made with fresh Dutch oven bread. At the bottom of the sack was half of an apple pie and half a dozen pieces of fudge. If Sherol Roy wasn't already one of my favorite people, she just moved to the top of the class. Taking a bite of fudge, I looked at Mutt, "That is some mighty fine fudge my friend Mutt; thinking I am going to adopt Sherol Roy and make her my honorary Aunt."

Mutt gave me that quizzical look of his when he didn't care what I was saying; he was just eyeballing the food in my hand. I tossed half of the first piece of fudge to him and just like I knew he would, he caught it in midair and down the windpipe it disappeared. Mutt couldn't voice it, but I could tell by the way he was licking his chops he thought it was some mighty fine tasting fudge also. After finishing off the chicken sandwiches, Mutt and I decided to hold off on the apple pie until supper time. With our bellies content for now, we headed back on the trail toward whatever awaited us in Hot Sulfur Springs.

The horses seemed to be making great time with Storm leading and Strawberry following tied off to my saddle. Mutt kept disappearing from time to time as he explored the wilderness that surrounded us.

I thought I should stop for the night a couple of miles short of Hot Sulphur Springs, not wanting to enter the settlement during late afternoon or early evening. This time of year in the high mountains, darkness comes early about four in the afternoon. I wanted to arrive in the morning to give me a chance to study the lay of the land with plenty of sunlight to see by.

While I was riding, my mind pondered some about the three remaining outlaws. If I had to encounter all three at the same time, which would be a good possibility, I probably would not survive the encounter. So far with my gunfights with Livingston, Edgar, and Biggers, I had been lucky where it had been one-on-one. That luck might not hold out the next time, and I had to be prepared for that outcome.

Rod Hammond, with his dark circles under his eyes, looked like a sick man the last time I saw him. His addiction to laudanum and his age would, I hope, make him slower on the draw. Sick or not Hammond had not lived this long without being the shrewdest of the remaining outlaws.

Before leaving Central City, I had read a quote in the Denver newspaper about Bobby Burke, "Burke had just about enough astuteness to open his mouth when he wanted to eat, but unquestionably no more." What the newspaper article failed to mention was that Burke's stupidity gave him the ability to not be afraid of dying, because he just didn't know any better. Stupid or not Burke was said to have cat-like reflexes with his six shooter.

Rick Alvardo, the half Ute Indian and half Mexican bandit, was of course the mystery man. Without ever meeting the man, Lucas warned me that Alvardo was the most dangerous, and I trusted Lucas' instincts like no other. Even Roger Baldwin had remarked that the other outlaws seemed to be a tad bit afraid of the man. All three men were dangerous as they come. My advantage I believed was that I was trained by a righteous avenger to become a righteous avenger even if the Lord may not quite see it that way.

About an hour before sunset, I found a suitable place to camp in a cluster of evergreens and aspens that would shield me from the wind. After unsaddling Storm and unpacking Strawberry, I rubbed down both horses and talked to them about how proud I was of their speed today. They both nudged with their noses wanting their sugar for their effort. I was happy to oblige.

Mutt returned just as I had got a cooking fire started, and he had a jack rabbit in his mouth for his supper and looking prideful on his capture. Rolling my eyes at the half wolf and with a chuckle, "Just this morning buddy, you were civilized and eating off a china dinner plate. Now look at you, didn't take long for the savage to come through again. I don't suspect you are going to share your dinner with me."

Mutt sat there pondering the question for a spell and then walked over and dropped the rabbit at my feet.

After our supper of roasted rabbit and apple pie, we each had another piece of Aunt Sherol's fudge whilst we watched the sun drop below the treetops in all of its orange and blue glory behind the mountains to the west.

As Mutt and I settled down in my bedroll, I could hear gunfire in the distance towards the west which did not surprise since I was only a mile or so from Hot Sulphur Springs, but it did worry me some since the men I was hunting and Kellie Shawn, Rey Chavez, and the Martinez brothers were all in that same direction.

Finding some solace from the warmth put off from my half wolf, I was soon asleep.

CHAPTER 22

Waking up as was my custom before dawn, I had to shake off a couple of inches of snow which had dusted my flannel blanket. My muscles were a tad sore this morning due to sleeping on the cold, hard ground. After stretching some to ease the kinks of sleep out of my body, I was able to stir some remaining coals into a sizeable fire to fry up some fatback bacon and beans from my supplies for my breakfast.

Mutt had disappeared and headed into the wilderness as soon as we woke up, probably trying to scrounge up some breakfast. And it wasn't long before he showed up with a small chipmunk that he had caught.

The light snow had stopped sometime during the night, and the menacing clouds moved on to places unknown. The half wolf and I watched the sunrise in the east as the burnt orange sun slowly made its ascent. Marble white, swollen non-snow like clouds rode the skyline just above the rising sun. Directly above the clouds the sky was dark blue. It seemed to me to be this close to the heavens that the autumn chill made nature's colors more vivid. The air was frosty this morning, which was to my liking. Living in the Rockies, I had become accustomed to days that were cooler.

Mutt finished his breakfast before I did and finished off two pieces of bacon that I had left over. After giving the "come to" whistle, both Storm and Strawberry made their way toward the campsite. As I took my curry comb and started to rub down and groom the horses' manes and tails, I thought about the gunshots I heard in the distance towards the west. Or at least I thought they came from the west. Sounds traveled differently in the high mountains; the acoustics were different at this altitude and sometimes it was difficult to tell the direction of the gunshots. I did not know the ins and outs of why this was, but I knew it to be true.

Since I was so close to Hot Sulphur Springs, the gunshots could mean nothing more than a couple of drunken souls shooting at the moon. My gut feeling was telling me something else. I was taught by Lucas not to dismiss a gut feeling, because more often than not, it has given you fair warning.

After packing Strawberry and saddling Storm, I took a few minutes to practice my draw. About a dozen times I palmed my Colt with what seemed like lightning speed. I felt fast and ready for anything that might await me in Hot Sulphur Springs.

Before stepping into the stirrup, I made sure that my Winchester was fully loaded. After the shootout with Biggers, I thought about taking the 12-gauge Greener and adding it to my weapon arsenal. After hefting it a few times, I discarded that thought. The Greener was bulky and heavy to use and thought it would slow down my reaction time. Roger Baldwin was happy when I gave it to him; he was grinning from ear to ear with what he called his new "home defense weapon."

As I rode toward Hot Sulphur Springs, I thought about the renegade Ute Indians that had fled to the isolated mountains to the north rather than spend the rest of their lives on a reservation, and I felt melancholy for them. It wasn't all that long ago that all the land that would take me many weeks to travel on horseback in any direction, be it north, south, east, or west, was the territory of the Ute Indians and their ancestors. Civilization was fast changing for all the Rocky Mountain's nomadic tribes. It was inevitable, but sad nonetheless.

It was not long before I could smell the smoke from numerous cook fires that told me that Hot Sulphur Springs was just over the next knoll to the west.

My hope was that I would find Senorita Kellie Shawn Arriaga, Rey Chavez, and the Martinez brothers safe and sound after purchasing the land that they sought. I then could warn them of the dangers from the last of the remaining outlaws of the Biggers and Hammond gang.

On top of the last knoll just east of Hot Sulphur Springs, I stopped the horses and Mutt and I looked onto the streets of the settlement. The town was larger than I expected with numerous wood framed buildings lining the main street. Further to the east I could see the steam rising above the town from the heated spring water from some long ago extinct volcano that gave the town its name. After a half-hour of studying from the distance, I saw nothing to indicate anything was off kilter within the town and gave Storm some rein and a slight jab of my right spur and headed cautiously into the town. As I entered the outskirts of town, I took the rawhide thong off the hammer of my Colt. I had a gut feeling I might need it and in a hurry.

Not sure on how to proceed at this point and not seeing anything that might look like a sheriff's office, I stopped at the livery stable on main street hoping to find some information about whether Kellie Shawn and her men had even come this way.

After I dismounted and with Mutt by my side, the long gray haired liveryman approached and said in a surprisingly deep voice, "Four bits per day, per horse to put up and feed your horses. Not sure what to do with your wolf there, but if he is friendly enough he can stay also."

The liveryman was obviously older because of his gray hair, but seemed fit and agile of a man much younger. He was about 6 feet tall and probably weighed in about 175 pounds. "My name is Chance Bondurant and not sure if I am staying just yet. I am actually looking for some information."

Mutt walked right up to the liveryman and offered his head to be pet, which the gray haired man did instinctively. I assumed this was Mutt's way of telling me this was a good man. Still tousling Mutt's fur, the liveryman spoke again, "Happy to meet you Chance, my name is Boone Glenn, and I was one of the original founders of this settlement. The last couple of days have been sort of horrific around here, and I hope you don't judge this town on those events. Most of the folks hereabouts are good Christian folks. Since we at present do not have a sheriff or any law here, I guess I am your best bet on information."

My gut feeling and Mutt's reaction to Boone Glenn was telling me this was a good man. Feeling this was the man I needed to be talking to, I began my piece, "I am looking for some friends of mine that may or may not have passed through here, a very attractive Mexican woman and three Mexican men. They would have been looking to purchase land somewhere near here to start building a ranch. I am also trailing three outlaws - two Anglos and one Indian-Mexican half-breed that may be trailing the Mexican woman. Have you seen or heard anything about these people?"

Boone stopped petting Mutt and stared at me for several seconds with a concerned look that started to spread across his face. "Friends of the Mexican woman you say?"

Mr. Glenn's whole demeanor had changed from welcoming to being very guarded. I replied, "Yes, very good friends. It is obvious Boone, from your reaction that you know something. I do not want to sound harsh or threatening, but I do not have time to beat around the bush. I need to know now what you know about my friends."

Boone's eyes narrowed some as he began to speak in his deep voice, "I fear son that I have bad news for you. The horrific events that I spoke of involved your friends and those very same outlaws that you seek. The Mexican gal and her friends were staying at the Stagecoach Hotel down on Nevava Street and using it as a headquarters to look for land every day. They would ride out every morning at dawn and would not return till towards suppertime. The Mexicans were well liked around town and paid their bills and were pleasant enough. The Mexican gal she was easy on the eyes of an old man such as myself. Anyway, two days ago the two Anglos and the half-breed showed up after the Mexicans had left town on their land search. The three newcomers asked about town in regards to the Mexicans stating the same thing you just did, that they were friends and were here in town to rendezvous with them. I knew something was not right because the Mexican men were well behaved and did not drink, but the newcomers sat in the Byers Saloon, downing whiskey and acting belligerent all day waiting for the Mexicans to return. When the Mexican gal and her friends returned just before supper, the older Anglo named Rod went into the street when all the Mexicans had dismounted their horses and spoke with the woman, and about five minutes later the other Anglo named Bobby and the half-breed named Rick opened fire in ambush with their Winchesters from both sides of the street shooting all three of the men. None of the three men had a chance to use their firearms. The Mexican gal was not armed and seemed in some sort of shock after seeing her three friends gunned down. The half-breed ran out into the street and grabbed the Mexican gal and claimed that she was his. While the half-breed held a knife to the Mexican gal's throat, the other two Anglos searched the saddle bags and the bodies taking any and all gold, coin, and the cash money they were carrying. They then tore apart the rooms of the Mexicans at the Stagecoach Hotel taking any valuables that they had. We have no law here in Hot Sulphur Springs and really never needed it before now. Everyone in town has scattered and stayed out of the way of those outlaws."

This news hit me hard; I was two days short of helping Kellie Shawn, Rey Chavez, and the Martinez brothers. I tried to calm my growing anger, knowing it was not going to help the situation as it was now. All I knew was no matter how long it was going to take me, I was going to track down and kill those responsible or I would die trying. Now the remaining outlaws of the Biggers and Hammond gang not only had to pay for what they did to my brother Jace and myself, but they also had to pay for what they did to Kellie Shawn Arriaga and my Mexican friends. Marshal Eric Robert said it the best, "We have to be the wolves that devour the evil," and by God that was what I was going to do. Trying to keep my voice even and failing in doing so I asked, "The girl, what happened to the girl?"

Boone could see and sense my anger and he was now uncomfortable in my presence. Although a good man, he was not accustomed to violence, and I could tell he wanted to be anywhere but here telling me the sad tale of my friends' fate. Boone's voice was softer and more worrisome as he continued, "Within an hour of the shoot-out, the half-breed took the Mexican gal and hog-tied her to her horse and headed north."

My mind screamed, "Kellie Shawn may still be alive!" With excitement in my voice, "Do you have any idea where the half-breed was headed?"

Boone said in a clear voice, "North is all I know. He started north, but the two Anglos Rod and Bobby are still in town. Last night both were drunk and shot up the Byers Saloon."

Those must have been the shots I heard last night. I tried once again to stop the flood of anger as it flooded my senses and I took several seconds before I responded, "Boone, think carefully; where exactly are these two men Rod and Bobby in town right now?"

Boone looked on down the street and then pointed twice, "Just before you rode in, one was still at the Stagecoach Hotel sleeping it off, and the other was already drinking whiskey in the Byers saloon down yonder."

My mind was already preparing itself for battle when I spoke again, "Boone, I am going to leave my horses with you while I go have a chat with those two. If something should happen to me, the horses are yours to keep, and they require a pinch of sugar every day."

Boone grabbed hold of Storm's and Strawberry's reins and then he said, "One other thing Chance, one of those Mexican fellows, the one named Chavez, is still alive, though barely and is down at Doc Steve Shamp's place."

CHAPTER 23

My mind tried to wrap around what Boone had just said, "Chavez is still alive." Grabbing my Winchester from the saddle scabbard, I told Boone, "Point me in the right direction to Doc Shamp's house and in the meantime, do not tell anyone that I am in town."

Boone was turning to lead my horses toward the corral as he spoke, "Understood about not telling anyone, and the Doc's house is the third one up from the Stagecoach Hotel, and you can't miss it."

Walking down the boardwalk toward Doc's Shamp house with Mutt by my side, I jacked the lever action of my Winchester placing a 44 shell in the firing chamber. Finding the Doc's house was an easy affair. He had a painted wooden shingle out on the front porch that read "Steve Shamp, Doctor of Medicine." Before knocking on the door, I looked both ways down the street to see if anyone had seen me. The last thing I needed was either Burke or Hammond to know I was in town. The street and the boardwalks were empty; I did not see a soul this morning. Everyone was scattered to the wind. The violence of the last couple of days was still fresh in everyone's mind and you could feel the fear that the town felt since the remaining outlaws of the Biggers and Hammond gang had made their debut here.

With no answer the first time, I knocked a little louder the second time and I heard a voice from behind the door ask, "Who is it? What do you want here?"

It was apparent that Doc Shamp was not expecting nor wanting any visitors. In a voice I hoped was reassuring, "I am a friend of the Mexican, Chavez; Boone at the livery stable sent me here."

Due to recent events in town Doc Shamp was being overly cautious as he cracked opened the door, but did not open it fully and said in a crackling voice, "Enter slowly, just know I have a sawed off shotgun pointed in your direction."

Slowly opening the door with my right boot, I raised my hands so the Doc could see me fully. I had my Winchester in my right hand and pointed toward the sky. My Colt was still holstered on my right hip. Doc Shamp still in a crackling voice, "Set your rifle just inside the door, leaning against the wall, and do it slowly."

As I did as the good Doc asked, my eyes never left him. Doc Steve Shamp was younger than I expected and probably only five years older than I was. He was not a big man at 5'6" tall and weighing in at about 120 pounds. His hair and goatee were light brown and groomed to the point of being called very short. Doc Shamp did in fact have a sawed off shotgun pointed in my direction, although it was heavy and either from the weight of the weapon or his nerves it was wavering slightly as he pointed it. I could see in his eyes, he had savvy and courage. Trying to ease the situation some, I said in a soft, calm voice, "I am truly a friend of Rey Chavez and mean you and him no harm."

Mutt slowly walked into the room and sat down in front of me. Doc stared at Mutt for a few seconds before asking, "Is that a wolf?"

Slowly reaching out to tousle Mutt's fur on his head to indicate all was well, "This is Mutt and he is a half wolf and half something else. All and all he can be a pain in the ass to me sometimes."

That statement brought a forced smile on Doc Shamp's face as he lowered his shotgun, "He seems friendly enough."

Chuckling slightly I said, "He can be a real gentleman when he sets his mind to it."

Doc Shamp pointed to a door, "Your friend Chavez is in there. You must know he is in really bad shape and not going to make it. He was shot three times in the chest, and the bullets are still in there. I am amazed he has lasted this long. I am just trying to keep him comfortable."

Opening the door slowly was not fast enough for Mutt as he pushed it open with his nose and entered first ahead of me. I followed, then Doc Shamp.

Chavez was lying on a table that was probably used for operations such as amputations. His face was ghostly pale, and he was naked from the waist up and covered with what used to be a pure white sheet. The sheet was stained with a large amount of blood in the vicinity of Rey's chest. Mutt immediately went over and jumped up on the table and then lay his head on Rey's shoulder, looking at his face. As Chavez reached out and put his hand on Mutt's head, he said in a hoarse and almost non-existent voice, "I heard voices and I prayed it was Senor Chance and Senor Mutt; you are a sight for sore eyes, my amigo. I prayed for an avenging angel and here you are. The Martínez brothers and I failed in our task of protecting the Senorita. You have to go after her and save her from that half-breed savage. You will do this? Yes?"

Chavez coughed a trickle of blood as pink bubbles danced across his lips for a few seconds. It hurt and angered me to see this good man like this. I pulled up a chair to get eye level with Rey and bent closer so he could see me better. "Never fear, my friend as soon as I am done here, I will go fetch the Senorita and kill the half-breed. You can't bother yourself with worrying about her anymore. She will be my responsibility now."

A smile appeared on Rey's bloodstained lips. He closed his eyes as if he was gathering all his strength to speak, "I knew it the day that you saved me from the cold and pointed your pistola at me that you were special, the chosen one. I dreamed of you when I was a young chico in Méjico. You are the tamer of wolves! Yes, I believe you will save the Senorita. Thank you my amigo, thank you."

Looking at this man, this bandit that I had grown to care about, I had more than a few tears formed in my eyes. Rey coughed a couple more times and more blood foamed up on his lips and started to ooze down the side of his face. Reaching out to touch his shoulder, I knew he would need human contact to ease his journey into death. Trying to talk without showing any emotion, I failed and my voice cracked twice, "It was my honor and privilege to have known you Rey Chavez. All those that I know, will know the true measure of my friend Rey Chavez."

Rey opened his eyes and looked at me and with a smile on his face and in a fading voice, "Chance, do not cry for me, for my father is calling me home to heaven. And just so you know my amigo, on this day of my death, it is only the second worst day of my life; the worst day was the day I got married."

I could not help myself; this not only brought a smile to my face, but I also actually laughed out loud. Rey's eyes were smiling. The entertainer to the end. Somewhat chuckling, "So tell me my friend, what was your wife like?"

Rey's eyes were still smiling as he gathered strength to keep talking, "Her name was Camila and was the most beautiful woman in all of Mexico City. She had a mean streak though; she was like living with a female panther. She was slick and moved like the wind she did, but with one swipe she could rip out your heart, your throat, or your testículos."

Still with a smile on my face and tears in my eyes, "So what ever happened to your wife, Rey?"

When Rey chuckled, he spit some more foamy pink blood but uttered, "A month after she ran off with that banker, he shot and killed her."

Not knowing how to act now that the story had turned so grim, "Whatever happened to that banker fellow that killed your wife?"

Rey coughed twice and there was more blood, but his eyes told a different story as they still were grinning. In a stronger and clearer voice, "I went to the square where they had built a gallows to hang him. No hood and his hands and feet were tied together as he stood upon the trap door. They asked him once again, 'Why did you shoot your lover?' The banker looked straight at me as I stood in the crowd and said, 'I was tired of her shit!'"

Rey reached out and grabbed my shoulder and squeezed hard and said, "Believe me, my amigo, I knew what he was talking about."

Still with tears in my eyes, but happiness in my heart for knowing such a man, "I will truly miss you Rey Chavez."

With one last squeeze and with his dying breath, "And I you, my amigo."

When Rey passed, Mutt sensed it and he let out a small whimper as he slowly got off the table as if his friend Rey was only asleep and Mutt did not want to disturb him. Mutt then sat by me and put his head into my lap.

I started to pet the half wolf as I looked upon the death of my friend, my amigo, Rey. It amazed me that I had not known Rey for all that long, but I realized he had left tracks in my heart on that day that I first met him. He was an amazing and interesting man. In the silence of death, I remembered my enemies. As I stood up and still looking at the body that had been Rey Chavez, I swore another oath, just as I had so many years ago when Jace was killed on that lonely mountain near Nevadaville. I would avenge his death and that of the Martinez brothers. I would track Rick Alvardo to the ends of the earth for what he has done to the Senorita Kellie Shawn Arriaga. I could only pray that I would find him before he killed her.

Turning to face Doc Shamp, "How much to bury someone in this town with a casket and marker?" Doc Shamp, who looked weary and sad, "Ten dollars would take care of that."

Trying to think ahead, "How much without a casket and marker, just to plant them in the ground?"

The Doc blinked his eyes several times as if he was confused and he stammered, "Two dollars is what the grave digger charges."

Taking off my money belt, I counted out ten dollars in cash and handed it to the Doc. "This is for your time and trouble taking care of my friend and giving him comfort to pass on."

I then counted out thirty-four more dollars in cash and coin and handed it to Doc Shamp. Doc counted the thirty-four dollars and with confusion in his voice, "Thirty-four dollars? I guess I don't understand."

While belting my money belt back on and checking the loads in both my Winchester and Colt, I said, "Thirty dollars is to bury my three Mexican friends with a casket and markers; the other four dollars are for the other two men I am going to kill today."

Taking off my Stetson, I shaped it some and then snapped it back on my head as Mutt and I walked out the door into the snowy streets of Hot Sulphur Springs.

CHAPTER 24

Stepping off the boardwalk into the street, I felt chilled. Looking skyward, I realized time was passing quickly today because by the position of the sun, it was already mid-afternoon. To the north were some dark clouds, the ones that looked as if they may contain snow. They were encroaching on Hot Sulphur Springs at a brisk rate. The temperature had already dropped enough that I could see my breath.

I heard a door slam, and as I looked westward toward the Stagecoach Hotel, a man just walked out into the main street. My luck was holding out because it was the smiling idiot Bobby Burke. He looked exactly the same right down to that same old beat up gentleman derby hat with a bullet hole in it - still bald, no facial hair or eyebrows. The man was a walking billiard ball. His Colt pistol was just as I remembered it, carried on his left side with the handle pointed forward in a cross draw manner for his right hand.

He was headed in the direction of the Byers Saloon, which was about a quarter of a mile down the road. I needed to force a confrontation with the outlaw now before he joined Hammond at the saloon.

Mutt and I started to walk in his direction and spoke loudly enough for him to hear, "Well, I will be damned if it isn't Bobby Burke!"

Burke slowly turned toward me with a look of confusion and that dumb smile still etched on his face. As Burke stood in confusion for a minute without speaking, I took in all things that mattered in this slice of time. The air was chilled, but the wind was silent. We were all alone on the street with no possibility of anyone else catching a stray bullet. Mutt had lain down on his belly and watched with interest from the boardwalk. He did not accompany me into the street, content to watch me handle Burke. I knew full well that if Burke somehow would out draw me, then Mutt would take him out; he was that type of dog and companion. I could smell the dusting of snow in the street and the strong odor of horse manure from the stables, which seemed fitting enough since this had turned into such a crappy day.

I could tell Burke was not comfortable with me approaching him, for he had always been the aggressor. By his stance he was not sure how to handle it. In the deepest baritone voice I had ever heard, Burke spoke, "Do I know you?"

I stopped about thirty feet away, surprised at how deep his voice was. "I would have thought one with your low mentality would have a lower voice."

Burke's eyes squinted as he replied, "What? You better move on stranger, you are starting to piss me off, and those that piss off Bobby Burke don't live very long."

Squaring my body so I faced Burke with my feet exactly the same width apart as my shoulders, "You don't remember me or my half wolf?"

Burke was still muddled in what was about to happen, but it did not stop him from squaring himself to face me, "No, should I?"

In a strong and even voice, "Do you remember two young boys and a half wolf dog near Nevadaville, Colorado? Did you read the newspaper accounts of the deaths of Livingston and

Edgar? Maybe you can't read, maybe you're like one of those "idiot savants," except without the "savant" part."

With Burke's speed with a firearm, I had to keep him off balance, and the insults seemed to be doing the trick. Burke's mind was all a flutter now. He had no idea what an "idiot savant" was, and it was possible he was so dimwitted to know I just insulted him - again. It seemed by telling him of Nevadaville that he did remember that. I wanted him…no, I needed him to know why I was going to kill him today. With some sort of recognition Burke responded in his deep voice, "You are the one that killed Edgar and Livingston?"

Looking him square in the eyes, "Yes, I am the one. I also killed Biggers several days ago at Grand Lake. And I plan on killing Hammond, Alvardo, and you!"

The smile on his face evaporated and Burke's mouth dropped open, "You killed Herman?"

I could probably tell him ten times, and his response would always be "You killed Herman?" I sort of felt sorry now for the man; Bobby Burke was not a product of his upbringing. Bobby Burke was born this way. Still the righteous avenger, I needed him to start to draw first. It was the only way this could be. Still looking him straight in the eye, "Ignorance Bobby can be cured. Stupid is forever."

Not sure if Bobby Burke understood that insult or not, but the outlaw had enough jawing and went for his Colt.

Burke was fast and he cleared leather, but I was a tad faster, fanning my Colt three times. The first two caught Burke center mass in the chest and as his knees buckled on the way down, the third glanced off the top of his skull tearing out a chunk of his scalp with it.

After Burke collapsed face first into the dirt of the street, Mutt joined me as I knew he would and promptly lifted his leg on the dead outlaw. Mutt must have been saving it up for some time; it was almost like a horse pissing on a flat rock.

I stood there waiting for a bullet to be fired by Rod Hammond from ambush to strike me. Since no bullet was forthcoming, I turned and made my way toward the Byers Saloon.

As Mutt and I walked toward the saloon, I was ready for Hammond to come out with his guns blazing, so much, in fact, I did not think I had the time to reload the three spent shells in my Colt. I still had my Winchester in my left hand and was prepared to bring it into action if I needed it.

With the town empty of people and the noise associated with that, I knew there was no way that Hammond had not heard the gunfight between Burke and myself. I was at a loss of why he had not responded yet to the death of one of his compadres.

Approaching cautiously, I started to feel the cold more as I moved more slowly towards what awaited me at the Byers Saloon. As I stepped up on the boardwalk, the wood snapped, crackled, and popped so loudly I was sure it could have been heard all the way to Grand Lake.

There were two broad glass windows just about five feet on each side of the bat wing doors that marked the entrance into the saloon. I was west of the first window. Turning my back to the wall, I took this opportunity to re-load the three empty chambers in my pistol then re-holstered it. I inched my way gently along towards the east and the first window, the whole time expecting a shotgun blast through the wall. I was tense, but focused on what was happening all around me. Mutt was content to move an inch at a time alongside me; he must have felt the danger too.

I was now close enough to be able to peer around and look through the window, still expecting a bullet or double ought buck at any second. I was no less surprised at what I saw and that was Rod Hammond as he sat with his back to the north wall facing the entrance and filling his shot glass full of whiskey. Hell, he looked like a man without a care in the world, enjoying a social drink. Looking around the room, I saw that no one else was in the saloon, not even a bartender. It was as if the town of Hot Sulphur Springs was a ghost town and the only people were Rod Hammond and myself. I was not sure what to make of all this. Deciding the time was a wasting, I walked by the wavy glass window to the bat wing doors. Using the tip of my Winchester, I pushed the right wing of the bat wing door open and then stepped into the Byers saloon.

CHAPTER 25

S tanding just inside the door, I was quickly accompanied by Mutt, who followed to my left side. Standing and letting my eyes adjust to the difference in light from outside to inside, I viewed my adversary Rod Hammond.

Hammond looked old and tired. It was obvious to me that his addiction to the opium spiked alcohol laudanum, combined with the heavy daily use of whiskey, had taken its toll on the man. The dark circles I remember around his eyes were now more profound and looked like a mask a bandit might wear. He had lost weight and looked almost skeletal on his lanky frame. His hair was still long and tied into a pony tail and almost white. I could not see how he was armed, sitting down as he was. Both his hands were visible, so I knew he was not holding a weapon on me from under the table.

Rod Hammond was not surprised when he saw me come through the door. So much, in fact, it never even slowed him down as he filled his shot glass from the whiskey bottle again. When he spoke, his voice was raspy either from the laudanum, whiskey, tobacco, or the combination of all three, "I was curious who might walk through that door after hearing the gunshots. Then a man with a half wolf walks in. You must be that fella Chance Bondurant and his tamed wolf from down Nevadaville way? Saw it in the newspaper that you killed Livingston and Edgar in stand up fights. Livingston was not too fast, but that one-eyed Dave Edgar was hell on wheels with his six shooters. I am impressed Bondurant, yes I am. I also saw in the newspaper that you were taught the way of the gun by the righteous gunfighter Lucas Eldridge. Some say you might even be faster than your mentor."

My goal here was to keep him talking long enough to find out where Alvardo might have taken Kellie Shawn. I would also like to recover any and all gold that the three outlaws had stolen from my three friends.

Squaring up my feet to the same width as my shoulders as I faced the aging outlaw, I spoke with a clear and confident voice, "One and the same Hammond, just so you know Edgar was not all that fast."

Hammond was still not alarmed or worried in the least bit as he asked, "I assume Bondurant, that you are the "angel of death" as you track down and kill the members of the Biggers and Hammond gang. And what of Bobby Burke? Is he dead too?"

I did not show any fear whatsoever; because I knew it was fate that brought Hammond and me together today here in the Byers Saloon. Feeling the need to answer his question, "And Herman Biggers several days ago in Grand Lake. Burke is lying down yonder in the street in a puddle of blood and wolf piss."

Hammond sort of chuckled and then raised his shot glass in a salute towards Mutt, "I see the half wolf has a sense of humor - I like that."

Still not knowing where Alvardo had taken Kellie Shawn, I asked, "Where did the half-breed take the Mexican girl?"

Hammond set his shot glass down as if to ponder the question some and looked as if he was in deep thought, "That Mex gal was a looker all right. Alvardo wasn't even interested in any of the money. All he wanted was that girl. I wasn't going to stop that crazy bastard. To be honest Chance, that Alvardo scares me a little. He took her north to the rugged mountains just this side of the "Great Divide" to meet up with some renegade Ute Indians that refused to go on the reservation. Said he was going to winter with them. You know his mama was a Ute Indian, didn't you?"

That was not good news. Alvardo was going to be with about sixty or more angry Indians. As I whittled down the Biggers and Hammond gang, I thought it was getting easier. Apparently I was wrong. Putting that information to the back of my mind for now, I tried to focus on what was happening at this moment of time. I wanted to know one more thing, "And the Mexican gold?"

Hammond started to laugh so hard he choked once. After regaining his composure, he said in his raspy voice, "Life is funny sometimes, kid. That is what is so damn humorous about this whole trip to this God forsaken shithole of a town. There was no gold beyond what the Mexicans were carrying to pay their expenses. They had a damn bank draft to pay for the land! Hell son, I don't even know what a bank draft is. How things are done anymore makes being a thief and bandit almost not profitable. Should have given it up years ago and become a saloon owner. That's where the money is, kid - gambling, whiskey, and soiled doves."

Hammond looked me up and down some and still did not seem to be worried at all, as if he might be speaking to his grandson about life in general, "Oh hell Chance, where are my manners? Can I pour you a drink? It is free today; it seems to me that the proprietor of this fine establishment has skedaddled, and we have the whole saloon and all the whiskey to ourselves today. Pull up a seat kid."

Still in an even calmer voice I said, "Not today Hammond, I will not find any pleasure today drinking with you; your company only gives me displeasure."

Hammond shrugged his shoulders and started to fill his shot glass again from the now almost empty whiskey bottle, "Guess that sort of disappoints me, Chance. I can understand how you feel though after Livingston shot your brother, and Herman shot your wolf. Of course you're probably not too damn happy about my blowing up the mountain side and caving it down on your head either." Downing another shot of whiskey, he looked at me and chuckled again, "You must have one hell of a story about how you got dug out of that mine. You must be one tough son of a bitch, Chance; you look dangerous and capable too."

This whole conversation was bizarre; I was here to kill this elderly desperado for wrongs committed to my family, friends and myself, and he acted as if we just had dinner and now we were having after dinner drinks. I need this to be right; I needed him to start to draw first. "You know Hammond, I am here to kill you, nothing more, nothing less."

That statement only made Hammond drain the last of the whiskey bottle into his shot glass. "Guessing it is too late to say I am sorry. I get it Chance, I am not a dummy like Burke. You need me to draw down on you first. You are the good guy and I am the bad guy. I just want you to know Chance, I was not always a bad guy. I got caught up in a way of life during and after the Civil War with Herman Biggers and William Quantrill. I know I paved a bloody path to hell, and yes son I deserve it. I also want you to know I feel honored to be here with you today Chance Bondurant."

Hammond stood slowly, still holding his whiskey glass in his right hand. I now could see how he was armed with the standard Colt pistol with the grip pointed backwards for a standard draw and tied down to his right leg just below the shot of whiskey he was holding. Hammond looked at me for several seconds not with anger, but resolution. He raised his whiskey glass in a salute to me then promptly downed it. Then he dropped the shot glass and went for his gun. Or did he? His action caused me to draw my Colt again with lightning speed, and I placed two in Hammond's chest where his heart would be, if he had a heart. In the blink of the eye that it took me to kill Rod Hammond, I realized he just dropped his hand, he never went for his gun.

Hammond's body fell onto the table in front of him and slowly slid off and fell to the ground. Mutt stood up to deliver his brand of justice and I said, "No Mutt, not this time."

For the first time ever, Mutt did as I asked. Mutt seemed to understand and went back to sit in the same spot that he had just vacated.

I knew I would live the rest of my life wondering about this confrontation with Rod Hammond. For whatever reason, it was either he was sick and already dying, or he finally felt remorse for the life he had led. It was obvious to me that Rod Hammond had me execute him today. One thing I felt was true that Hammond had said, he probably had been a good man before the Civil War. That still was not an excuse for what he became afterwards.

CHAPTER 26

Stepping over the body of Hammond, I bent and picked up the shot glass that Hammond had used to drink his last drink. Holding it up to my face, I looked at my distorted reflection in the glass, and wondered what just happened here with Rod Hammond the outlaw.

Stepping back again over the dead outlaw, still with the shot glass in hand, I went behind the bar and grabbed a bottle of whiskey. After laying a dollar on top of the bar to pay for the bottle, I found a suitable seat with my back to the wall facing the door and sat down, took off my Stetson, set it and my Winchester on top of the table, and then poured myself a drink. Mutt joined me at my feet and lay down and promptly went to sleep.

I had just finished my second shot of whiskey when the town folks started to filter into the Byers Saloon behind Boone Glenn and Doc Shamp. Everyone looked at me, but no one spoke to me. It seemed as if they were as confused as I was on what just happened in here. I had no doubt I would read many different versions of the killing of Rod Hammond in the newspapers and dime novels for years to come. Maybe by that time I might understand why Hammond did what he did.

Pouring my third and last drink of the day, I raised it in a salute to the second to last of the Biggers and Hammond gang. After downing the watered down version of whiskey, I stood and snapped my Stetson back on my head, grabbed my Winchester and with Mutt following, walked out through the ever-increasing crowd. Stopping in front of Doc Shamp, I handed him another eight dollars in paper money. The Doc took the money and seemed confused about it, "What am I supposed to do with this, Mr. Bondurant?"

Looking back at Hammond, who now in his death seemed at peace, I then pointed at the man with two of my bullets in his chest, "Add it to the other two I gave you. Guessing Rod Hammond there deserves a wooden box and a marker too."

The Doc's and Boone's jaws dropped open as Boone spoke first, "Rod Hammond? You mean of the Biggers and Hammond gang? We had no idea these were those famous outlaws."

With a slight nod of affirmation, I replied in a quiet voice, "One and the same, you will find Bobby Burke of the same bunch out yonder on the street. He gets the two dollar burial; my generosity only goes so far today."

With no law in Hot Sulphur Springs to answer to, I stepped out onto the boardwalk when I realized the day was just about done as the sun was setting down to the west. In the orange afterglow of the setting sun, I could see my breath as I pondered my next move. This day of death had taken its toll on me, and I was hungry and tired. Boone Glenn had followed me out of the Byers saloon and stood next to me on the left side. "Mr. Glenn, looks as if I will be staying the night."

Boone in a respectful voice replied, "Figured as much, Mr. Bondurant. I have already unpacked and unsaddled your two mares. Gave them a pinch of sugar after a good rub down and currying."

That brought a smile to my face. "You are good man, Boone; Mutt and I saw it right off. If you will excuse me, sir, I am headed to that mighty fine hotel for hopefully some food and a bed. Good night, Boone."

On my way to the Stagecoach Hotel, I realized I had forgotten to reload my Colt and did so before reaching the Stagecoach.

With the half wolf, half something else dog right behind me, we walked in, and I was in no mood for some hotel clerk giving me crap about Mutt this evening as that fellow did in Rollinsville. The clerk behind the desk was a small man, maybe 5'6" and weighing in at a 150 pounds or so. He had thinning short blonde hair and was wearing round spectacles that kept falling to the end of his nose as he tried looking over them at me. The clerk was looking hard at Mutt, and he asked, "Is that your pet or did the wolf just follow you in?"

The thought crossed my mind, "here we go again" and in a not so friendly voice, "He is my dog if that is what you are asking. Mutt is no pet, he thinks of himself as his own man."

The face of the bookish man behind the hotel counter lit up with a huge smile. "He does, does he? I will not be so erroneous and call him a pet, but just so you know pets and dogs that think they are their "own man" get to stay for free."

That of course brought a smile to my face. "Guessing you and I are on the same page then. My name is Chance Bondurant and the gentleman that looks like a wolf is named Mutt."

The hotel clerk stuck out his hand to shake, "I am the proprietor of the Stagecoach Hotel, and my name is Curt Weber, but folks hereaboust just call me Wally."

Shaking his hand, I started to laugh, "Wally Weber? I am sorry Wally, but "Wally Weber" strikes my funny bone. I apologize."

We were still shaking hands and grinning like a couple of jackasses that just got done eating some cactus when he leaned in to whisper to me, "My wife - HATES - it when folks call me Wally. I encourage it though, just to irritate her some."

Wally turned out to be more than helpful in supplying me with a supper of venison stew and some homemade Dutch oven biscuits that his wife, who hated him being called "Wally," had fixed for the guests at the Stagecoach that evening. Mutt even got his own bowl of stew along with some deer bones.

After supper Mutt and I retired to a room on the second floor. My mind was a jumble of all that had transpired today with finding out about the Martinez brothers' deaths and having been with Rey Chavez when he passed on. Of course the tension and the aftermath with both shootouts with Burke and Hammond, I needed much sleep and tried to put in the back of my mind that Kellie Shawn Arriaga was being held captive and on the run with Rick Alvardo. There was no doubt in the morning I would be back on the trail in the same direction as the Senorita. I promised Chavez that Kellie Shawn was now my responsibility. And I meant that. Lying down on the bed without undressing or even unbuckling my holster, I fell asleep with Mutt lying next to the bed.

Jolting awake at dawn, I felt as if I had not even slept. Swinging my legs over the edge of the bed to place them on the floor, I accidentally landed them on Mutt who rolled out of the way, then proceeded to give me the ole' stink eye in return. The stink eye didn't last long as Mutt came over and lay his muzzle on my lap. He knew my mind was going here and there, and he felt my uneasiness as I pondered our next move.

Alvardo will be heading north of Lulu City and the Kawuneeche Valley, where, according to Marshal Eric Robert, the renegade Ute Indians were headed to last out the winter far from any white man's influence. With winter fast approaching, I could expect no help from the military or the law and I would be on my own in trying to rescue Kellie Shawn from the last remaining member of the Biggers and Hammond gang.

Trying to put everything into perspective, I started to look at my chances and the pros and cons of getting Kellie Shawn back without either of us getting killed. The cons were Rick Alvardo was a very skillful and deadly foe who was not afraid of combat or death; Alvardo would have more than a two day head start on me; and old man winter was just around the corner and more likely than not would kill Mutt and me in those rugged and high altitude mountains even before we got anywhere close to Alvardo and Kellie Shawn. Even if the wolf dog and I were to not die a wintery death and make it as far as the Kawuneeche Valley, we still had to locate the renegade Utes and Alvardo when they did not want to be located. Then, if fate would have it and I did in fact happen to locate the renegade's camp, then of course on top of Alvardo, I would have to deal with sixty or more pissed off Ute Indians that the last thing they wanted to see this winter would be a white face.

The cons of the situation were bad, real bad when I put them in some sort of order in my mind. Now I had to think of the pros of what I was going to do - I was still thinking - and not much came to mind except I had the half wolf dog as my traveling companion. Looking at Mutt as I tousled his hair as I spoke to him, "Well, it is like this Mutt, if we go after Kellie Shawn, it is more than likely we will die a wintery death or death at the hands of Rick Alvardo or even death at the hands of sixty or more Ute warriors skilled in the way of torture of their enemies. That being said, my friend, are you dumb enough to follow me to a certain death?"

Mutt tilted his head, looking as if he was mulling it over some. After about a minute his tail started wagging and he barked one time. I took that as a "yes" and with a smile I added, "A lesser man and dog would not have the courage to do what we are going to attempt to do. A smarter man or dog would call us crazy for the attempt. All I can say, my friend Mutt, is we are wasting time and daylight, so we need to get moving."

With no need to get dressed and after shaping my Stetson some, I snapped it on my head and grabbed my Winchester and walked out of our rented room.

I ate a filling breakfast of venison steak and chicken eggs for Mutt and myself that had been prepared by Wally Weber's wife Molly. I almost busted a gut when Wally introduced his wife Molly. After settling up my bill for the rental of the room and my meals and with enough grins to go around, I said my goodbyes to Wally and Molly Weber.

Stepping out onto the front porch of the Stagecoach Hotel, I took in a lungful of crisp cool autumn air and looked toward the sky. The sky was pleasant overhead this early morning, but dark clouds were forming in the northeast, which would be the same way as my travels.

After reaching the livery stable, I found that Boone Glenn had already saddled and packed Storm and Strawberry, and both mares were chomping at the bit to hit the wilderness trail again. After settling up with Boone, I stepped into my stirrup and mounted Storm and with Strawberry tied off to my saddle and Mutt by my side, we headed northeast into the wilderness.

CHAPTER 27

Not knowing the exact direction and trail that Alvardo was heading was a disadvantage and since I was three days behind him, finding his trail would be darn near impossible. If by accident, I did find the outlaw's trail, just trying to follow it would be time consuming, and Alvardo and his captive Kellie Shawn would even gain more distance on me. My one slim advantage was that I knew roughly the region that Alvardo was headed, so instead of trying to trail him, I would simply head to that area and hope and pray that Hammond had been telling the truth. The path from Hot Sulphur Springs to the Kawuneeche Valley could be traveled by two different routes. First one was to head north to Rabbit Ears Pass and stay on the eastern side of the "Great Divide" and then head east towards the rugged mountains surrounding the Kawuneeche Valley. The second one was to backtrack roughly the same way I traveled from Grand Lake to Hot Sulphur Springs and stay within the Middle Park high mountain plateau until I reached the area around Grand Lake and then head north until I reached the Kawuneeche Valley.

Once I reached the valley, I would then search for the renegade Utes and Alvardo and Kellie Shawn.

I decided to back track instead of heading north to Rabbit Ears Pass simply because I knew what type of terrain was that way and I thought the trail could possibly be traveled faster than going straight north. Smiling to myself, I thought, "How tough can it be to find sixty or more Indians in the remote mountains?" Guess I will find out if I survive the trek and the trail to the valley.

By mid-morning the weather had stayed pleasant with no wind and the dark storm clouds stayed in the northeast. Looking around the mountain sides, I decided that autumn had breathed its last breath for this year with nary an aspen tree among all the evergreens that had any of its golden leaves left. I already missed the sound of the quaking aspen leaves that created "the tree whispers," nature's melody.

At midday Mutt disappeared into the wilderness, probably hunting up some grub. I stopped long enough to water the horses on a small creek that was not more than a foot wide along the trail.

After eating a half a pound of elk jerky and drinking a full canteen of water, I pondered about what I knew about Kellie Shawn Arriaga. I thought of what had happened so far with the death of Kellie's bodyguards and friends and being kidnapped by Alvardo and the possible unspeakable horrors she was now going through just being his captive. A lesser woman's mind would snap and never could be repaired again, but in just the short time I had gotten to know Kellie Shawn, I realized she was no ordinary woman by any means. If a woman could survive this ordeal, it would be Senorita Arriaga. Along with her physical beauty, she was tough as nails with a strong personality. My biggest worry was that her strong personality would become more than a pain in the butt to Alvardo and just like in the story told by Rey Chavez about his wife on his death bed, "I became tired of her shit," he would kill her because she was too bothersome.

Remembering Kellie's words and the one kiss that we shared on that day not so long ago, I could not help but worry about this woman. Kellie had invaded all my thoughts and dreams since I had met her and I questioned if in fact I was in love with her. Love for a woman was nothing I knew about, but what I did know was that having thoughts of Kellie made my heart flutter. Speaking to the wind and hoping it would carry my message, "I am on my way Kellie; I am on my way."

By mid-afternoon Mutt had returned and seemed to have a full belly since he was not looking at me to provide something for him to eat. As much as Mutt the dog had become domesticated enough to accept humans into his life and pack, I realized that Mutt the wolf was still a child of the savage wilderness. I was just happy that he accepted me as one of his own.

About one hour after sunset, I could smell the cooking fires coming from Grand Lake. I had already decided to stay the night there and leave for the Kawuneeche Valley in the morning. It would be good to see my friends Roger Baldwin and Sherol Roy again. I also needed to stock up on supplies, not knowing how long I would be in the wilderness and what I would be against if and when I located Alvardo and the renegade Utes.

After I arrived at the livery stable, Howard Smith the owner stepped right up and took the reins of Storm and of Strawberry. As I dismounted he asked, "How long will you be staying, Mr. Bondurant?"

Tired and weary from the ride today and the emotional turmoil of what happened in Hot Sulphur Springs, I almost felt at home here in Grand Lake. Looking at Smith, I answered in a very tired voice, "Just one night Howard, and I will be leaving at dawn. I will pay extra if you can have Storm and Strawberry ready for me by that time. Howard was looking at me as if he wanted to say something, but held his tongue. I was a little confused why he did not tell me what he wanted to say. "Howard, I get the feeling you want to say something, but decided not to. Go ahead and tell me what's on your mind."

Howard was still holding my mares' reins and cleared his throat some before he began, "It is just all the folks in the settlement have been talking about you today, and I was surprised to see you back so soon."

Now I was confused, "Why would everyone be talking about me today?"

Howard stammered some, "Word came over the telegraph wire about you killing those two members of the Biggers and

Hammond gang, Burke and Hammond. After you killed Biggers here in town and after what happened in Hot Sulphur Springs, folks are speculating that you are the fastest man with a gun that ever strapped on a holster. Folks think you are maybe even faster than Johnny Ringo or Lucas Eldridge. The telegraph wire has been humming all day long with newspaper reporters trying to locate you to get an interview for their papers. The telegraph operator Linda Saylor has been listening to all the traffic, and it seems that newspaper reporters from Denver, San Francisco, Kansas City and even as far as away as Chicago and Philadelphia, have been yammering on the wire hoping to find you. You are the most famous man that most of us simple folks have ever met."

What Howard had told me disturbed me. I never needed or wanted a gunfighter reputation. After Russell Gulch with Livingston and Edgar, and now with what has happened in the last week, I could see why people would be interested, but all I was doing was trying to rid myself of some inner demons. Lucas had warned me about this, but at the time it sort of seemed surreal. Now that it seemed to have happened, I was not actually liking it at all. Right now all I wanted to do was find Kellie Shawn Arriaga and if she would have me, spend the rest of my life with her on some quiet and remote ranch somewhere in the Rocky Mountains. Howard was standing there still looking at me as if he was waiting for me to answer, "Thanks Howard, for speaking your mind. If I gave you a list of extra supplies that I will be needing, do you think you could wake up whomever you need to have it delivered here before daybreak? And would it be possible for my horses to be ready at dawn?"

Howard spoke as if now he was on a mission, "Yes Sir Mr. Bondurant, I will have Storm and Strawberry fed, groomed, saddled, and packed with your new supplies for you at daybreak, you can count on that."

I spent a few minutes after borrowing a pencil and a piece of paper from Howard, and I scribbled down the items I would need and handed it to him with forty dollars in paper money."

Looking over the list, he said he thought he could get all the items I wanted and that the forty dollars was plenty. Howard then led both horses into the barn to unsaddle and unpack them for me.

After Mutt and I left the livery stable, we made our way to the Baldwin Hotel.

Sherol Roy and Roger were happy to see us both, and Sherol fussed over us as if we were relatives she had not seen in a coon's age even though it was just three days ago. Needless to say Mutt and I felt welcomed amongst our friends, and Sherol fed us some leftover roasted chicken, Dutch oven biscuits and fried taters for supper and a slice of apple pie for our dessert. It was a meal fit for a king and his wild beast.

Even though Sherol and Roger had probably heard about what happened in Hot Sulphur Springs, they never asked about it and that reinforced my love for these kind folks. I did tell them what my plans were of the future in heading north and tracking down Alvardo and trying to rescue Kellie Shawn Arriaga. Both of their smiles evaporated knowing full well it might be the death of Mutt and me. They also both knew me well enough by now that trying to talk me out of it would not change my mind and I would stay on the same course that I had chosen.

Mutt and I retired to our room for some much needed sleep. I savored the crackling of the fire as it danced and sizzled across the wood in our pot belly stove, for it would be a long time before I slept in a heated room again. Rolling over onto my side with Mutt nuzzled up to my back, I watched the flames from the open cast iron door of the stove create swaying shadows on the walls and ceiling. It was not long, watching the flame shadows move back and forth, before sleep found me.

I woke up before dawn, and the fire had died and the room had grown cold. Standing to look out the broad glass window, I could not see anything because the window had frosted over with a thin layer of ice. The ice was a reminder that winter was now here and what I was going to try and do was more than just a little foolish. Foolish or not, Kellie Shawn was my responsibility now if she knew it or not. I also had to deal with the last outlaw from the Biggers and Hammond gang.

After dressing and strapping on my holster, I palmed my 44 Colt several times to check my speed and it slid easily and fast into my hand, and I felt confident in case of needing to draw my sidearm. Gathering my few belongings and with my Stetson and

Winchester in my hand, Mutt and I walked out into the dining area, and Sherol already had a plate set for both of us, mine on the table and Mutt's next to my chair. Roger, Sherol, and I did not talk as we ate our breakfast of flapjacks, maple syrup, eggs, and venison sausage. I think we all were sad to say goodbye, I know I was. I truly had learned to care about and love these folks.

After settling up my bill and standing on the front porch of the Baldwin Hotel, I shook Roger's hand, and Sherol gave me a hug. I could see tears start to form in her eyes as she turned back toward the front door. With nothing more to be said, I headed toward the livery stable.

Howard Smith looked as if he was lacking in sleep but was good to his word and had secured all the supplies and had Storm and Strawberry packed and saddled for me. He handed me a written receipt and a ten dollar gold piece that was my change from the forty dollars. I kept the receipt and handed back the ten dollar gold piece to Howard for his trouble. He looked as if he was going to refuse it and I said, "Don't even think about it, Howard."

After shaking hands with Howard, I stepped into the stirrup and squared myself into the saddle as I reined Storm toward the north. Making sure that Strawberry's reins were secured to my saddle, I gave Storm some rein and a slight jab of my spur and headed into the breaking dawn of a new day.

CHAPTER 28

I could see my breath and the breath of both Storm and Strawberry as we made our way through the ever thickening evergreens toward the northwest. Mutt was lagging behind this morning and for some reason keeping a watchful eye toward the timber to the east and the rising sun.

As the sun slowly topped over the evergreens and aspens, the shadows of the trees began to grow longer. The sky was clear and blue above, but storm clouds were forming in the north in the direction I was heading. The smell of autumn's death was heavy this morning as the droplets of dew had marinated during the night into the aspen leaves that lay on the forest floor as they decayed before the onslaught of the winter snows. Autumn with its smells, color, and cooler temperatures was by far my favorite time of the year. My mom used to tell me that the Lord created autumn just for the beauty of it, and it was hard to find fault in her reasoning.

By mid-morning I had traveled roughly about six miles from Grand Lake and had entered from the south into the Kawuneeche Valley. The "Great Divide" towered above me on the eastern side with its snow-capped peaks. Looking toward the heavens and the darkened clouds that hovered over the "Divide," I could see that winter was in full swing at that altitude as the winds with no trees above timberline to slow it down, created a blizzard and a complete white out. No man nor beast could survive that; the deer and elk had moved down to the lower elevations long ago as their instinct had told them to do.

Watching the storm brought home the realization that no matter what happened in the days to follow, that if I survived, that I would have to winter here on the valley floor or at the least in the Middle Park plateau region. There would be no crossing back across the "Divide" and making it back home to Central City. Like it or not I was stuck here in this wilderness. So were the renegade Utes, Alvardo, and Kellie Shawn.

Kawuneeche Valley was a long, narrow valley that was surrounded by some of the most rugged and remote mountains in the world, or at least that is what Matt Lee, the mountain man, used to tell me. He used to say that the Great Smoky Mountains back east where he was born were small foothills compared to the Rocky Mountains.

Thinking of Matt Lee got me deliberating about the old mountain man and whether or not he was still alive because I had not seen him in over a year. Without telling anyone he was leaving the night before, he woke me up one morning and walked me out to where he had his horse saddled and pack horse packed and with a fatherly touch on my shoulder, he said, "I reckon Chance my boy, there is nothing more that Lucas or I can teach you. The rest of the lessons come from just living your life. You have learned well and will go far. You are smart enough to know to keep the leather thong off your hammer when your gut tells you that trouble is a brewing; to always sit with your back to a wall facing the entrance; to never kill a man out of anger, but instead with determination when you are right; and that a woman can be your blessing or your demon, so you best choose the right one." As he stepped into the stirrup to mount his horse, he turned to me as he said, "Keep in mind youngster that I love you like a son, but I don't have the seeds to plant roots. It is just that I have to drift with the wind, son, towards the mountains; it was what I was born to do. I call it my "Wandering." One last thing Chance, when you are in the wild, keep your eye along the skyline and watch your topknot." Having said that and with one last goodbye, the mountain man named Matt Lee headed into the Rocky Mountain highlands.

If Lucas was like an older brother, then that grizzled old mountain man was like a second father. If I was to survive this winter here in the winter wilderness and find and rescue Kellie Shawn, I would have to use every skill and then some that I had learned from both Matt Lee and Lucas Eldridge.

The horses, Mutt, and I had been moving north on a narrow trail with thick dark timber on both sides when we emerged into a meadow, and I finally saw why Mutt was keeping his attention toward the east. It seems a bull moose and his harem of six cows had been traveling in the same direction as we were. They had been trailing on the eastern side of the timber, whilst we had been on the narrow trail in the center of it. They were about a quarter of a mile to my east and as I had stopped to watch and admire this magnificent herd of animals, the bull stopped and looked my way. He was huge with an antler rack was at least 6 feet across. The bull was probably close to 6'5" tall and weighing in at 1200 pounds or so. His brown hide already had that winter prime look about it and seemed heavy and dark. Moose were not like a deer in the fact that deer were spooked easily and took to flight with just as much as a rustle of leaves. Moose were cagier and would stand still until they figured it out and moved on with a slow gait. This bull was probably already done with the rut for this year, but I was still going to keep my distance, not wanting to have a run in with an animal that outweighed me by 1000 pounds. After the bull decided I was no danger to him or his ladies, he started his harem slowly moving in a northeast direction to put more distance between myself and his herd, which was fine by me.

By mid-afternoon after finding a suitable place to camp with a small brook with fresh water and a stand of evergreens on three sides to block the wind, I decided I would stop for the day and eat a good meal and try and plan for the days to come.

After unsaddling and unpacking both Storm and Strawberry, I decided to hobble both of them during the remaining daylight hours so they could graze and not wander too far and then set up a picket line and tie them off for the night and keep them close to the fire. Having the knowledge that there were at least 60 renegade Indians somewhere in the direct vicinity and that my horses would be too much of a temptation not to steal, I needed to keep a closer eye on them both; without them I would be in some serious trouble when the weather turned bad.

Mutt wandered off searching for some supper as soon as I was getting the horses hobbled. Looking through my pack, I found the three leg hold traps or what some folks called jump traps that Howard Smith had scrounged up for me in Grand Lake with the rest of my supplies. I went about finding a few small trails that some rabbits had been using and set my traps; setting the traps on trails that the rabbits had been using saved me from having to bait the trap. If I was going to survive the winter here, I needed to start living off the land some and the sooner the better.

Having set my traps, I found some downed timber and proper rocks to build a campfire. After starting the fire, I added some more wood to get some nice coals for cooking my supper. I found a perfect log for sitting on and dragged it up next to the fire, and having done that, I sat for a spell watching Storm and Strawberry graze as the sun slowly started to drop behind the mountains in all of its orange glory. Just as I was about to grab some beans to fry up, I heard not one, but two of my leg hold traps snap. Grabbing my Winchester in case I trapped a bobcat instead of a rabbit, I went to check on the traps and found two nice fat jack rabbits, enough rabbit for supper and breakfast. Nothing better than roasted jack rabbit on a chilly autumn night in the Rockies.

After gutting and skinning the rabbits, I cleaned my 12" Bowie knife and carved out two nice roasting sticks. With both of the rabbits roasting on the fire, the aroma made my stomach start to rumble in anticipation. As soon as the rabbits were done, Mutt wandered into camp with a large tree squirrel clenched in his teeth. "Glad you brought your own supper, Mutt; I reckon it's nice to have company so we don't have to dine alone." Mutt just turned his wolfish head sideways looking at me as if I had somehow lost my mind whilst he was hunting up his supper. Mutt couldn't talk, but he had a full range of facial tics and expressions.

After finishing off one rabbit in record time, I started to brood over what to do next. Mutt, after finishing his supper, came over and lay his head in my lap and as I started to pet his black tipped gray fur, he closed his eyes.

Locating the Kawuneeche Valley was easy enough; locating the Ute Indian renegades winter camp was not going to be an easy affair since they did not want to be located. This has been their ancestral home since the dawn of time. The mountains surrounding this valley were rugged and remote, and the Utes would know it better than anyone else - every hidden valley or gulch. They also would know where to obtain water when it was scarce. I believed my one advantage in locating the renegades, Alvardo, and Kellie Shawn was that the Indian encampment would need a steady meat supply to feed sixty or more people. That steady meat supply would have to come from this valley where I now found myself. All the deer, elk, moose and other critters would have headed here to these lower elevations to survive the cold and snow. Sooner or later I would run across a fresh kill or tracks that would hopefully lead me to where their encampment was. Once I located them, the next problem would be figuring out a way to get Kellie Shawn. With no clue on how I was going to accomplish that at this point in time, I put it in the back of my mind to ponder on at a later date. I needed to take it one step at a time.

I hoped beyond hope that Kellie Shawn was still alive and surviving the mental and physical torture I knew was being handed out to her by Rick Alvardo. It was a possibility she might be broken beyond repair once I found her. Had to put that last thought in the back of my mind; I could not concern myself about what time and fate can't change. "Would've, could've, and should've" needed to be put out of my mind forever. I had to focus on the now and what was happening at this moment in time.

Now that I was in the Kawuneeche Valley, starting tomorrow I would start exploring it and looking for signs of the renegades. Rolling out my bedroll and using my saddle as a pillow. I lay down. Almost a full blue moon had started to rise in the east, and it was something to behold. Blue moons seemed like magic to me. Maybe it was a sign of the coming final ending of the retribution against the last of the Biggers and Hammond gang. As I closed my eyes, my last thought before sleep overtook me was, "I am on my way Kellie, I will find you if it is the last thing I do!"

CHAPTER 29

I decided I needed to move my camp every couple of days so I would not fall into a familiar pattern in case the renegade Indians were watching me as I tried to find them. Each camp had to have several things going for it before I could use it. First, it had to have some shelter from the wind to keep Storm, Strawberry, Mutt, and myself from the bone chilling wind chill. Next, it had to have some sort of fresh water supply, and it also had to be easily defendable in case of attack. Matt Lee and Lucas had told me that the Utes almost always hunted in groups of three. I felt that if a hunting party did happen to run across me that I would be facing no more than three hostiles.

For four days I explored the northern end of the Kawuneeche Valley without any success. I could not find even one broken tree limb or track left by a horse or a man on foot. Finding 60 Indians that did not want to be found was proving to be more difficult than I thought it would be. I was lucky to have Mutt and his wild instinct and that hunting nose that the good Lord gave him to help me in my pursuit. I was confident that I had not missed anything as I searched for any sign of the Indians passing through the woods. I had to exercise patience and work the area slowly and not leave any sign that I was here in the valley. The weather had remained mild and cold with no snow yet even though each day the dark clouds that formed overhead threatened it.

As I searched for any indication of the renegades, I also went about setting my leg hold traps for small critters such as rabbits, squirrels, and chipmunks. Even though there was plenty of big game in the valley and they would be easy pickings for me with my Winchester, I was hesitant to shoot an elk or deer, fearing that the renegades would hear the rifle shot.

On the fifth day in the valley, I started to explore more of the western side looking for any mark that might lead me to the renegade winter campsite. About midday I tied off Storm and Strawberry and started to explore on foot, ascending a steep incline following a game trail wondering where it was heading when I came across a large cavern.

Now caves are a funny thing; they can be the perfect shelter from severe weather for man or beast. A cave can keep the wind at bay if faced in the right direction and when heated with a campfire, it can become very comfortable in the winter because the rock surrounding you holds in the heat. They also can be a death trap as I almost found out in the Bondurant mine when Jace and I were braced for the first time by the Biggers and Hammond gang. Most of the time a cave will have only one entrance, which can be good or bad depending on whether you have enough ammo, supplies, and time to defend it, or it can be your adversary if someone has a stick of dynamite as Rod Hammond had and uses it to bring the roof of the cave down on your head.

I settled down behind an evergreen with Mutt to observe the entrance for a spell, thinking I might need this cave sometime in the near future. As I sat there keeping an eye on the cave, Mutt and I finished off a good half pound of venison jerky and drank a full canteen of creek water. After about an hour of observing, I felt assured that no person nor animal was using the cave at the present time. One clue was that Mutt had promptly fallen to sleep. The half wolf obviously was not smelling or sensing any danger within the walls of the cave.

Waking Mutt up out of his slumber, I started slowly to approach the cavern. It had a large entrance, which was a good nine feet high and seven feet wide; a horse could easily walk into the entrance without a rider. Holding my Winchester out in front in case I needed to fire it suddenly, I was watching Mutt for any sign that he sensed anything out of the ordinary.

Reaching the entrance, I slowly peeked in expecting a mountain lion or grizzly to finally show its furry hide and tear me from limb to limb. When no such critter decided to make me its supper, I walked into what seemed like an empty cavern as far as the day light extended. About ten feet past the entrance, the cavern become larger and much darker. Locating a wood match from my leather possibles bag, I then shucked the Lucifer down the back leg of my Levi Strauss blue jeans to light the cave. After two tries it burst into flames, providing enough light to see the entire cavern.

In the flickering shadows and before the match burnt my fingers, I saw most, if not all of the cave, which was easily 30 feet by 40 feet. I shucked another wood match down the back of my leg, and it caught and lit on the first try, and this time I also saw an old ring of stones that had previously served someone as a campfire. Before the second match sputtered and went out, I saw an abundance of dry wood that the person using the ring of stones had stored. Seeing what I needed to see and not wanting to waste anymore wood matches, I made my way back to the entrance. Hanging back far enough into the cave to allow my eyes to adjust from the darkness of the cave to the daylight outside, I studied the trees and the surrounding countryside looking for anything off kilter. Even though I had not seen any sign of anyone, be it an Indian or white man since I had been in the Kawuneeche Valley, I needed to keep treating it as hostile territory. It helped having Mutt and his keen senses and knowing the half wolf would smell, see, or sense danger way before I realized it.

Once outside the cave and back hidden within the evergreens, I looked back at the cavern and realized it was difficult to see it from almost any direction. It was pure luck that I stumbled on to it. I had a gut feeling that sometime in the near future this cave was going to serve me well.

It was already mid-afternoon, and the sun was just about ready to drop behind the snowcapped peaks to the west. The days and daylight were short now and with each passing day, they become shorter. Mutt and I made it back to Storm and Strawberry and after stepping into the stirrup, I mounted Storm and gave her some rein as we made our way back to the campsite for the night.

Working our way back to the campsite looking for any sign of the renegades, I checked my traps and had two rabbits - one jack and one cottontail. The cottontail was the first I had seen in this country and was surprised when I had it in my trap. Looking at Mutt I said with a chuckle, "looks like rabbit... again."

Mutt gave me his "I like rabbit" look; of course, that was the same look he had with any type of food. The half wolf, half something else dog was many things, but finicky was not a trait he possessed when it came to grub.

After seeing that the horses were rubbed down and fed, I then tied them to a picket line close to the fire. I fried up some beans from my supplies and along with our roasted rabbit, Mutt and I had a tasty and filling supper. A piece of Sherol Roy's fudge would be tasty right about now, but of course I ran out of that long ago.

Rolling out my bedroll and dropping my saddle at the head of the roll to use as a pillow, I held the blanket so Mutt could get underneath it with me and after he found his spot and cuddled up next to my side for his and my warmth, we both quickly drifted off to sleep.

Watching the moon and the shimmering stars in the eastern sky as they began to be engulfed by the dark clouds blowing in from the northwest, I started to plan my day for tomorrow. I would continue to explore the western edge of the valley tomorrow looking for any sign of the renegades, which would hopefully lead me to Kellie Shawn. If in a couple of days after exploring the west side and having not located any indication of the renegades, I would move back north to where my gut told me the Ute renegades were. The only reason I felt this way was because it would be the farthest away from any white man's settlement.

Lying here by the campfire, I was starting to doubt myself to date. Should I have tried to track Alvardo out of Hot Sulphur Springs? Did Alvardo in fact meet up with the Ute renegades as Rod Hammond had stated? Are there any Ute renegades at all like Marshal Eric Robert had said? If in fact the renegades were real, did they head into these remote mountains as it was believed? So many questions and I have yet to find one shred of evidence to support any of this. I had to keep following my gut instinct, and that gut feeling told me that the renegades, Alvardo the half breed, and Kellie Shawn were close. Or was I wrong about that? I was starting to make myself sick thinking I would be too late or never find Kellie Shawn Arriaga.

I looked back to the heavens as the moon and the flickering stars of hope disappeared behind the clouds. My rational thinking told me I was lucky it had not snowed yet. Just as I thought that, two fat snowflakes fluttered from the dark and landed on my face and melted.

CHAPTER 30

I awoke with a jolting start as Mutt slid silently out from beneath the blanket and crouched down next to me with his head toward my feet as if he was ready to spring into action. Grabbing my Colt 44 from under the saddle, I watched Mutt trying to get an indication of what was wrong and what he was sensing. Mutt never gave false readings; he never barked nor was startled unnecessarily. Watching the half wolf eyes, I knew there was someone or something out just beyond my vision.

Now Storm and Strawberry started snorting and throwing back their heads as they were alerted to whatever danger was afoot. Slowly pulling back my blanket with my Colt in hand, I eyed my Winchester which was leaning within reach next to the log I had been using as a sitting stool next to the now almost extinguished fire.

Following along Mutt's line of sight, I finally saw what had disturbed him and the horses. I could see a Ute Indian warrior dressed in buckskins and with long black hair tied in a braid with three eagle feathers tied to the end of his braid. He was not wearing war paint or dressed for war. I believe he and probably two others that I could not see yet were a hunting party and had come across my camp by pure chance and were looking to steal Storm and Strawberry.

The way the Ute Indian was still advancing, I do not believe he had seen Mutt and thought in the low light it was just one man sleeping. Not wanting a battle, but looking as if it was going to be forced on me, I started to focus on what was about to happen. It was probably an hour or so before dawn, and there were a couple snowflakes lingering and floating in the chilled air. The moon and the stars were hidden behind the clouds above, and there was little or no light except what was given off from the glowing embers of my campfire.

Still watching the Ute Indian advancing and knowing there was an empty chamber under the hammer of my Colt for safety, without any noise I slowly rolled the cylinder one click so there would be a live shell under the hammer.

Mutt's eyes never left the renegade by the horses as I caught more movement out of the corner of my eye to the left of the first Indian about ten yards. It was a second muscular Ute Indian with long black hair tied into two braids advancing on my camp, and he had a lance with several eagle feathers tied right behind the head and killing end of the lance. That was two, now where was the third Indian?

In the low light it was difficult to see, and the third Ute Indian was not visible to me. Mutt was fully aware of the second and probably the third Indian, but it was an unspoken command that my half wolf would take care of the one by Storm and Strawberry, and I would take on the second and the third renegade if there was a third.

As the first Indian started slowly to untie Storm, the second Indian started to bring his lance up above his shoulder to launch it in my direction. I yelled "now" and Mutt with no more prompting sprang into action as I did, and all in one action I fired my Colt, grabbed my Winchester, and rolled to my right away from the campfire.

At the end of my roll that brought me to my knees and suddenly to my feet, with one glance I saw that the Indian's lance was sticking out of the ground where I had been lying, and the Ute that had launched the killing strike was down and not moving. Mutt had the first Indian down on the ground and with a well-placed backward kick by Storm, it caught the Indian on the top of his noggin as Mutt was chewing at his throat.

The third renegade Indian had joined the foray seconds after it began and realizing his buddies did not fare so well in the first couple of seconds, turned tail and started running back from where he had come from. I knew my life and probably the life of Kellie Shawn depended on the third Indian not making it back to the Indian camp, but I also needed to know the location of their winter camp. I started to sprint after him lifting my Winchester and yelling several times, "Stop!" The final member of the hunting party turned raider made it to his horse and quickly jumped on it and pulled his own Winchester from a saddle scabbard, pointing it in my direction. Not wanting to kill this man, but not having a choice, we both fired at the same time. Firing from the back of a moving horse is never easy, and his 44 slug went wide right. I had come to a standstill and had a second to plant my feet before I fired; my 44 slug caught him in the right side of his face, and he flopped off his war pony and was dead before he hit the ground.

Grabbing the third Indian's war pony's reins, I started slowly walking back to my campsite on high alert, glancing at and listening to the forest trying to decipher if there were any more hostiles near that I had missed. About half way back to camp I found the other two renegades' horses tied to a branch of an evergreen tree. After reaching my camp and not knowing what else to do, I tied all three of the Ute Indians' war ponies off to my picket line that Storm and Strawberry were tied to.

I checked on the two now dead renegades, and the one that Mutt attacked and was finished off by Storm was a mess. The renegade Indian turned horse thief had his throat torn out savagely by the half wolf and would have died from that wound alone if Storm had not speeded his death by a brutal kick to the top of his head, which by the way was bent to the side after his neck snapped. The renegade that tried to lance me was shot through his chest left of center with the slug entering through the front and ricocheting off a bone and exiting his right side. He was probably dead before he hit the ground.

Killing these three warriors of the Ute Indian nation was something I was not proud of. It was a battle I wished had never happened, and there was nothing now that could be done about it. The renegades tried by force to kill me and steal my horses. Even if they had only succeeded in stealing my horses, it still would have been a death sentence for me in this remote wilderness with winter coming on.

Walking over to the half wolf, I bent down and ruffled his fur some, "Thanks Mutt for saving my hide. Not sure that I would still be alive if you had not warned me. I love you buddy."

Mutt seemed pleased at my praise, and his eyes widened as he gave me that wolfish grin he had. Shaking my head and with a small laugh, I told him, "Don't get a big head about it Mutt, just for the record that's your job." Mutt's grin evaporated and that made me laugh even more as I roughed up his fur some more.

Sitting down on the log next to the fire, I used my bowie knife to stir the still hot coals of my fire to get more air flow, and a small flamed jumped up. I added some small wood chips, and my fire began to grow and once the flames were big enough, I added some more wood. I was not worried about giving away my position anymore; the shots I fired would have done that. Having not to worry about hiding this morning, I decided to cook a decent breakfast and then move out and find another campsite.

The sun was now starting to peek above the mountain tops of the never summer mountains and looking toward the Indian ponies in the new light of morning, I saw that the Ute hunting party had been somewhat successful in that they had a small deer already gutted and skinned, packed on the back of one of the war ponies. The dead Indian renegades at least had provided me with grub for my breakfast and for the next couple of days. Carving off two large venison steaks, one for Mutt and one for myself, I started to roast the steaks on a couple of roasting sticks over the fire.

The snowflakes I felt last night before sleep had not amounted to much with just a light dusting on the ground. As I looked skyward, the dark clouds were starting to roll in again and this time it didn't only look like snow, but it felt like snow. It was that time of year in the high country, and I realized it was way over due for some heavy snow. The temperature dropped rapidly this morning and I was sure that the snow was soon to follow.

After the sudden intense tension and the heat of the battle with the three renegades, I was finally able to ponder on what all of it meant while Mutt and I ate our breakfast of venison steak.

It was obvious that these were the Ute renegades that refused to go out on the reservation in Utah just like Marshal Eric Robert had mentioned. It also meant that my gut instinct was correct in that they were close. With so much big game in the valley, the hunting party would not have to travel far for the food they needed to survive the winter. If the shots that had been fired this morning were heard by those still in camp, I was hoping that they would only think it was the hunting party bringing down a deer or an elk and not be alarmed. To date all the evidence pointed to the fact that everything that I had heard so far was true. What I did not know yet was if Alvardo and Kellie Shawn were in the Indian camp.

With all three of the renegades dead, there would be no questioning to find the answers I sought. It would have been doubtful any questioning would have produced any responses since the Utes probably didn't speak English, and I sure as hell didn't speak Ute.

Looking at the two dead in the campsite and glancing out at the body further out, I was wondering what to do with the bodies? These men were fathers, husbands, and sons to all that loved them, and I did not want to disrespect their warrior creed by doing the wrong thing. Giving them a Christian burial was probably erroneous and disrespectful. Remembering some of what Lucas had taught me about how the Ute Indians viewed the death of loved ones, I knew they took extreme care to ensure that the ghost of the deceased did not return, although according to Matt Lee they believed that the soul lingered near the body for several days. They also believed all Ute souls went to an afterlife similar to this world. Bodies were washed, dressed, and wrapped and buried in a rock-covered grave in the mountains. I was not sure how I should handle the bodies, but thought it was the best course of action to let them lie where they had fallen in battle for them to be found by some of their own and then given the proper burial by Ute customs.

The next question was, of course, what to do with the renegades' war ponies. They were too many to keep hidden when one was trying not to be found. Most men probably would have shot all three knowing the horses as soon as they were released would head home to their camp. And the more I thought about it, that could be the perfect solution in finding the renegades' campsite. I decided to release two of the war ponies when I was packed and ready to move my camp and keep one until later so I could pick a time that was of my choosing to release the third and follow it to the Ute winter campsite.

Since the renegade Indians were armed with Winchesters like mine, I located all 44 ammo from the Indians' packs that I could use in both my Colt and rifle. Along with their remaining ammo, I took the remains of the deer and all the food and grain for their horses they had been carrying, which was not much.

I knew it would probably be less than a day before the others came looking for the three hunters when they never returned back to their camp. My best option was the cavern that I had located yesterday for my next campsite; it offered protection and it could be defended more easily with only one entrance. The cave would be perfect for hiding Storm, Strawberry, and of course the Ute Indian horse until I decided it was time to release it.

Having come up with a plan of action for the rest of the day and after saddling Storm and packing Strawberry, I released two of the Ute Indian war ponies. Stepping into the stirrup and getting squared up in the saddle, I gave Storm some rein and started her moving with Strawberry and the third pony toward the north and the cavern.

Traveling today would be much slower through the evergreen forest to hopefully not leave much of a trail so we wouldn't be tracked easily. Once the dead warriors had been found, the Ute renegades would be looking for the ones responsible for their deaths.

As luck would have it about a half mile from my old camp, it started to snow, and not a lazy snow, but a hard snow with big puffy snowflakes. Winter had finally made its appearance on the floor of the Kawuneeche Valley. The snow could not have come at a better time; it was snowing hard enough that it would cover my tracks and make it almost impossible for the renegades to track me once they found the bodies of the three warriors.

CHAPTER 31

The snow was getting thicker and heavier as the morning wore on. It was now sticking to the shoulders of my rabbit fur lined duster and fox fur winter hat. And as the air was getting colder, my hands had grown icy and started to turn blue, so I finally had to stop and dig out my rabbit fur gloves, which I hated to wear, because it made it difficult to draw a weapon if I needed it in a hurry. Looking back every once in a while to check my back trail, I did not see any pursuit, and any trail I was leaving was quickly being covered by the snow.

By midday I had made it back to the area that the cave was near, but with the fresh snow being a good five inches deep now, it had changed how everything looked, and I was finding it difficult to find the game trail that led up to the cavern. I spent nearly an hour going back and forth trying to jog my memory or see something that would indicate the path I needed to take, narrowing it down to three possible game trails. Not knowing which one was the correct trail, I would have to try all three. My gut feeling was it was the middle trail so heading Storm in that direction, we started up the game trail.

Within a half hour I knew that I was on the correct trail and sure enough, we emerged at the edge of the evergreens, and the entrance of the cavern was before me. I took a few minutes to study the cave to see if any person or critter had taken it as their home since the last time I was here. There were no tracks in the fresh snow on the outside of the cave, and it seemed to be as empty as it was before.

Pulling my Winchester from the saddle scabbard, I gave Storm some rein and a slight jab of my right spur to urge her forward. Once I got within several feet of the entrance, I dismounted and tied the horses off just outside the cave entrance and with Mutt by my side, I entered the cave. The cave was even darker near the entrance this time because it was a much drearier day with low light outside. After finding a wood match in my possibles bag and after shucking it down the back of my leg, I lit the match on the first try. I worked my way over to the ring of stones and after locating enough wood chips and tinder for the makings of a starter fire, the match sputtered and went out. After lighting another wood match on the back of my leg, I used it to start the wood chips and tinder on fire, blowing on the smoldering chips to give it air. Fire needed three things - fuel, air and an ignition source. Once I provided all three, in no time I had a substantial fire going and started to add some smaller wood logs to it.

I walked out of the cave to retrieve the horses and in the short time I had been in the cavern, the horses had accumulated a good three inches of snow on their backs. This storm was really settling in for a spell. After leading Storm, Strawberry, and the Ute war pony into the cavern, I set up a small picket line and tied the horses off to it. Before unsaddling and unpacking the horses, I thought it best to gather more wood for the fire while I still had some daylight left. There was an ample supply of down firewood for a couple of days left by whomever had built the ring of stones, but I reckoned you could not have too much firewood to sit out a snowstorm such as this one. I added two more logs to the fire to keep it going whilst I went about gathering more wood.

Mutt went with me and got the right idea of what I was doing and once he figured out how to carry a log in his mouth, he made twice as many trips as I did with one log at a time. After half a dozen trips gathering wood, I watched the day and daylight fade into the night.

With the last load of wood stacked, I stood at the entrance of the cave and looked out into the darkness, watching the snow fall soundlessly from the sky. If not for the dire circumstances that I now faced, I could be happy in this moment. There was nothing as beautiful as an autumn snow storm in the Colorado Rockies. I could not help but think how fragile a snowflake was and how easily it melted when it touched my skin, yet when combined with literally hundreds, if not thousands of other snowflakes, it could change how the world looked. Snowfall is a lonely and silent event; it changes how you see your world without one sound. Loneliness and snow walked hand in hand this evening in this remote wilderness I now found myself.

After unpacking Strawberry and the war pony and unsaddling Storm, I knew all three had probably grazed well this morning and last evening before the snow storm began. Giving each a portion of grain and a pinch of sugar, I then spent some time and rubbed each one down and groomed their manes and tails. The war pony mare was 16 hands tall and a fine-looking pinto that had splotches of only black and white. These types of pintos were commonly called piebald. The word pinto was Spanish for painted.

Carving up the rest of the deer that the renegades had provided gave me enough meat and venison steaks for at least a week, and the snow and cold temperature would help keep it from spoiling. The butchered deer also provided the half wolf some bones to chew on which would make Mutt a happy fellow for a few days as we waited out the storm.

I added more wood to the fire, and the cavern was heating up enough that I was comfortable enough with taking off my winter duster and wearing only my heavy long sleeve blue cotton shirt with jeans. I laid out my duster and fur hat and gloves close enough to the fire to help them dry out.

After making the horses and the cavern as comfortable as possible, it was time for some supper of venison steak, fried beans, and camp fire tortillas. This day had been stressful and physically tiring with the battle with the renegades and the flight from the battleground to this cavern, and the good food helped myself and Mutt settle down for the evening.

Once I laid out my bedroll and my saddle as a pillow, I checked my loads in both my Winchester and Colt and counted my 44 ammo. With what I was able to scrounge up from the renegade Ute Indian packs and what I had brought with me came to the grand total of 612 rounds, more than enough to start a small war if needed. Of course going to war with the remaining 60 or so renegades and Alvardo would only end up with me dead and Kellie Shawn still a captive.

My plan was simple. I would release the Ute war pony and track it to the Ute winter camp. Once I located the campsite, I would observe to make sure that Kellie Shawn was in fact a captive in the camp and then decide on the best course of action to take. If I could somehow sneak her away and make it back to this cavern, maybe - if luck and fate was in our corner - we could winter here and get out of the Kawuneeche Valley come spring and head to Grand Lake. Another option I had was that I had enough money in my money belt to buy Kellie, which was a poor option if Alvardo did not want to sell her and it would be impossible if the Indians decided to kill me and take what was mine anyway. Once locating the winter camp, I would have to make decisive and split second decisions as the slim opportunities presented themselves. Then there was that "rocky mountain retribution" that Alvardo had coming. As of now my priority had changed in that Kellie Shawn Arriaga now came first and the "retribution" came second. Of course, if the opportunity presented itself, I would not hesitate to kill Rick Alvardo; it would not be wise to have such a dangerous adversary on my back trail once I had Kellie Shawn.

A smart man would wait out the winter and wait for the military. Nobody has ever accused me of being smart! I had made a promise to myself and Rey Chavez that I would go and fetch the senorita and make her safe. Chavez and the Martinez brothers had given their lives in the service of Kellie Shawn Arriago, and that meant something to me. I was either going to save her or die trying myself.

My mind was all a tumble with thoughts of Kellie Shawn. I could not help but ponder, after knowing Kellie for only less than 24 hours, how one kiss could lead her to become such a fixture in my mind. I had been so focused on the moment and the quest to recapture her, that I had not given it much thought on the "why." Why was I risking an almost certain death to rescue a woman that really I hardly knew? Yes, she was very beautiful, and yes, she made me laugh, and yes, I felt at home with her, and yes, I could see myself spending the rest of my life with the spitfire Mexican girl bandit. Even those moments of silence with her while we watched the sunset and groomed the horses felt right; I felt as if we were one. Thinking these thoughts and starting to put them in some sort of order in my mind, I guess the answer was very simple - I had fallen in love with Kellie Shawn Arriaga.

There was no doubt as soon as the weather broke, I was going to find Kellie Shawn and make her mine. Rolling onto my side, I held the blanket up so Mutt could lie down and cuddle up next to me.

CHAPTER 32

S now fell for a full day after I reached the cavern, and fortunately for me it was not a hard snow after the first couple of hours. The total snowfall amount was about a foot and a half, not enough to strand me in the cave, just enough to make travel difficult and dangerous.

During the time spent in the cave, I cleaned and oiled my firearms and sharpened and oiled my Bowie knife and made sure both the Colt and the Winchester were fully loaded and ready for battle.

Storm, Strawberry, and Mutt all got some extra loving from me with extra grain and sugar for the horses and Mutt getting his fill of bones from the deer that the renegades had provided.

It was difficult for me to do, because it went against my nature, but I purposely gave the Indian war pony only the bare essentials to keep it alive, not wanting the Ute pinto to get accustomed to me and my other animals so when the time came, it would make tracks back to what was the mare's normal living conditions with the Indians.

My gut feeling was telling me that I was close to the Ute winter camp and would have no difficulty in locating it with the war pony's help within the hours of daylight. Even though it would be possible to track the Indian horse at night because of the snow, the last thing I wanted to do was to stumble into camp of 60 irritated Indians with my white face during the night.

If the snow had not covered the tracks and the three bodies of the renegades that Mutt and I had killed and they had been found, then there would be a huge possibility that a couple of war parties would be out and about looking for the ones responsible for the death of the Ute warriors.

After leading Storm, Strawberry, and the Ute Indian war pony outside of the entrance of the cavern, I stopped and took in a lungful of icy chilled air that made me feel invigorated. The morning sun in the east was just starting to break above the evergreen tree tops, and the probing rays of dawn were glistening across the mantle of undisturbed fallen snow. No longer was the smell of decaying autumn leaves devoted to the wind; only the smell of pine needles, tree bark, and freshly fallen snow now scented the air. Looking at what was out in front of me and what lay in the valley below, I pondered how anyone could not believe in the "Lord All Mighty." How could you explain the grandeur of all that surrounded me if the earth and nature had not been touched by the Lord himself? Stepping into the stirrup, I settled into my saddle and looked at my half wolf that was beside me and asked, "Mutt, are you ready?" The half wolf, half something else dog tilted his head as if to say, "What's the hold up? I am ready, are you?" Nodding my head "yes" I replied, "I reckon so!" I gave Storm some rein and a slight jab with my right spur, almost feeling guilty as we broke trail across the pristine landscape that was before us.

Half an hour later we reached the end of the game trail that led to the cavern, and I dismounted to try and cover the tracks leading up the trail by brushing the snow over them. Hopefully, someone that may follow this trail would not see the deception if they were in a hurry. After remounting, I reined Storm in the direction of my last campsite and battleground with the three Ute renegades. My plan was to release the war pony there, the last place it had been with its owner and the other two war ponies.

By mid-morning the temperature had risen some but still cold enough to keep wearing my winter duster and fox fur hat. I took off my fur lined gloves and kept flexing my fingers to keep them warm and mobile in case I needed to draw a weapon fast.

I knew I was for sure in hostile territory; my senses had to be vigilant and on high alert. It helped to have Storm, Strawberry, and the half wolf that would sense anything amiss before I did.

An hour before midday I located my old campsite, and it looked completely different under a foot and a half of snow. If not for the marks left on the evergreen trees from my picket line that was used to tie up the horses, I would not have believed it was the same place. Kicking through the snow, I found the remains of my old campfire stones just to make sure. The bodies of the Ute warriors were gone, and there were no fresh tracks in the snow, so they had to be found prior to the snowfall or shortly after it began.

Untying the reins of the Ute Indian war pony, I took off her makeshift Indian halter and raised my arms several times to shoo her away. She stepped gingerly away for about ten yards then looked back like, "What the hell?" I raised my arms again and shooed her again. This time she bolted and at a fairly fast trot took off to the southwest.

Knowing the war pony could be easily tracked in fresh snow, I began to clear out the area around my old campfire. I gathered just enough downfall wood for one cooking fire, thinking I may as well finish off the renegades' venison while I still had a chance to do so.

The smell of the roasting venison steaks set my stomach to rolling since I had not eaten this morning before leaving the cave back yonder. I made some campfire tortillas like the Martinez brothers had showed me thinking it would have been nice to have some of that dried Habanero chili to season the steaks with. After Mutt and I finished off the steaks, I decided to grain the horses and give each a pinch of sugar before I rode them into harm's way.

An hour passed and I was impatient, so I mounted Storm and slowly started to follow the war pony tracks as they meandered their way southwest.

By mid-afternoon I was happy to note that the war pony's tracks did not wander back and forth anymore and now were pretty much in a straight line, which hopefully told me that the pinto had a certain destination in mind. With the trail and snow broken in front of the war pony, Mutt was on point and leading the pack when he stopped suddenly and lowered his body to the ground with his ears perked up and pointed. As soon as he did that, Storm's ears raised also as she started to sense what Mutt was sensing. My present position was not desirable since I was smack dab in the middle of an open meadow with no protection from being seen or shot from someone in the surrounding trees. Pulling my Winchester from the rifle scabbard, I spoke softly for only Mutt to hear, "What? Could not give us a little more warning there, Mutt? We are out here in the open, buddy!"

Mutt turned his head to look at me with a facial expression like, "Hey, there is only so much I can do." Then he turned his eyes back to the front and ahead toward the trail in front of us and ignored me.

For several minutes of Mutt checking the broken trail before us, I scanned the tree line all around us waiting for the report of a gunshot and the killing bullet that would end my life. Mutt finally stood and started moving forward, but at a much slower rate. Still glad to be alive and finally moving, I gave Storm a slight jab of my spur.

Feeling some release of tension as we entered into the evergreen tree line to the southwest, I dared to look on our back trail expecting to see 60 livid and killing mad Ute Indians hoofing at a full gallop in our direction with their Winchesters pointed and their bows ready to sling some arrows in my vicinity. There were no renegades, and the meadow was as silent as the fallen snow. Thank you, Lord!

Mutt continued on for another 20 yards into the forest of evergreens, and then he depressed once again to his belly, his ears perked up, and his black tipped gray hair on his back standing straight up.

After Storm, Strawberry, and I came to a complete stop, I listened to the trees and the mountain, hoping to hear anything that the half wolf was sensing. After several seconds I could not hear anything, but I could smell it - wood smoke and it was obvious it was in front of us and the war pony tracks were leading us straight to it. So far, so good. With the help of Mutt and the renegade pony, I had located the Ute renegade winter camp. Now what the hell was I going to do?

Chapter 33

The wind, coming from the west, was in my face, meaning that the wood smoke had been carried farther than if the wind had been at my back. If the wind had been at my back blowing to the east, I may not have smelled any smoke until I was right on top of the encampment. Since the wind was blowing towards me, I hazard to guess that the Ute winter camp was anywhere between a quarter of a mile to a half mile to the west in front of me.

My guess was that the Ute renegade camp would be in some sort of meadow to be able to house that many Indians, possibly on the edge of the stand of deep evergreen timber I now found myself. Urging Storm forward and westward another 30 yards, I found a game trail heading to the south. Turning Storm south and up the game trail for roughly 50 yards, I stopped and dismounted. With Mutt, I walked back to the original trail left by the Ute war pony and cut a substantial evergreen limb with my Bowie knife and used it to brush snow and cover my tracks heading south. My intention was if one of the Utes followed the pinto's tracks backwards, they may not see that I followed and headed south. Any tracker worth his salt would see it right off, but it might be a youngster or an experienced tracker they sent to investigate.

Heading south through the timber, I only came across tracks of deer and elk and the occasional rabbit in the snow; there were no tracks of any shod or unshod horses, meaning that the renegades had not sent any hunting or scouting parties in this direction which was good news for me. I was hoping to be able to find a suitable location to observe the camp and determine if Kellie Shawn was in fact a captive there.

The sun was now starting to dip below the snowcapped mountains to the west as the night started its descent upon the Rocky Mountain frontier and the Kawuneeche Valley. Deciding the night would give me cover to move closer to the campsite, I kept moving as silently as I could with my troop of animals. Mutt of course was silent as the wind, but the horses snorted every time their snouts butted up against an evergreen tree limb heavy with snow. I would just trust that there was plenty of normal camp activity and racket that would cover the sound of my horses. In a half hour of time I found the edge of the deep timber and could see the Ute winter camp in its entirety stretched out before in a large meadow. After finding a good observation position, I walked both Storm and Strawberry back in the dark timber about 50 yards or so and set up a picket line to tie them off. I then left the horse saddle and pack saddle on for now, but I fed them some grain and a couple of pinches of sugar each.

After taking care of the horses, I reached into the pack on Strawberry to fetch a blanket, my fur lined gloves, and last year's Christmas present from Lucas and Devon which was a pair of binoculars that was invented by some Italian fellow named Ignatio Porro so I could more easily observe the comings and goings of the Ute renegade camp. I also retrieved a pound of venison jerky and a full canteen of water. After I checked the loads in my Colt and Winchester to make sure they both were fully loaded, Mutt and I slowly made our way back to the edge of the timber.

I scooped out enough snow about a foot deep and five feet wide so that Mutt and I could lie down in a somewhat comfortable position in a shallow trough in the snow. Being down in the trench would help keep us out of the wind and give us some insulation against the cold. Mutt, after watching me lie down on my stomach with the blanket on my back facing the renegade camp, took the opportunity to get some shut-eye, and he cuddled up next to me, which gave us both body heat from each other.

My vantage point was better than I could have imagined; it was located almost straight south of the camp 75 yards on a ridge that was a good 50 yards higher than the renegades' camp. I could see at least 40 teepees which told me there were more than 60 Indians that had refused to go to the reservation in Utah. I lost count of their horses at 80 in their makeshift corrals made out of down evergreen timber.

It was obvious that no one in camp sensed my presence up on the ridge above them as they went about doing their nightly chores and eating their suppers, so I was safe for the time being of being detected.

As the night wore on, the moon lifted and made its arc across the cloudless sky which gave off plenty of light by which to see. The only problem was that with the dancing and flickering light of the numerous campfires, combined with the moon creating shadows, it made it hard to distinguish any facial features. It was easy enough to tell the differences between men and women by how they were dressed or how they walked, but trying to recognize a face on this night was not going to happen. During the day it would be easier to tell the faces apart.

Mutt was the smart one out of the two of us; he was still sleeping and I decided it was better getting some shut-eye now and try my luck in the morning to see if Rick Alvardo and Kellie Shawn Arriaga were in the camp down below.

After eating a half of a pound of venison jerky and drinking half of the water that was in my canteen, I closed my eyes. Sleep was difficult not from the cold because in our hollowed out observation pit in the snow we both were very comfortable, but instead from the difficulty of trying to shut down my mind that was trying to reckon out the next step to take. After tossing it back and forth for several minutes in my mind, I resolved the next step would make itself known when it was ready. After realizing I had no set plan of action and anything I did come up with was probably going to get me killed anyway, I drifted off to sleep.

The smell of roasting meat woke me up as it made my gut rumble. Mutt woke up at the same time, and he slowly got out of our shallow dugout observation pit and made his way into the timber. I assumed he was hunting up some breakfast for himself as I finished off the last of the venison jerky that I had taken from Strawberry's pack last night. As soon as I finished my breakfast and the last of the water in my canteen, I pulled out my Italian binoculars and started to study the renegade camp again.

The Ute Indians below seemed content in their winter encampment knowing that they for the length of the winter would be free from any harm by the military. Looking at how they went about their daily lives, it was obvious to me that the renegades were not thinking beyond this moment in time. If they were worried that the spring would bring the military and those that will force them onto the reservation, they were not showing it.

The Ute women of course were doing the heavy lifting and chores around camp. They were tanning hides, gathering wood, cooking and roasting meat, cleaning and making new clothes, and taking care of the kids. When the Utes were on the move and ready to break camp, the women did all the chores associated with that also. The Ute women were dressed in normal winter clothing consisting of long buckskin dresses and leggings to keep the cold out. Their dark black hair was always long and in one or two braids.

As a warrior society, the Ute Indian men usually slept later than the women and spent most of their winter daylight hours trying to keep warm either in their teepees or around the many large campfires sprinkled around the campsite. The ones that had gathered outside were warming themselves by the campfires, probably planning the day's activities, such as forming hunting parties to hunt for the much needed meat to keep a camp this size from starving in the middle of winter. The men were dressed similarly as the women were in buckskin. There were no breechcloths this winter, but plenty of buckskin pants with leather leg trimmings for decoration. They wore full long sleeve buckskin shirts with beads sewn here and there for decoration along the back of their arms. Almost all had eagle feathers tied at the end of their long dark braids. The more eagle feathers a man had meant he was either an elder or prominent warrior among their tribe.

As I scanned the whole camp with my Italian binoculars, I noticed all the men were dressed the same - except one. The one man that was dressed differently, I focused in on him and him alone. He had his back to me and was wearing Levi Strauss blue jeans and a dark brown winter duster almost an exact duplicate of my own. On his head he had what looked like a coyote fur hat that covered his ears. After I watched the man for a minute or so, he finally turned his face and body in my direction. Rod Hammond had been correct; I had found the last surviving member of the Biggers and Hammond gang. Even though it had been a couple of years since I last saw him, the man in the winter duster down below was Rick Alvardo in the flesh.

Knowing that if Alvardo was in the renegade camp and if Kellie Shawn Arriaga was still alive, she would also be there as a captive. My heart was now rising in my throat as I started to scan only the women as they went about doing their chores hoping beyond hope that Kellie was still alive.

A sudden movement caught my eye as two of the women down below started to scuffle with one another. At first it started as a couple of shoves to the chest of one of the women. The woman being shoved had more than enough abuse after the second shove and with both fists plowed into the first one knocking her down. Knocking the first woman down did not seem to be enough punishment as the second woman fell on top of her and proceeded to give the first woman an epic ass kicking. The fighting of the two women drew the attention of the warriors and Alvardo, which seemed to amuse the Ute Indian men. Alvardo was not amused as he rushed over and grabbed the woman giving the ass kicking and pulled her off her defeated adversary. After separating the two women, Alvardo slapped the second woman hard enough to knock her down. The second woman stood slowly and stumbled twice as she regained her senses as she advanced on Alvardo. Just before she spit on the outlaw, I could see her face fully as she turned to spit. Senorita Kellie Shawn Arriaga was alive.

CHAPTER 34

Lifting my Winchester, I sighted in on the chest of Rick Alvardo. After being spit on by Kellie Shawn, he slapped her once more and then turned his back to my position and headed back to the campfire that he came from. Keeping the sights of my rifle on his back, I held my fire. Lowering my Winchester, I realized it was not in my nature to shoot a man from a distance let alone in the back, no matter how evil or how much the man deserved it.

Alvardo's second slap had knocked Kellie Shawn down again. A second woman dressed in a long buckskin dress helped Kellie Shawn up to her feet. Kellie had at least one friend amongst the women, maybe a fellow captive.

As much as I hated seeing Kellie abused in such away, her reaction against both the first woman and Alvardo told me her essence and mind had not been broken yet. Kellie Shawn Arriaga was one hell of a woman with a resilient personality and spirit. I was now even more determined to get her out of there even if it cost me my life. The way my heart had almost crushed when I realized it was in fact Kellie down below told me all I needed to know. I was madly in love with the Mexican girl bandit; there was no doubt about it at all.

My half wolf returned with what looked like a content face, meaning he had found some wayward animal for grub. Ruffling up his hair I told Mutt, "Kellie Shawn is down below, we just got to find a plan of how to get her out of there safely without all of us getting killed." Mutt turned his head in such a way that looked as if he was deep in thought.

Thinking it was way past time to check on Storm and Strawberry, I made my way back through the timber. I unsaddled and unpacked both horses and rubbed them down and then fed them some more grain and gave each a good portion of sugar. After walking both horses to get the kinks out after being on a picket line all night, I let them have their fill of water from a small brook that had not frozen over yet not ten yards from where I had them tied off for the night. After combing out both their manes and tails, I re-saddled and re-packed them both in case I needed to move in a hurry.

After refilling my canteens from the same brook that the horses drank from and not wanting to risk a fire and being detected in hostile territory, I grabbed another pound of venison jerky and headed back to the edge of the timber to keep observing the renegade camp, and hopefully a plan of action and the rescue of Kellie Shawn would present itself.

In a full day of watching from afar and observing every move that Kellie Shawn made throughout the renegade camp, I noticed that she was never alone or without an escort. It was clear she was a captive among the Utes and being used as a slave to do the jobs the other women did not want to do. I could only imagine the horror of her nights when she was alone in the teepee with Alvardo. Kellie was a prisoner within the winter camp, but also a prisoner in the surrounding remote wilderness that she was not familiar with far from her brother Jesús Arriaga and with no way to contact him. The cold and snow of the winter months ahead were better than any prison wall, because if she had somehow made good an escape, it would almost be a certainty that she would perish in the mountains without food, weapons, a horse, or shelter of any kind. It was nothing short of amazing that Kellie Shawn's spirit was still intact after seeing her bodyguards shot down in ambush and being dragged through the wilderness, not knowing if each day would be her last.

It broke my heart to think of these things that I knew to be true. It also saddened me that after observing Kellie this day, I could see no way of sneaking her out of the renegade camp and away from the outlaw Alvardo without being noticed. I was also worrisome again that Kellie would become too much trouble for Alvardo and he would simply just kill her like in Rey Chavez' story of his wife's lover killing her and saying, "I was tired of her shit!" It seemed like it was going to be an impossibility to rescue Kellie with any type of stealth. I was afraid that any delay - be it a minute, hour, or day - that Kellie Shawn's life was hanging by a mere thread. Someway, somehow I needed to get the woman I loved out of there and into my arms.

After watching the coming and goings at the camp for a full day, I saw numerous hunting parties return with elk and deer strapped to their pack horses which were turned over to the women of the camp to prepare to be roasted to feed the hungry camp. Watching so many warriors come and go from the renegade camp drove home the fact how fortunate I was that I somehow had not been detected yet. It would only be a matter of time before some hunting party cut my trail and would follow it and locate Storm, Strawberry, Mutt, and myself. Every passing daylight hour was counting down to the time when I would have to fight or flee the area. I was still at a loss on how to get Kellie safely out of the renegade camp.

At dusk when the sun was starting to drop down below the mountains to the west, another hunting party returned in the dwindling light. This hunting party was different because it consisted of two Ute warriors and a white man. The white man was dressed as you would expect a mountain man to be dressed - in furs and a heavy white beard just below his coyote fur hat. The white man was not a prisoner nor captive; he seemed to be leading the hunting party. I trained my binoculars on him, hoping to get a better feel for the man, but in the low light of the dusk I could not see any of the men's faces of the hunting party clearly. After several minutes of studying the last hunting party, I started to get a headache from straining my eyes looking through the Italian binoculars in the dwindling light, so I gave up for now.

Once the sun finally made its last appearance for the day, I made my way back to the horses again and went through the routine of un-packing and un-saddling and letting them stretch their muscles for a spell. Once Storm and Strawberry were watered and fed some grain and some sugar, I then saddled and packed them again. Both horses were tired of this routine and stomped their hooves and threw their heads back and forth to let me know they were ready to be back on the wilderness trail. This waiting game was getting on their nerves just as much as mine. Come sunrise I was going to have to make a decision on how to proceed.

After slowly making it back to my observation pit, I ate another half of a pound of venison jerky and fed a half pound to Mutt. We both drank heavily from my canteen until it was empty. I rolled onto my back and lifted the blanket for Mutt to crawl under and add his body heat for the night.

Lying there listening to the wind rustle the evergreen needles above my head, I felt the temperature start to drop, and with the slight wind came some snow, not a heavy snow, but a light snow and within a half hour, there was a good dusting on top of the blanket that Mutt and I were using.

My mind was a jumble of what to do and how to go about trying to rescue Kellie Shawn Arriaga. After seeing so many hunting parties moving about today, I realized time was my enemy and it would not be long before I was discovered. After observing Kellie's movement all day throughout the camp as she did the chores with the other Ute women, I now knew she was never alone and under constant observation either by the Ute Indian women or Rick Alvardo himself.

From my conversations with Lucas and Matt Lee, I knew the Ute Indians were a warrior society, but they also were honorable and respected courage. If the situation was normal, I could probably just ride up and be accepted as a friend. Times were not normal, and these Indians in this camp were fed up with how the white man in general had treated them. They were considered renegades and come spring the Utes would have the might of the US army coming to force them on to the reservation in Utah. More than likely there would be bloodshed on both sides. I was more than certain that the Ute Indian renegades would see me as an enemy.

The more I pondered the problem, the only solution and the only chance that I thought might work to save Kellie Shawn was the simplest of all plans and that was to just ride down there and see what would happen. I might be able to buy, trade, or fight for Kellie Shawn. Sneaking her away was not going to work, I reckoned. I was just going to have to ride up to the camp in the morning and let fate rule the day.

Having decided on a plan of action, even though it was probably going to get me killed, I felt better. Looking skyward and saying a small prayer, I would just have to put trust in the Lord that if Kellie Shawn Arriaga and I were meant to be together, then he would make it possible for that to happen. Having cleared my mind of any more doubts on what I was going to do tomorrow, I burrowed down under the blanket and cuddled up next to the half wolf and fell asleep.

CHAPTER 35

Waking up at dawn, I watched as the sun was starting its daily climb in the sky in the east; the wind had died and the air was silent, no sound, none as if the mountains knew this day was a day that may present only death. And as if to seal that thought and my fate, the tree above me came alive as a flock of six midnight black crows landed on the evergreen tree limbs above my head. The largest crow stared at me, looking down as if it was studying me. Looking above, I locked eyes with the crow and the crow's eyes never wavered, never left mine.

This was no ordinary crow; I saw its intelligence flicker back and forth across its ebony eyes. With a sudden flurry of flapping its wings, the large crow broke the silence of the morning with a "caw, caw, caw" that was meant only for me. I pondered if this was an omen of what was going to happen today. The large crow cocked its head back and forth several times as if it was waiting for a response from me and after deciding none was coming since I did not have the skill-set to understand his message, he and his compadres took flight and headed north to parts unknown.

Regardless of what the crow's message was, it changed nothing. I could wait no longer. I would take the trail that would lead me into the Ute renegade camp that Kellie Shawn was being held captive and Rick Alvardo's "retribution" was fast approaching. Having thrown caution to the wind, I realized in the end the only thing that might be accomplished this day was my death. My fate and that of Kellie Shawn would be decided today.

Mutt, sensing that our lives would forever be changed today, lay his muzzle on my chest and looked into my eyes. Ruffling and roughing up his black tipped fur on the top of his head, I told him, "Today of all days you must listen to me! When I ride into the camp, you have to stay behind in the timber. If I ride to my death, then you must live. Do you understand?" Mutt rolled onto his back and gave me two whimpers. He was not happy, but he understood.

Taking time this morning once again to un-saddle and un-pack Storm and Strawberry, I rubbed them down with a curry comb and combed out their manes and tails. After both horses had their fill of water from the brook, I fed them some more grain and a pinch of sugar. It was as if both horses sensed something had changed, and they no longer pawed the ground with their hooves and tossed their heads in anticipation for the trail. Storm and Strawberry knew something was amiss and probably could tell by my manner this morning that any sensible caution had been set aside. Come hell or high water fate, and destiny was going to take a hand today.

After eating a cold breakfast of venison jerky, I was ready for what was to come today. Mutt seemed a little jittery, but I was ready. It did not take long to get both horses ready for the trail and after stepping into the stirrup to mount Storm, I looked to the heavens and for an early winter day it was going to be a pleasing sort of morning, not too cold, just barely cold enough to see my breath. The forever blue sky over the never summer mountains was cloudless, and the sun felt good as it warmed my face. The wind had picked up slightly and brought the scent of the evergreen needles and the freshness of the snow to me. I took in a lungful and it made me feel strong and powerful.

Mutt was pouting and hung back behind Storm and Strawberry and seemed uneasy and unsure of what I was going to attempt to do today as I gave Storm some rein and a slight jab of my right spur as we headed back the same way we had come. After finding the original trail that the war pony I had released made, it was obvious that this was the main trail for the recent hunting parties as they came and went to the renegade camp.

Looking to the west in the direction of the Ute camp, I took another deep breath and filled my lungs with some fresh clean mountain air. I headed west to whatever fate and the good Lord had waiting for me at the end of this trail.

Once reaching the end of the dark timber, I was only 50 yards from the renegade camp and could see the entrance that the trail took. So far I had not been spotted by any of the Ute Indian men or women.

After studying the camp for a minute, I dismounted and went up to Mutt knowing in my heart this might be the last time I would ever see my friend. Dropping to one knee, I grabbed his face in my hands and brought him close to me so my eyes were only inches from his. Trying not to show emotion in my voice, and I failed in doing so, I spoke to the half wolf, my voice cracking with emotion, "You need to listen to me for the first time in your life. By riding into that camp yonder, it is probably a one way ticket and you can't go, my pal. They will kill you on sight and I will not allow that to happen. If I do not come back in a full day, you must leave and find a lady wolf and make some tiny wolf pups and live the life that I will not be able to live. This is my fight this time and mine alone. Do you understand?"

Mutt, my half wolf and half something else dog, lowered his face but kept his eyes locked on mine. His reaction told me he understood and was saddened by this turn of events. With the Lord as my witness, I loved this dog, this half wolf that chose to be my friend. Not wanting Mutt to see me tear up, I turned quickly and remounted Storm.

Giving Storm her head and some rein, I gave her a slight jab of my right spur as I headed toward the entrance of the Ute winter camp and the unknown. Looking back only once, I saw Mutt standing on the edge of the timber and not following which made my heart jump a beat.

Halfway in between the camp and the timber, I heard some hollering and whooping as I had been spotted, and it was making a commotion within the camp. It was not long before five war ponies, no make that six war ponies, were heading at a fast gallop in my direction. The two war ponies in front had warriors with lances with eagle feathers tied behind the killing point of the lance leveled and pointed in my direction. One rider was on my right and the other had taken up a position on my left. I just kept going forward at the same pace; I could not show fear nor even flinch even if they ran me through with their lances. Just mere seconds before the lances would pierce my body, the Indians brought them closer to their bodies and each rider and lance missed me by an inch or two.

As if six warriors were not enough, more war ponies and warriors started to spill from the campsite in my direction. I also spotted what looked like the white man I had seen last night galloping my way.

The second wave of two Ute warriors at a full gallop held war clubs and as they raised them above their heads, the one on the right swung and barely missed my noggin as he flew on pass. The one on the left swung his war club and if by accident or design, he connected to my right temple, and I saw stars and blackness as I was stripped out of the saddle in a somersault and thudded to the ground.

The sudden meeting of the ground caused the air to rush from my lungs when I landed face first on my stomach in the snow. My first thought as I tried to refill my lungs with much needed air was "this plan was for shit." That was when I heard the howling. Sitting up, even as the blood was flooding my right eye, I could see Mutt as he paced back and forth on the edge of the timber howling in anger toward the heavens. The half wolf was anxious and distraught at what had just transpired as he quickly paced back and forth not knowing what to do.

Out of the corner of my eye, I saw two of the warriors bringing Winchesters to their shoulders to fire at Mutt. I tried to yell "NO!" as they fired. Using their lever action of their rifles as fast as they could, the renegades kept firing at Mutt. The first couple of shots missed and kicked up snow in front, the next volley was closer, and the third found home as I heard Mutt yelp and stumble and saw him go down.

Everything was happening faster than I could imagine as I watched Mutt go down in the distance. I was so distracted by what just happened to Mutt that I failed to see some of the other warriors had dismounted until they started to beat and kick me.

All I could think of during the beating was I had failed Kellie Shawn and Mutt. Each kick brought more stars as the irate Indians targeted my head and just before blackness overtook me, I heard a voice say, "Hold on, I know this man."

CHAPTER 36

W hen I woke up, my head was pounding and I reached up and touched the wound on the right side of my skull from when the buck hit me in the head with his war club. And what I felt was not good, it was a sizable knot about the size of a large chicken egg and in the middle of the knot was a gash about four inches long and still oozing blood. As a matter of fact my whole body hurt; touching my face I found at least six different tender spots from where the warriors had kicked me in the face. Thinking and trying to remember what had happened, it was obvious from the pain of even a slight movement that I had taken a severe beating and it was a wonder that I was still alive.

Looking around at my surroundings, I could tell that I was in a teepee and from the light and the smell coming through the teepee flap that served as a door that it was mid-morning.

I would not admit it to anyone if they asked in this camp because I needed to be fearless to survive here, but a tear formed in my eye thinking of my half wolf and the last vision of his going down with a dying yelp. I loved that dog and he died on my watch. Mutt, my friend, died because of me, the fool. Never for the rest of my life would I be able to forgive myself for that.

Now that my senses were starting to come back, I pondered the question of, "Why am I still alive?"

Seeing movement to my right, I saw the orange, cherry glow of burning tobacco at the end of a corncob pipe as someone inhaled on it in the darkened shadow. Trying now to focus on the person in the shadow, I was finding it difficult due to the blood that was still in my eyes or I was just still hazy from the beating I took.

Finally there was a voice from the shadowy figure, and it was a voice I recognized, "Well Chance my boy, I have been here enjoying my pipe whilst you were taking a nap and trying to figure out if you are the bravest or the dumbest son of a bitch I have ever known."

Even as sore as I was, that statement brought a slight chuckle to my throat, "I gather Matt Lee, that it was you that stopped those wild savages from spilling my brains out there in the snow."

Moving into the light of the campfire where I could see him fully now, I could see that he seemed to not have aged since I last saw him. Matt Lee was probably one of the toughest men I have ever known and he stood at 6'2" tall and weighed about 200 pounds and it was all muscle. Matt Lee never told me how old he was; Lucas thought he might be in his 50's. I never knew if Matt Lee was his given and full name or his first and middle name with no last name given. Everyone called him Matt Lee and so did I. His hair was solid gray, and his beard was snow white which gave away his age more than the way he moved. Matt Lee was a legend and was a man respected everywhere he went in the Rocky Mountain frontier...and he was my mentor.

Matt Lee took another pull on his corncob pipe and still chuckling, "It was me; I couldn't let them beat you to death without knowing what made someone who I thought had more meat in his brain pan than most do such a foolish thing."

Looking at Matt Lee as he once again inhaled on the corn cob, "I thought you gave up the pipe, that you were afraid it was going to kill you."

Sitting down on a log next to where I was lying, Matt Lee replied, "Hell, I did for a while and I got to pondering about why I gave up something that gave me so much pleasure and I reckoned if ole' father time, wild injuns, or critters never killed me, why was I afraid of a little tobacco smoke. Enough about me Chance, you did not answer my question. What the hell were you thinking?"

Finally, I was able to push myself into a sitting position as I faced Matt Lee. "I have been on the trail of a man that is in this camp; his name is Rick Alvardo."

Matt Lee looked deep in thought as he replied, "You mean the half-breed? He is an evil one for sure and probably needs killing more than most. Why were you trailing Alvardo?"

Talking made my face hurt, but I continued, "Remember how Lucas came to find me buried in the Bondurant gold mine after the Biggers and Hammond gang blew it up after shooting and killing my brother? Rick Alvardo is the last remaining member of that gang."

After Matt Lee took another draw on his corncob pipe he said, "Alvardo is a slimy back shooting no account, but I had no idea he was a member of that notorious gang. I have not been down to a town or a camp in quite a spell, and you are the first white man I have seen in six months and had not heard any of the latest comings and goings in the Rocky Mountain frontier. So I reckon with what just spilled out of your mouth is that the other five members of the outlaw gang somehow have made an early departure out of this life?"

Shaking my head "yes" to answer Matt Lee's question prompted him to talk some more with a slight chuckle, "Well, if you downed those five desperadoes, those who write the newspapers must say you now have a gunfighter reputation on par will ole' Lucas. I also should point out a fact you may have not thought of; by your riding into a Ute renegade camp with 60 or more fighting mad injuns on the prod all by your lonesome, makes you seem as if you are not the sharpest tool in the shed."

That brought a smile that made my face hurt, trying not to laugh because every muscle and every bone in my face hurt from when those young bucks tried to cave in my face and skull. After stifling my laugh and with a more serious tone, "That's why I always liked you Matt Lee, you have a way of pointing out the obvious. I had another reason not to wait till spring. The woman captive that Alvardo has, I mean to take her and rescue her from him. When I was watching the camp from up on the hill, I saw him abuse her more than once, and I know her well enough that sooner or later she would push him over the edge, and he would kill her. I will not allow that to happen; I came here to kill Alvardo."

Matt Lee stopped smoking his corn cob pipe altogether and with a slight chuckle before he got serious said, "I reckoned it just goes to figure there was a woman involved for you to do something so imprudent as to ride in here with your weapons holstered. You got a set of balls Chance, and they are bigger than most. I knew right off the first time I saw you. The Mexican gal besides being a looker, she is a fiery one, that's for sure. I figure she would knife Alvardo sooner or later in the dark of the night. When you abuse and give a lesson in meanness to a critter or a person, don't be surprised if they learn their lesson and teach you a lesson. Let me do some thinking on this for a spell so we get the girl, kill the outlaw, and still stay alive."

Shaking my head "no" I said, "Not your fight Matt Lee, it is mine alone."

Matt Lee started talking and it was more to himself than me, "I understand that dipshit; you let me do the thinking for you on this one. It seems to me you are thinking with your heart and not your brain pan. So far all you have accomplished is getting your dog shot and that ugly mug of yours caved in."

Matt Lee's last statement sort of made me annoyed, but he was right. Just for him to mention Mutt brought a tear to my eye, and I had to turn my head so he didn't see it. Mutt my half wolf, half something else dog was killed on my watch, and I was to blame and would have to live with that for the rest of my life. I loved that half wolf more than I wanted to let on. Mutt was more than just a dog; he had been my friend and we had understood each other. We were a team and could read each other's minds.

The minute of silence that had fallen in between Matt Lee and myself was broken when an older Ute Indian woman entered into the tepee. Her hair was long and black as coal with streaks of gray interwoven into one braid that reached all the way down her back to her waist. She wore a long buckskin dress that was adorned with colorful beads and what looked like feathers from a crow. Her features were soft and beautiful and not as hard as most Indian women. When she looked at me, she did not smile but when she turned toward Matt Lee, her face broke into a large grin showing her pearly whites. Matt Lee pointed toward the woman and said, "Chance, I would like for you to meet "Walks With Ghost," my wife."

"Your wife? I never knew you were married." I was sort of dumbfounded by this bit of news. Matt Lee, the famed mountain man that was respected by those that knew him and a man that put fear in the hearts of his enemies, was married. Who would have thought?

Bowing my head in acknowledgment to "Walks With Ghost," she did the same. "Walks With Ghost" is an unusual name even for an Indian name. Must be quite a story behind that name."

Walks With Ghost smiled and pointed at Matt Lee as he tittered some before he spoke, "Before our nuptial her name was Crow, but shortly after we got hitched the tribe started calling her "Walks With Ghost."

I knew I must look somewhat befuddled and confused as Matt Lee continued, "The Utes call me "Ghost," henceforth the name "Walks With Ghost."

Still trying to decipher what Matt Lee was saying, "Ghost? I don't understand."

Matt Lee's alias, known as "Ghost," looked deep in thought as he recalled a time long ago in his past, "A tale from a lifetime ago and for another time, Chance. Right now we need to focus on your situation and how are we going to get your Mexican gal freed from Alvardo."

"Mexican gal" seemed like a poor way to describe the woman I loved, so I wanted Matt Lee to start thinking of her as a real person. "Her name is Kellie Shawn Arriaga and she is the sister of a well-known bandit in Mexico named Chucho el Roto, whose real name is Jesús Arriaga."

Standing up and right before he left to go out the entrance of the tepee, Matt Lee responded, "Mexican bandit royalty? This Rocky Mountain frontier love story of yours gets better and better. Chance, you need to let Walks With Ghost tend to your wounds and bruises right now to get you in the best shape possible in the shortest amount of time. I have an idea and I am going to go talk to my brother in-law."

I shook my head "yes" meaning it was okay for Walks With Ghost to treat my numerous aches and pains, "Brother in-law? Why are you going to go talk to your brother in-law?"

Crouched with one foot out the deerskin flap that acted as a door to the tepee, Matt Lee looked over his shoulder back at me when he said, "Yes, Walks With Ghost's older brother is my brother in-law – Chief Piah, the head honcho of this band of renegades."

CHAPTER 37

Walks With Ghost cleaned my wounds and applied two different types of salve to my wounds and bruises. After doing her doctoring on me, she gave me a large bowl of rabbit stew from the cook fire in the center of the tepee, which tasted wonderful since I had not eaten much in the last couple of days except venison jerky.

While Walks With Ghost was tending to my needs, it was a pleasant surprise to find out she spoke very good English and that Matt Lee had also taught her how to read and write in English also.

I asked her many questions about her husband; some she answered and others she said were for Ghost to answer. It was apparent to me that she loved her man with her whole heart and spoke of his greatness as a warrior and husband with glowing esteem. She also spoke of her loneliness the many times he was gone for long periods of time; sometimes he would be gone for more than a year. She understood and accepted his long absences which she called his "Wanderings." It was the same term Matt Lee had spoken of on the last day I saw him when he rode away from Central City. Matt Lee, alias the "Ghost," was always one of the most interesting men I knew, but now I find out that there was much more to the man than I ever knew. If I lived long enough, I must know his whole story.

Walks With Ghost also explained that Matt Lee had all of my possessions like my weapons and money belt, and my other possibles here in the tepee, and she assured me that Storm and Strawberry have been well treated and turned into the renegades' remuda, but were still my horses.

After two hours of being gone, Matt Lee returned and opened the deerskin flap and told me to follow him. Stepping out of the warmth of the tepee into the cold air made me feel invigorated as I took a lungful of the winter air. I felt naked without any of my weapons and especially my Colt pistol. All the Indians, the women, warriors, and kids followed me with their eyes as I walked along with the man they knew as Ghost. Matt Lee looked at me as we walked and said, "I spoke with Chief Piah at length about why you were here and about Kellie Shawn being your woman. I also told him about the death of your brother and why you were trailing his nephew in the first place."

Stopping, I grabbed Matt Lee's arm and turned him toward me, "Are you serious, Alvardo is Chief Piah's nephew? Which means he is your kin by marriage. You got any other good news, Matt Lee?"

Matt Lee in all seriousness said, "Look around you Chance, the Ute tribe is a closed society with little or no influence from the outside world. Hell kid, they all are related in one form or another. I did not realize until speaking with Chief Piah that the half-breed Alvardo was a nephew. Chief Piah and Walks With Ghost were siblings of Falling Rain who was Rick Alvardo's mother. She was captured by a Mexican and before her son was born, she killed the man that had fathered her unborn child. After Falling Rain's son's birth, she found her way back to the tribe and Alvardo although a half-breed was raised among the Utes. The good news from what I gathered is Chief Piah never thought much of his nephew and thought him to be rotten through and through. I don't believe it would hurt too many of these renegades' feelings if Rick Alvardo's life ended prematurely."

We started to walk again, and I started to think what I had said to Matt Lee and would be shortly telling Chief Piah about Kellie Shawn being my woman. I could only hope that Kellie Shawn felt the same way.

In front of us was the largest teepee in the camp and was obviously a home of a man of great importance. As we entered through the deer skin flap, Matt Lee went first, and then I stepped through the opening and if I ever had doubts about Kellie Shawn Arriaga being my woman, they were quickly dashed once I entered.

There were only three people in the teepee when we entered - Chief Piah, Rick Alvardo, and Kellie Shawn Arriaga. Chief Piah was sitting shoulder to shoulder with Alvardo, and Kellie Shawn was sitting down Indian style directly behind the last remaining outlaw of the Biggers and Hammond gang.

Chief Piah looked like the classic example of one that led and commanded men; he could have been a general of a Roman legion or a commander of the French army. His mere presence commanded respect and honor. His hair was long and almost white with streaks of gray in it and braided into two braids with four eagle feathers woven into the braids on each side. He wore doe skin pants and a long sleeve doe skin shirt that was fringed with colorful beads and small eagle bones. His elaborate breast plate foretold of his importance as Chief among the Utes. The breastplate was made of eagle bones for a warrior's wisdom and clarity, with a few grizzly claws thrown in for strength and power. He seemed ageless and strong and in command of all that was around him. His face showed the wrinkles of countless summers and winters that he had lived, but also of knowledge and insight of one that had seen it all. I had no doubt that Chief Piah could be a deadly adversary if the need should arise.

Rick Alvardo, the man that I had hunted and trailed to this spot, looked much the same since the last time I saw him on Bald Mountain when Jace was killed. Like me he had been brought to Chief Piah's teepee unarmed. The outlaw was a tad smaller than me, but he was a hard and angry looking man about 170 pounds and 5'10" with long midnight black hair drawn into a ponytail down to the middle of his back. He wore Levi Straus blue jeans and a buckskin shirt with very little fringe. His body was chiseled with muscle and looked very powerful in all his movements. His face was stone and spoke of the unhappiness of being born out of rape, lust, and hatred. He was a man that probably never once in his life had a happy thought or even smiled. The man that had ridden with the killers of the Biggers and Hammond gang that had caused the death of my little brother Jace was also the same man that had also captured the woman that held my heart. There was no doubt that the evil man that now sat less than ten feet away from me was a man that I was going to kill or die trying.

Kellie Shawn Arriaga, although her face was battered and bruised from the fists of the man I was going to kill, still was a stunning and beautiful woman. Her midnight black hair was braided into one braid that resembled that of a Ute Indian wife. She was petite, but not frail or fragile looking even in her present condition. She still had the look of a strong woman who knew her own mind as she turned her head to look at me with her eyes that were blue with a hint of green that told me the story of how she had braved the storm that had been her life since her kidnapping. Her eyes revealed that her mind was still intact and probably stronger from what she had endured like a wild mustang still unbroken. She was a woman to ride the river with and I wanted her so.

Kellie Shawn's jaw dropped when she first saw me, and her eyes widened in total disbelief. After about a minute when her mind caught up with what she was seeing, a flood of tears came as she jumped up and ran into my arms, and as she started to speak, her voice broke with emotion several times, "I asked the Lord to send an angel to rescue me, and I prayed every night that it would be you, Chance. How I had wished we had never parted ways that morning, for I knew it then as I know it now, I had already fallen in love with you. The only salvation that I had was knowing that you were still out there and once you had heard what had happened that you would find me. I never lost my faith; I was never broken as long as there was a possibility that you would find me."

Alvardo had enough, and he stood angrily as if to rush me there in his uncle's teepee as I was still holding on to Kellie Shawn. Matt Lee palmed his Colt with lightning speed and pointed at the outlaw's head which brought the now fuming Alvrado to an immediate halt. "Sit your ass down Alvardo, you will not dishonor this man's teepee with bloodshed here. There will come a time and it isn't right now."

Chief Piah never moved a muscle as his eyes and mind took in everything that was happening as the tension mounted as the stare down between Matt Lee and Alvardo continued. Alvardo's eyes showed extreme loathing as he looked first at Matt Lee and then at me as he stood on the wrong and deadly side of the Ghost's pistol.

Chief Piah spoke in his native tongue to Alvardo which I had no understanding of. Alvardo turned and nodded a very irritated "yes" to his uncle and then slowly sat back down.

Holstering his pistol, Matt Lee took hold of Kellie Shawn gently by her elbow. "Ms. Arriaga, do you know my teepee and my wife Walk With Ghost?"

Kellie Shawn, still looking at me, shook her head "yes" as she replied to Matt Lee, "Yes, your wife has always been the only Ute woman that has treated me with respect."

Matt Lee looked directly at Alvardo, but speaking to Kellie Shawn in a low, but firm voice so there would be no misunderstanding, "Kellie Shawn while you are in this camp, you will forever be under my protection from now on. No one will harm you ever again. I want you to go to my teepee; my wife is waiting for you."

Kellie Shawn still held me tight, not wanting to let go as she looked into my eyes and held them as I spoke, "I had second thoughts riding away from you that morning. After the first time I saw you, I knew in my heart you were the one for me. Seeing you here Kellie Shawn has brought all the heartache I felt since I learned of your capture and the guilt I would have felt if you had died. I loved you that morning as we watched the sunrise and if possible, I love you more even now, always will. Our fate is now in the hands of the Lord and being played out here right now with our future still not being shown to us. No matter what happens in the hours and days to come, you are now safe from Alvardo. If my life is to pay for your safety, so be it. My friend Matt Lee will protect you, so now go to his and Walks With Ghost's teepee until I can join you."

Kellie Shawn stood on her tiptoes as she kissed me full on my lips. No doubt in my mind or anyone that just witnessed our exchange of words and gestures that we were meant for each other. My heart was beating so fast in her presence that I thought the sound could be heard by all of those in the Kawuneeche Valley.

Before Kellie Shawn left Chief Piah's teepee, she turned to face Alvardo, "You and the others killed those that I cared about; you beat me, you told me I was nothing, and you forced yourself on me at night. I was biding my time to get a hold of a knife or a dull deer antler, and I would have killed you just as your mother killed the man that did the same thing to her. Just know asshole, I am stronger than you. I never broke."

Having spoken her mind to the man that had savaged and brutalized her, Senorita Kellie Shawn Arriaga walked out of Chief Piah's teepee with her head held high. I could not have been any prouder of this woman than I was right now.

CHAPTER 38

A s soon as Kellie Shawn had left the teepee, Chief Piah without speaking indicated that Matt Lee and I should be seated across the fire from him and Alvardo. I found it difficult to sit not only because of my wounds and bruises, but also because I was anxious from the tension that filled the air. Looking at the man who was with those that killed my brother and had up until today abused the woman I loved, I knew the feelings that were flooding my mind could be my undoing, so I concentrated on calming myself. For whatever might happen in the minutes and days to come, I needed to not let my emotions rule my behavior. I forced my mind to focus on my training at the hands of Lucas Eldridge and the man now seated to my right Matt Lee.

Once I did that, my heart and mind quit racing and everything in the teepee came sharply into focus; my eyesight became more acute; my sense of smell increased; and even my sense of touch was more apparent.

Chief Piah studied me for several minutes before he spoke in perfect English, "Ghost told me some of your life outside of the Kawuneeche Valley and that you lost your woman. How is it that this Mexican woman is your woman if she is here with the son of Falling Rain?"

Fair enough question. One thing that I had learned from Lucas and Matt Lee about the Ute Indian mind is that they respected honesty and thought of things in black and white with no gray areas. "The Mexican woman Kellie Shawn was not my woman yet; I had not decided on taking her for my own just yet. Falling Rain's son killed those that had been sent to protect her and took her before I had an opportunity to claim her as my own."

Chief Piah looked confused by my answer, "Is this not the warrior way to take her for your own if you are stronger than those that have her?"

Nodding my head in understanding of the Ute way, "That is the warrior way and ancient way of the Utes, but in the land of the Mexicans where the woman comes from and in the land of the Whites where I come from, it is not the way. In our lands the woman and the man must both agree on who the woman belongs to. It is both the Mexican and the White custom. You saw for yourself Chief Piah, how the Mexican woman acted when she saw me. There is no doubt that she is my woman."

Chief Piah nodded his head "yes" as he replied, "She was pleased to see you that was plain for all to see. I invited you here Bondurant and the son of Falling Rain because Ghost asked me to decide who the Mexican woman belongs to. And if not for Ghost, who is an honored and respected warrior among my people, I would not sit for council on this question. Before I decide what must be done with the Mexican woman, I must ask you Bondurant one question, Were you the one that killed three of my warriors several days ago?"

I had been waiting for this question to come up and had thought hard about the answer I was going to give. "Yes, I killed two, and my half wolf and horse killed the third. Your warriors tried to add my belongings and horses to their teepees. They fought valiantly and died a respectable warrior's death. I left them where they were slain so all of the Ute nation would know they died a glorious death. It was my honor to have fought them."

My answer on the death of the three renegade warriors seemed to please the old Chief, and nothing more was said about their deaths. After a full minute Chief Piah spoke again, "The Mexican woman belongs to Falling Rain's son, but she can be traded for or bought according to our customs. You also have the right to fight for her, but let it be known according to our ways, the fight will be to the death. So Bondurant, what will it be?"

Not even hesitating one second, I spoke with a confident voice, "I choose to fight for the woman. Does Alvardo have the courage to fight me?"

Alvardo smiled as he shook his head - yes. Chief Piah, looking first at the outlaw and then at me before he spoke, "Then it shall be a fight to the death today an hour before sunset. The weapons will be in the old way - tomahawks and knives from horseback."

Alvardo stood and did not seem happy with the choice of weapons or maybe the method of battle and stormed out of Chief Piah's teepee. I stood slowly to show respect toward the Chief, but also because I was sore from the beating I took yesterday when I rode into the camp. Chief Piah nodded towards me which I took as permission to leave and make ready for battle. Matt Lee grabbed me by my elbow and led me out of the teepee.

After that Matt Lee, once we were out of earshot away from any other of the Utes, turned me toward him to make sure I was paying attention. "Listen up Chance, I have studied this Alvardo since he has been in camp knowing it was a good possibility I would have to fight the son of a bitch someday. I know he is totally blind in his left eye; I suspected it and two days before you showed up I stood just to his left so that he could only see me out of his corner of his left eye. I tossed a small log at him and he never flinched or saw it coming before it hit him. I made out like it was an accident, and then I did it again with the same result. He is totally blind in his left eye; you can use this to your advantage. It is probably a wash since you are somewhat beat up already, but it might level the field. Do not hesitate to kill this man in battle; if you show mercy at all, they will split Kellie Shawn and yourself from crotch to eyeball. Do you understand me?"

Nodding my head "yes" to answer the question, I looked toward the sky and the sun and was able to gauge that there was an hour to ready myself to fight Alvardo. With time short, I started to ponder the disadvantages and advantages of fighting Alvardo.

One disadvantage was he was a more experienced fighter when it came to hand-to-hand combat or combat from horseback. It was said he was an expert in the use of knives and tomahawks. I was also not in tip top shape after the severe beating that I took at the hands of the young bucks yesterday. Since he was smaller than I was, he also might be quicker, so I had to take that into consideration.

I started to count down my advantages; first and foremost was I was younger than Alvardo, and I was bigger and possibly stronger. He was blind in his left eye if Matt Lee was right. I was trained by Lucas and Matt Lee in hand-to-hand combat with knives and tomahawks, but never in an actual battle with these skills. After I viewed both sides of the pros and cons of my impending battle, it almost seemed like a wash, so I hoped that fate looked favorably on the love between Kellie Shawn and me. Looking toward Matt Lee, "Matt Lee you need to promise me that if I fall in battle that you will kill Alvardo and that Kellie Shawn is protected."

Matt Lee smiled when he spoke, "It would be my pleasure to cut the little shit's throat for you if he kills you. I do not think that will be the case though; In the heat of the battle just let your instinct take over, clear your mind, and let what you learned from Lucas and myself flow from you. You have been well-schooled in this type of combat. It will come naturally to you. We need to ready your horse as well. Which horse will you take into battle with you?"

Thinking of what Matt Lee had said about letting my instincts take over seemed like the wisest course and it was the way I had been trained. Thinking that and really doing it were two different things altogether though. Answering Matt Lee's question, I replied, "Storm, I need to ride Storm; we know each other so well that I can ride her without using reins if needed just by using my legs. I have been thinking of what Chief Piah said and didn't say. He never referred to Alvardo by name; he always called him Falling Rain's son. I found that odd since it is his nephew. What was your take on that?"

Matt Lee looked at me and said, "I caught that also. By not naming Alvardo by his name or not mentioning that he was his kin, I reckoned it was the old scalphunter's way of telling us that there would be no ramifications if his nephew got himself killed today."

After reaching the renegades' remuda, I simply gave the "come to" whistle and both Storm and Strawberry made their way in my direction. Giving Storm a rub down with a curry comb as Matt Lee located my saddle, I spoke to Storm softly, and trying to get her to understand that what was about to happen was a life or death struggle so she could prepare herself for the encounter. Not sure if she understood, but all playfulness disappeared in her demeanor as I saddled her.

Matt Lee also retrieved his tomahawk because to fight from a horse, it was prudent to have a tomahawk that was longer to make your arm reach further. Matt Lee's tomahawk was three inches longer than the one I had. My Bowie knife was sufficient since it had a 12 inch blade and razor sharp.

Stepping into the saddle, I mounted Storm and kept my Bowie knife in its sheath and held the tomahawk in my right hand. Matt Lee had also saddled his Pinto and would ride next to me until we reached the area that now had been staked out for the fight. Matt Lee was continuing to give me pointers as we rode to the south end of the encampment, "Remember Chance, let your instinct and training guide you and that Alvardo is blind in his left eye. Sometime during the battle you or he or both will become dismounted, so if this looks like it might happen, you have to take him off his horse at the same time. A man on a horse has never lost to a man on the ground in this type of warfare to the best of my knowledge. The horse is the deciding factor."

Alvardo was already mounted and waiting for me 50 yards away as I approached, more than enough distance for both of us to get our horses to full speed. Matt Lee still mounted and by my side explained there were no rules and there would be no quarter given in case a combatant was injured. There would be no mercy on either side. This was a fight to the death.

The last remaining member of the Biggers and Hammond gang had chosen a horse roughly the same size as Storm, so there should be no advantage in weight. I tried to focus on all things that mattered at this moment of time, but it was difficult as I searched the bystanders that had lined the southern end of the Ute camp to watch the half-breed outlaw and I fight. I finally found Kellie Shawn standing next to Walks With Ghost; I hoped and prayed this was not the last time I would see her. With one last look at the woman that held my heart, I cleared all thoughts of her from my mind. Reaching deep inside and locating the killer and the killer instinct that resided within my soul, I summoned forth the animal that lived just below the surface in us all.

Feeling the tension of Storm's muscles as she now understood what was happening, I knew she welcomed it. Storm was pawing the ground with her right hoof and throwing her head in anticipation of the battle that was coming. With a whoop, whoop, Alvardo started first and spurred his pinto mustang into action. With a "HIYA," I gave Storm her head and rein and a hard jab with my right spur as Alvardo and I raced toward each other like a couple of locomotives.

CHAPTER 39

Both horses were at a full gallop at the halfway point. I felt the power and strength of Storm's muscles as they rippled as we sprinted toward Alvardo. I had pushed Storm by using my legs to the left of Alvardo's pinto and his blind side and with the reins in my left hand, I raised the tomahawk in my right hand.

Alvardo was an excellent horseman as all Ute men were, and he was able to push and shift his pinto to put Storm and myself on his right side just a few yards before our encounter. Having to switch hands and use the tomahawk in my left hand made me swing and miss as Alvardo easily ducked under my now awkward swing and by not connecting, the momentum of my swing almost took me out of the saddle.

Alvardo's swing with his tomahawk did however find flesh. He had not targeted me, but Storm as we blew past. Pulling back on the reins and using my legs to turn Storm, I found myself covered in sprayed blood, Storm's blood. On the first pass Alvardo was hoping to take my horse out from underneath me and had cleaved Storm in the long part of her snout just below her left eye. It had been a glancing blow but an effective one as it tore out a hefty chunk of flesh, leaving an eight inch long wound that was bleeding profusely.

After turning Storm and now facing Alvardo once again, I realized that Storm was bleeding so badly that it would not be long before the fatigue of blood loss would take her stamina, and she would soon start to falter.

Giving Storm rein and her head again, I gave her my right spur as we started rushing headlong again toward Alvardo and his fast approaching pinto. This time I would stay on his right side and move to his left just before the horses would encounter each other as he had done on the first pass.

Halfway I could feel Storm's strength and fortitude start to seep out of her body as the blood flowed from her wound on her snout and was delivered by the wind fully to me as we charged on.

Just before the horses met, I pushed Storm only using my legs to my right and Alvardo's left. From either a mistimed move or because Storm's strength was so depleted from blood loss by that time, Storm and the pinto ridden by Alvardo collided head to head and chest to chest in a horrific impact.

As I was de-horsed for the second time in two days, the sound of a bone snapping filled the crisp winter air. Meeting the ground and the snow with a solid thud that took the air right out of my lungs, I rolled to my side to push myself up, but failed in doing so. Not having the air to do so, I collapsed back down into the snow. Gasping for air and trying to refill my lungs, I tried to locate Alvardo in my line of sight.

Finally, with enough air now filling my lungs, I was able to push myself to my knees and look around to see the wreckage that was left of the horses after the sudden impact at a full speed gallop. The pinto's leg was what I had heard breaking as she was down on her side and blowing her nostrils with such fury that blood was being sprayed all over the snow from internal injuries. The pinto's right foreleg was broken so badly that the bone was sticking out through wounds in the flesh in three different places. Storm was staggered, but still standing. Her eyes were glazed over and with blood flowing from her wound on her snout and the after effect of the impact of the pinto, I was amazed she was still alive, let alone still standing.

After the few seconds that it took to see the aftermath of Alvardo and I running our horses into each other at full speed, I started to take inventory of my body. Although covered in blood which was both Storm's and my own, I was able to move all my body parts, which told me for the love of God I had no broken bones.

After slowly standing, I realized I had lost my tomahawk in the wreck between the horses, but still had my Bowie knife in the sheath on my side. Pulling my Bowie and its 12 inch razor sharp blade, I once again tried to locate Alvardo.

Seconds after unsheathing my Bowie, I saw Alvardo slowly start to stand not 20 feet away and to my right. Like me, he was still trying to regain his senses and was rocking on his feet as he tried to take stock of what just happened. He also was awash with blood, mud, and snow. How he still had possession of his tomahawk was beyond me after a collision that left his horse crippled and dying in the snow, but there it was still in his right hand. Realizing my advantage that I was also in the outlaw's blind spot, I tried to move quietly more to his left side.

Stealth was not going to happen today because my muscles and body had been so injured that it was not responding the way it normally would. Any slow maneuver into his blind spot would only give me away. Reaching deep inside to find the fortitude and strength, I was able to gather enough for one last all out push as I rushed Alvardo with my Bowie in an underhand grip.

Alvardo sensed my closeness as I shortened the gap in between us as he swung the killing edge of his tomahawk in a round house swing to his right, which I deflected above my head with my left forearm striking his right forearm, making the razor sharp edge of the tomahawk miss flesh and bone.

His miss and my forward momentum brought my chest to the chest of the outlaw as I thrust upward through the flesh and just below the center peak of Alvardo's rib cage.

As my Bowie knife tip pierced Alvardo's heart, his strength slowly vanished as he dropped his tomahawk with his right arm slumped to his side. With my left hand now freed and the tip of my Bowie knife still within his heart, I grabbed the outlaw's face by his jaw and brought him closer to me so he could look me in the eye so he would know the misery that he had caused to the ones I loved had finally been avenged.

Face to face I watched the life fade from the eyes of the one that had hurt, killed, and raped so many. When Alvardo's eyes went blank, his body slumped and I pulled my knife from his heart and let his body drop into the snow at my feet.

Staggering backwards, I now looked at what use to be the evil that was Rick Alvardo as he lay in the bloodstained snow. Knowing he would never be able to hurt, rob, kill, or rape anyone ever again brought no satisfaction to me. One thing I did know as the fatigue and the injuries of the battle dropped me to my knees was that my "Rocky Mountain Retribution" was at its end.

Turning and falling to my back in the snow, I felt the wetness either from the blood or the melting snow as it seeped into the back of my shirt.

My mind was in a whirlwind of fog as my life played out in front of my eyes. Everyone's face that had played a part in my life appeared before me as I lay in the snow of the battlefield in which I was just a combatant.

Images of Lucas, Devon, Mom, Dad, Mutt, Herman Biggers, Storm, Bobby Burke, Strawberry, Walks With Ghost, Ronda Joy, Dave Edgar, Matt Lee, Rod Hammond, Chief Piah, Chucky Livingston, Rey Chavez, Eric Robert, Sherol Roy, Roger Baldwin, Rick Alvardo and of course Jace flooded my mind. The memories moved so quickly that when I was just able to recognize the picture in my mind, it had moved onto the next person until I got to Jace. Jace's memory and his image lingered and seemed to glow as it floated above me. My mind told me he was an angel and I reached out to touch his face one last time before he took me home. Reaching out and just before I touched Jace's heavenly face, he faded and was no longer there. As the darkness hovered in my mind, the face of my brother had been replaced with that of Kellie Shawn, the woman I loved. As the shroud of darkness started to close, I could see Kellie Shawn's tears as she was speaking, but there was no sound as the darkness overwhelmed me.

CHAPTER 40

I woke up, not from the pain and injuries that were punishing my body, but from the caress of tender loving lips as they brushed against mine. Slowly opening my eyes, I saw it was the woman that now held my heart. I hoped this was not a dream and that my life would forever now hold moments just like this.

As Kellie Shawn started to slowly pull away, her eyes were closed and I quickly closed mine so she could not see that I was awake. I could still feel her presence as she sat next to me, bending over my chest. I could feel her looking at me and I silently counted to ten before I spoke, "Kiss me again."

A hearty laugh filled the air as Kellie Shawn pushed my face gently with her hand, "I knew you were faking it."

Opening my eyes once again and with a smile etched across my battered face, "Kiss me again my love."

As she lowered herself once again, I looked deep into her blue eyes with the hint of green and saw what I wanted to see. She was forever mine and I was forever hers. Stopping halfway she smiled and said, "You know Chance, it really isn't the kiss, it is the moment before the kiss - the wanting and the desire that makes it all worthwhile."

The moment was lasting too long as I reached up and put my hand gently and lovingly behind her head and pulled her to me and kissed her. I knew as we held each other in the quiet after our kiss that from this moment on that without Kellie Shawn in my life, I would be nothing, and with her by my side we would be something, and with our hearts now as one we would be unbeatable.

After a few minutes I looked around and realized we were in a teepee, but it was not Matt Lee's and Walk With Ghost's teepee. I turned to look at my woman and smiled because she was already staring at me. With a smile and a chuckle I said, "Where are we? I don't remember this place."

Kellie Shawn slowly and mindful of my injuries slid out gently from my arms and stood up and looked stunning and desirable in her buckskin dress which was inundated by the campfire light as she stood over me and with a smile and a wave of her right hand, she answered my question, "This is now our home or until the winter snow melts and we can leave the Kawuneeche Valley. Chance Bondurant is now an honored guest and famed warrior among the Ute Indian nation. And with your victory over the one man that every Ute Indian hated just as much as you go the spoils of war. You now own everything that Rick Alvardo owned, including his weapons, horses, and the teepee you now find yourself."

Looking around and taking in the surroundings of my spoils of war, my eyes once again landed on my lady love. Laughing, I asked her, "Are you impressed?"

With her blue eyes with the hint of green smiling, she replied, "Not really, I don't believe that I look good in buckskin."

Lifting the buffalo robe that was covering my nakedness and with longing in my voice, "You may be right, I think you might just have to take it off."

Watching Kellie Shawn undress until she was wearing only the shadows of light that sprang forth from the fire, I realized that she was right about one thing - it is the moment before the wanting and the desire that makes it all worthwhile.

EPILOGUE

Five days after my battle with Falling Rain's son, the last remaining outlaw from the Biggers and Hammond gang, Kellie Shawn joined me as we stood at the renegades' makeshift corral as snow started to fall. I gave the "come to" whistle, and Storm and Strawberry made their way to stand in front of us. I used the curry comb and brushed and rubbed down Strawberry as Kellie Shawn applied some pine needle salve to Storm's wounds she had received during the battle.

Storm's wounds were healing fast in the cold mountain air and was feeling frisky as we started to grain both horses with an added pinch of sugar. Out of the corner of my eye, I caught some movement at the edge of the dark timber.

Stepping aside from both of the horses, I kept my eye on the timber hoping to catch the movement again. Kellie Shawn joined me as we watched through the snowfall toward the distant tree line.

There it was again something dark moving towards us, hopping and lurching at a fast pace through the snow. The dark cloudy light of the early winter morning and the glare of the snow was making it difficult to see. Palming my Colt, I slid the empty chamber over one notch so I had a live shell under the hammer.

Storm and Strawberry were now aware of the movement and started to toss their heads and paw the snow with their hooves. The horses were excited, but not alarmed as the dark shape rapidly moved closer.

Kellie Shawn realized what was going on before I did as she turned to me with her mouth wide open and tears starting to fill her eyes.

More confused now, I looked again and the tears now started to overflow my eyes as the half wolf and half something else dog got closer. Mutt, my friend, was very much alive and was headed in our direction.

AUTHOR'S NOTE

If you, the reader, has made it this far, that means you have finished reading my book "Rocky Mountain Retribution," and I would just like to take a line or two to thank you for purchasing my work, and I hope you enjoyed the book.

It is my hope you have found Colorado to be a living and breathing character as much as Chance and Kellie Shawn - I love Colorado and everything it offers.

I also wanted to assure you that the Colorado geography, along the path my hero Chance Bondurant and the beautiful Kellie Shawn traveled through the Colorado Mountains, does in fact exist - every mountain, mountain range, mountain pass, town, mining camp, river, and creek.

The fictional final showdown between the outlaw Alvardo and Chance happens in the Ute renegade camp in the very real Kawuneeche Valley, which is located on the western side of the continental divide in Rocky Mountain National Park along Trail Ridge Road just north of Grand Lake, Colorado.

I took some liberty in using the modern names in some cases or the more historical names if I thought it fit the story better. I wanted folks who were locals or familiar with this Colorado area to be able to follow along on Chance's adventure more easily in their mind and to be able to travel if they wanted to on horseback, foot, or even by car or 4 wheel drive the same path of Chance Bondurant in his quest for retribution.

The cover photo, as with my first novel "Rocky Mountain Reckoning," is one of my own taken in Rocky Mountain National Park.

ABOUT THE AUTHOR

Kurt James was born and raised in the foothills of the Colorado Rocky Mountains. With family roots in western Kansas and having lived in South Dakota for 20 years, Kurt James naturally has become an old western and nature enthusiast. Over the years Kurt James has become one of Colorado's prominent nature photographers through his brand name of Midnight Wind Photography. Along with being a member of Western Writers of America, his poetry has been featured in the Denver Post, PM Magazine and on 9NEWS in Denver, Colorado. Kurt James' poetry is also featured at Creative Exiles, a collection of some of the finest poets on the web. Kurt James Reifschneider is also a feature writer for Hubpages with the articles focused on Colorado history, ghost towns, outlaws, and poetry. Inspired at a young age by writers such as Jack London, Louis L'amour and Max Brand, Kurt has formed his natural ability as a storyteller. "Rocky Mountain Retribution" is Kurt James' second novel in his Rocky Mountain Series, but not the last novel of the western frontier of the wild and dangerous Colorado Rocky Mountains.

https://www.facebook.com/authorkurtjames/
http://hubpages.com/@kurtreifschneider
http://www.creativeexiles.com/author/kurtjames/
https://www.amazon.com/Kurt-James/

Made in the USA
Columbia, SC
13 November 2017